The Bargain

The Bargain

By Desiree Holt

Resplendence Publishing, LLC
http://www.resplendencepublishing.com

Resplendence Publishing, LLC
P.O. Box 992
Edgewater, Florida, 32132

The Bargain
Copyright © 2010, Desiree Holt
Edited by Michele Paulin
Cover art by Les Byerley, www.les3photo8.com

Print format ISBN: 978-1-60735-257-0

Warning: All rights reserved. The unauthorized reproduction or distribution of this copyrighted work is illegal. Criminal copyright infringement, including infringement without monetary gain, is investigated by the FBI and is punishable by up to 5 years in federal prison and a fine of $250,000.

Print release: April 2011

This is a work of fiction. Names, characters, places and occurrences are a product of the author's imagination. Any resemblance to actual persons, living or dead, places or occurrences, is purely coincidental.

As always, to my beloved David who was the inspiration for Cole Cassidy. His strong personality and loving care will always be with me.

Chapter One

"That is the most asinine thing I've ever heard." Jake Varner stared at Cole Cassidy sitting behind the massive, scarred desk, and eyed him with a critical look.

In the last year, Jake had watched his partner's normal vitality slowly leach out of him. The fire in his eyes had been replaced by a constant look of torment and anguish, and the famous Cassidy manner had become abrupt rather than smooth. The two of them had built Alamo Construction into one of the top builders in south central Texas. Theirs was a longstanding friendship. But now Jake wondered if his friend and partner had completely taken leave of his senses.

"What's asinine?" Sean, Cole's younger brother, walked into the office. "What am I missing?"

"My partner's screwy idea, that's what." Jake frowned, turning back to Cole. "I think you're out of what passes for your mind. That sounds like the insane raving of a desperate man."

"I *am* desperate." Cole's mouth tightened in a grim line. "Do you think I'd be thinking of this otherwise?"

Sean dropped into one of the chairs opposite the desk. "Will someone please tell me what the hell's going on around here?"

"*Your brother* has decided the only way to fix the mess he's made of his life is by asking Tara to marry him."

Sean gawked. "Tara? Your secretary? Marry you? Are you nuts?"

Cole sat upright in his chair. "What? Am I so repulsive? Will she run away from me?"

"If she's smart, she will."

"I thought you said you were off marriage," Jake reminded him. "Your first try at it didn't win any prizes."

Cole recoiled as if from a blow. The painful imprint of his late wife, Maggie, still lingered like a festering sore.

Regret flashed at once on Jake's face. "Sorry about that. It was a stupid remark, and I apologize. But Christ, Cole..."

"I know you think I handled things badly with Maggie." Cole's face was stiff as a mask. "You would have acted differently, but I'm not you. I created a mess, I was responsible for it and I had to do what I thought was right."

Creating a mess was a mild description of what had actually happened. On a long overdue vacation, he'd ignored the fact that his body didn't metabolize alcohol, gotten himself royally drunk and screwed his brains out for a week. With a woman he'd let pick him up in the bar. He'd paid the price ten times over for the lost week of lust with a predatory female he'd let his dick coax him into taking to bed.

Disgusted with himself and his absence of control, he'd returned home and tried to wipe the whole thing from his mind. He considered himself lucky to climb out of the hell he'd allowed himself to fall into.

Until she'd come up pregnant.

Greedy and determined, Maggie Renfro had forced the marriage issue, and Cole was too honorable to walk away from her. Or the baby.

* * * *

The marriage had been a catastrophe from day one. That was the only description for it. That he managed to keep things together until the baby was born was a miracle in itself. But his first sight of Molly had made his heart open like a flower. Life was brighter, warmer and more joyful. Every day, he raced home from the office to spend time with her. When he held her in his arms, inhaled her special baby scent, touched his lips to the skin as soft as peaches, he could convince himself Maggie was a small price to pay for this kind of happiness.

He stood there now, cradling her in his arms and ignoring his half-drunk, raging wife—until a few vicious phrases penetrated his brain and shattered him completely.

"She's not even yours, you arrogant bastard," she taunted, angry that he'd lost his temper over her drinking binges. "Joke's on you. I had a little problem, and there you were, rich, ripe and ready to be plucked. I knew the baby would get you."

"Do you even know who the father is?"

Her answer devastated him.

"Don't know, don't care." Her mouth twisted in a sneer. "I don't even remember who all I slept with besides you. No telling whose genes are running around in your precious baby girl's body."

"Stop it. Stop it right now." He shook with anger, afraid he would do her bodily harm.

She ran from the room, and he didn't try to stop her. He fed the baby, changed her and put her to bed, staring down at her for a long time.

Hours later, he was roused from sleep by the policemen at his front door. Maggie was dead. She'd been drunk enough to crash her car into an overpass, and the gas tank had burst into flames. He'd hoped against hope the DNA test he'd insisted on at the time would prove Maggie's words a lie, but the results left his heart with a wound that wouldn't heal. So now here he was, with a child he both loved and hated. No one was more disgusted with his behavior than he was, but as the months went by, he couldn't seem to get past the pain and betrayal.

* * * *

"I didn't realize you and Tara were, um, you know...." Sean searched for the right word.

"What, dating?" Cole shook his head. "We're not. But I've known her for two years."

And she's the first woman who's made me hard, made me even think about sex, since Maggie drunkenly crashed her car and killed herself. How come I never notice before that just standing next to her makes my cock stand up and take notice?

"As your goddamned secretary," Jake pointed out. "That's hardly a basis for marriage."

Sean scratched behind his ear. "Okay. I feel as if I came in at the middle of a movie. Did I skip over the beginning?"

"Yeah," Jake put it. "We both did. This moron can't seem to get control of things at home, so he thought he'd make a bargain with Tara. Somehow he just expects her to say sure, she'd love to marry him, play mother to his child and fall into bed with him." He snapped his fingers. "Just like that."

"Skip the falling into bed part," Cole said. "Been there, done that. I don't plan for sex to be any part of this marriage."

Liar!

But he tamped down that thought at once.

"Excuse me?" Sean's eyebrows rose nearly to his hairline.

"I'm proposing a business arrangement." Cole sat forward and leaned his elbows on his desk. "A bargain, if you will. She'll run my household, serve as my hostess and be a mother to that child. In return, she will have financial security for life."

"No sex," Jake repeated.

Cole slammed his hand on the desk. "I'm not looking for sex, for God's sake. After the fiasco with Maggie, I don't think I'll ever take a woman to bed again. My body isn't even interested."

Liar!

"Jesus, Cole." Sean shook his head. "What makes you think Tara will even do this? What if she's already...you know...interested in someone? She's liable to have you committed instead. Besides, this company can't run without her."

"In the two years, she's worked here, she's never dated anyone. I...checked."

Jake burst out laughing, "My God, you had her investigated."

Cole's lips thinned. "I had to be sure there weren't problems to deal with."

"So this is going to fix things for Molly?" Jake stared at him as if he'd grown two heads. *"That's* what you think?"

"The child doesn't have my DNA," Cole said through gritted teeth, "but she has my name. I can't expect her to pay for something that's not her fault. I certainly wouldn't just walk away from her, no matter how hard it is being around her."

He forced back the familiar pain that stabbed at him whenever he thought of the little girl. God, would his punishment never end? No one knew the silent tears he cried because his arms ached to hold her. The problem was, every time he looked at her, he saw Maggie's mocking face.

"People usually get married for other reasons," Jake argued. "Like falling in love?"

"Love isn't on my agenda. Ever. At least with Tara, I know her. I'm comfortable with her. She's efficient and competent and will just...handle things. If I have to bring another woman into that house, I want it to be someone I can stand being around." He raked his fingers through his hair. "I'm sorry if that makes me sound like a jerk.""You're taking a big risk here," Sean pointed out. "Tara could walk away from both the proposition and her job."

"As I said, it seems like a pretty straightforward bargain to me." He flipped open a file he'd been fiddling with. "Her father has some severe health problems. Before long, his health insurance will run out. This arrangement will relieve that strain from her. A bargain. Financial security in exchange for a commitment to the child."

Jake raised an eyebrow. "Do you even know if she likes kids?"

Cole shrugged. "As far as I can tell. I've seen her with a lot of the employees' children, and she seems to relate to them well. Although..."

"Although what?"

Cole shook his head. "Nothing. Forget it." He forced himself to wipe away the memory of the sadness he sometimes saw on Tara's face when she held a child

The Bargain

in her arms. The thought that she longed for a child of her own had been part of the impetus for focusing on her. So why hadn't she married?

God, was she a lesbian? He hadn't even considered that.

He shook off his depressing thoughts and looked up from his desk, realizing the two men in his office watched him carefully.

"It's been a month," he said very slowly. "In that time, I've had four different housekeepers. None of them could manage the job. The most recent one just walked out last night, said she decided she didn't like kids after all."

"What about an agency?" Jake asked. "Plenty of other people seem to have good luck with them."

Cole shook his head. "I think I must be snake bit. The good ones don't seem to come my way. And that child cries all the time." He raked his fingers through his hair. "Jesus. I have to do something."

Everyone was silent for a moment, his brother and his partner still watching him carefully.

"When do you plan to make your big pitch?" Jake asked at last.

Cole sighed. "Tonight. I'm going to ask her out to dinner."

"Tonight?" Jake's jaw dropped. "Without any preparation or anything?"

He shrugged. "I'll just present it to her in a reasonable manner. Tara's very level-headed."

"*Present* it to her?" Sean raised his eyebrows. "*Level-headed*? At least, you didn't expect to just stop at her desk and drop it on her as if it were a letter you'd want typed up. Anyway, what do you really know about her, except what you see at work? And the fact that a gorgeous woman like her doesn't date? What else did your little investigative foray turn up?

"Gorgeous?" Cole frowned.

"My god, are you blind as well as dumb? Tara is positively stunning."

"If you say so. Anyway, I discovered she was married before. Yeah, big surprise," he said as both men raised their eyebrows. "Her husband was killed in a carjacking about a year before she came to work here. Her parents live here, but that's it for family. She's not in a relationship, and she apparently has no close friends. What else do I need to know? Anyway, my mind's made up, so leave it at that."

"What makes you think she'll accept your invitation?" Sean wanted to know. "If she doesn't date, why would dinner with you appeal to her?"

Cole frowned. "What else would she be doing?"

Jake grimaced. "Nothing like making her feel last minute."

Sean blew out a breath. "I know she'll be flattered to learn you have such a low opinion of her social life."

"Maybe she doesn't like men." This from Jake.

"I thought of that, but then why did she get married?"

"Maybe she still grieves for her husband," Sean put in. "Maybe she's even still in love with him."

Cole pushed himself away from his desk and went to stand at the window, his hands shoved into his jeans pockets, watching the early evening traffic in downtown San Antonio.

"I'll talk her into it," he insisted, as much to himself as to the two men. "I have to. It's not as if I have any family I can depend on. And no way in hell would I turn this child over to anyone associated with Maggie. So. I'm out of options. This is all I have left."

"You'd better get to it, then." Jake pointed to his watch. "It's almost five o'clock."

"I'll do it right now, if you'll both get the hell out of my office."

Sean threw one final word of warning over his shoulder. "You have to tell her the whole story."

"I can't," he said. "She'd run in the other direction. And I wouldn't blame her."

When the two men had left, Cole stood in the doorway, watching Tara finish some last minute chores. From the first day he hired her, he'd been impressed with her competence, her efficiency, her warmth as a person. She worked magic in his office. He needed the same thing at his house. And maybe Molly could satisfy the longing he saw in her eyes in rare unguarded moments.

When he walked up to Tara's desk, she turned to him, smiling.

"Whatever it is, we're closed for the day," she joked. "I understand the boss refuses to pay overtime."

In two years, she and Cole had developed an easy give and take relationship, a good thing since her entire life was devoted to her job.

He was definitely the total alpha male. His presence was so powerful that usually when he walked into a room he owned it at once. Any room. Yet she never felt dominated by this man, as large as he was, or intimidated by him. She'd made it her business to learn the things that pleased him at work, and in turn, he gave her enormous responsibility. They were always comfortable with each other, so when she realized tonight he seemed slightly ill at ease and edgy, she wondered the reason for his behavior. This awkwardness was strange.

"Cole?" She raised an eyebrow.

He shoved his hands in his pockets, exhaled and clumsily blurted out, "Tara, I was wondering if you're free to have dinner with me tonight."

"I beg your pardon?" Her eyes widened and her jaw dropped. Dinner with Cole?

His smile looked forced. What was going on here?

"You know," he said, slightly joking, "where two people sit down at a table and share a meal. You've done that before, right?"

"You want me to have dinner with you?" She was still gaping.

"I can promise you a good steak and fine wine. Is that an incentive?" He named one of San Antonio's top restaurants, located on the famous Riverwalk, the city's hot tourist spot.

The shock of the invitation faded, and Tara felt curiosity tickle at her. In the month since the death of his wife, Cole had driven himself even harder than before, working longer hours, his conversations curiously devoid of any mention of either his late wife or his motherless infant daughter. His social calendar contained only business obligations. And they met for an hour every morning to go over business details. So why the sudden interest in dinner with her?

"I'll admit steak *is* my weakness. But why the sudden invitation. Something special come up?"

He raked his fingers through his hair. "You might say that. There's something I'd like to discuss with you, and I thought it might be nice place to get out of the office."

Why did he sound so anxious?

"Well," she chuckled, "I guess it beats the usual frozen dinner. Right?"

An unexpected look of relief washed over his face. "Good, good. I'll call the restaurant."

She looked down at the jeans and tailored blouse she usually wore to work. Fancy clothes didn't make it in a construction office. No one dressed up unless there was a special event. "I'll need to go home and change, unless we're going someplace casual. It won't take me long. Or are you in a hurry?"

"No, of course not. And I need to change, too. How about if I pick you up at seven? Will that give you enough time?"

"Seven it is."

He offered up silent thanks as he followed her out of the office.

Chapter Two

Please let me get through this.

Tara had been in an agony of indecision while getting dressed, discarding items, then pulling them back out again.

This just a business dinner. That's all. Don't think it's anything else.

But she couldn't get rid of the flutter in her stomach. Just looking at Cole Cassidy made her nipples harden, her pussy dampen, and the muscles in her entire body tighten. It had taken a lot of discipline to put out of her mind the erotic dreams that left her shaking and go to work each day as if her boss were just a cardboard figure.

Yeah, right.

It wasn't as if she was looking for a relationship, for heaven's sake. Been there, done that. She and Mike had been on the verge of divorce when he'd been killed, and she'd sworn off men after that dismal experience. But that didn't mean she couldn't indulge in fantasies about one fantastic, erotic night with Cole Cassidy.

If she didn't get over this, she'd have to look for another job. Maybe her mistake was taking the job even though her body went into sensual overload after the first time she'd seen him. But the pay Cole Cassidy offered was good and the work really interesting.

When he got married, it put him safely out of her reach. But now he was a widower with an infant daughter. So of course the dreams had come back with stunning force.

Cut it out and get dressed or you won't have a chance to find out what he wants.

Finally settling on a silk blouse and skirt she knew matched the blue of her eyes, she'd been fastening her earrings when the doorbell rang promptly at seven. She swallowed a gasp at the sight of Cole in a dark gray shirt, white on white shirt and paler gray tie. God, the man was too sexy for his own good. For *her* good.

"Ready?"

His smile was a little strained, and all her original nervousness surged forward again. She swallowed and forced a smile. "Absolutely."

Soon, they were at the restaurant. The maitre d' showed them to a corner table, bowed them into their seats, shook open their napkins and quietly handed them menus. Tara's palms sweated and her pulse raced, as much from nervousness as from sexual attraction, as she looked at the man across from her. She tried to ignore the strained look on Cole's face and let the quiet, elegant air of the restaurant work its magic on her. The polite tinkle of crystal sounded faintly in the air, punctuated by the genteel clink of silverware. Underneath it, muted conversation hummed at tables where carved tapers flickered in Waterford candlesticks, bathing the diners in a warm, amber glow.

"I've always loved this place," she said, thinking she should attempt conversation. "I don't get to come here as often as I used to, though. Thank you for choosing it." She rearranged her napkin in her lap and wet her lips. "And you're right about them serving the best steak in town."

"Score two points for the good guys." Cole grinned back at her, but the expression looked forced.

The knot in Tara's stomach grew to enormous proportions. This must be something terrible for him to be so uptight. Was he going to fire her? Surely, he wouldn't take her out to a fancy dinner to do it.

"Too bad none of the men you date are smart enough to bring you here," he added.

She looked across at him then down at the table, her mouth suddenly dry. "I don't date, Cole."

"I'm sure that disappoints a large part of the male population."

Tara smiled politely, avoided commenting and focused on the menu. She gave the waiter a weak smile as he took her order. A strained silence stretched between them as they worked their way through the meal, Tara taking tiny bites of food, Cole merely pushing his around on his plate.

Cole stared at his dinner companion. She was such an obvious choice for his plan, the most together woman he had ever met. Very little rattled her. She was equally at home with corporate clients as she was with the construction crew. He saw her as the perfect combination of silk and steel. And he was sure she wouldn't demand any kind of personal relationship with him. Yes, she was exactly what he needed to stop his life from unraveling further. Except he'd avoided the subject all through the meal, suddenly unsure of how to begin.

Now, the meal was over, and he was still stalling.

"Coffee?" He raised his eyebrows.

"Yes, thank you." She looked at the waiter. "Some of your fabulous Spanish coffee, please."

Her choice surprised Cole. He wouldn't have expected her to order something quite so exotic. He tucked this little fact away among all the other little things he didn't know about her, things he would have to learn. He hoped none of them held a trap for him to fall into.

"Just the French roast for me," he said.

He leaned back in his chair, studying Tara, and Sean's words popped into his mind. His brother was right—the woman was stunning. She was maybe five foot four, but the heels she wore tonight added another three inches to her height. And her figure! Why hadn't he ever noticed it before? All he'd seen when he'd looked at her was a female in jeans and shirt who efficiently handled everything he and Jake threw at her.

But the work clothes apparently had disguised a body with lush, feminine curves and a graceful line of neck and chin. The light from the candles on their table reflected the tawny highlights in her abundant, coffee-colored hair, whose thickness she ruthlessly tamed into a French braid every day. It warmed her almost translucent skin, accenting her high cheekbones and delicate lips. Her eyes were warm brown pools of liquid chocolate with tiny flecks of gold in the irises, the most expressive part of her face. The light jasmine scent she wore drifted across to him and teased at his nose. An image of her graceful legs as she'd walked out of her house zapped his mind, but he suppressed it with great determination.

Shit. She's beautiful. I should have insisted we go someplace casual so she couldn't change out of her office clothes. She'd still be an anonymous female with excellent skills.

Maggie had been a carbon copy of all the other women in his life—exotic women who were striking and out of the ordinary. In contrast, Tara's beauty was understated but incandescent. It should have made her less attractive to him, but unfortunately for his plans, she stirred something long buried in him. He had an unexpected urge to release her coffee-colored hair from its braid, let it tumble about her shoulders and run his fingers through it.

Damn! An unexpected stirring of desire, a heaviness in his groin that hadn't been there for a long time, shocked him.

What the hell?

"Have I spilled something?" Tara asked, checking her blouse and brushing at an invisible spot.

He frowned. "No. Why?"

"You're staring at me with the most peculiar expression."

"Sorry." He twirled his wine glass, the liquid nearly sloshing out. "Just lost in my own thoughts."

"They must be pretty heavy." She grinned. "You look as if the world is weighing on you."

"I'm sorry." He sat up straighter in his chair, his mind working furiously. He was nervous as hell, a condition he wasn't used to. He couldn't afford to make a mistake with this. Or let his unexpectedly awakened libido lead him astray. He wiped his perspiring palms on his pant legs.

Tara hadn't realized how difficult it would be to come out of her self-imposed shell and use her rusty social skills. Her catastrophic marriage had made her withdraw into herself. At work, she could look at all the men—Cole, Jake, Sean and the others as sexless individuals. She did her job, and they were part of it. Period. But Cole's overpowering presence crowded her, and all she could think of was how she could go back to pretending he didn't make her panties wet or invade her dreams hot and naked. And how she would do her job after this. Maybe it would be better after all if he fired her.

Something was making him uneasy tonight, though, and it piqued her interest. It was so unusual for him. Whatever it was, she wished he'd get to it. And quickly.

"Tara."

"Yes?" Okay. Was this finally it?

He cleared his throat. "You'd say we're a good team in the office, wouldn't you? We've developed a good working rhythm? We almost have a better relationship than some marriages."

What? Where was this going

"You do such a great job," he continued. "I don't know how I ever got things accomplished before you came along. Alamo owes you a great deal."

"Thank you." She pushed away the remains of her coffee, suddenly losing her taste for the sweet drink and took a deep breath. "This is very nice, your compliments are wonderful, the dinner was great and I'm enjoying the evening. But I have no idea what's on your mind. What's going on here, Cole? What's so important you had to ask me to dinner?"

Cole swallowed the last of his coffee and set his cup down with careful precision.

"You're right. It's time I got to it."

Tara waited, forcing herself to sit quietly, even while her pulse began to accelerate. Something was definitely up, and something about Cole's attitude unnerved her.

He cleared his throat again. "I know that you lost a child when your husband was killed, and I can't tell you how sorry I am."

How the hell did he know that? It was carefully guarded information. *I wanted a child, but not Mike's. Not something I can tell a stranger.*

"What I wondered...that is, I wanted to know..." He shifted uncomfortably in his chair. "If the opportunity to have a child were presented to you, would you take it? Would it interest you?"

Tara stared at him. Now, she was *really* confused. What did this have to do with work?

She blinked. "Excuse me?"

The air between them was suddenly so thick a saw couldn't have cut it.

Tara dropped her napkin on the table and pushed back her chair back. "I think I'd like to go home now."

"Wait, please." Cole reached across the table and placed his hand on her arm. "I'm doing this badly. Just hear me out, okay?"

She nodded but withdrew her arm, the heat of his hand searing her skin through the silk fabric of her blouse.

"You know I have a two-month-old infant," he began. "I haven't done very well with her since Maggie's death. The circumstances are somewhat difficult."

"Difficult?"

What could be so difficult about raising a child? she wondered. Not to mention the fact she had a hard time imagining this sexy as sin man with a child to begin with.

"My fault, nobody else's," he continued. "I can't seem find a housekeeper, and my situation's desperate."

Tara frowned. "Did you want me to check out some agencies? Really, Cole, you didn't have to take me to dinner to ask me that. I'd be happy to help."

Cole shook his head. "No, that's not it at all. I know people who've had really serious problems hiring through an agency. I don't really trust strangers, and I don't think I'd be comfortable having one live in my house. It hasn't worked so far."

"Cole, please. Enough. Just get to the point here."

"I'm sorry. I don't usually botch things this badly. Okay, here's the deal." He took a deep breath and exhaled. "Tara, I'm asking you to marry me."

Tara stared at Cole, speechless. If he'd asked her to take off her clothes, she couldn't have been more shocked. Of all the things she might have expected, this wasn't even on the radar. Cold liquid dripping on her skirt startled her, and she realized she'd knocked over her water glass.

"I'm sorry." Her face flamed, heat suffusing her skin.

Cole jumped up from his seat, agitation lining his face. "Here. Let me help you."

She brushed away his hand, blotting at her skirt with her napkin. "Thank you. I can handle it. I'm sorry for being so clumsy."

He stood so close to her his arm was touching hers. The spicy scent of his aftershave, the heat radiating from his body, his overpowering masculinity threatened to suffocate her, and for a moment, she couldn't catch her breath. This was not the time for arousal to take over her senses. She needed a clear head to understand this totally unexpected situation. Then he moved, and she breathed again.

"Please don't apologize." His voice was tight. "I know this has to be a shock to you."

"Now there's an understatement for you." She waved her hand at him. "Please sit down. I'm fine."

No, I'm not, but it won't help if you hover over me.

She took a deep breath, steadying herself. "Cole, is this some kind of joke? If so, it's not very funny."

"I assure you there's nothing humorous about it." His voice was earnest, pleading. "I want to make a bargain with you. Exchange of goods for services."

Her head was spinning. "A bargain?"

He nodded. "I have a child who needs permanence in her life. I can't give it to her. I can't tell you why so you'll just have to accept that. I know you've been worried about your father and his health problems. And I'm sure he's concerned about taking care of your mother, since he can no longer work. Alamo Construction has done very well, as you know. I propose to take care of your parents financially in exchange for you serving as the child's mother. And my hostess on occasion."

Tara's pulse accelerated. Hostess. His hostess. What else would he expect?

"As I said, this would be strictly a business arrangement," Cole went on to assure her. "You could hire someone to do the cleaning and laundry. I certainly wouldn't expect that of you. It would be nice if we could have dinner together, maybe share some time on the weekend, but that's strictly up to you."

"Dinner." She tried to follow everything he said. "Weekends."

"Yes. Sometimes, I go out to visit Jake and Lindsey at their ranch. Jake and I have known each other since our days at the University of Texas, and we've been a good fit as partners in the business. You've probably been able to see that."

"Yes. That's true." Lindsey Varner was a sweet-faced blonde, and she and Jake were so obviously in love the air around them nearly crackled with flames when they were in the same room.

"She's really domesticated Jake. I think you'd enjoy spending time with them if you wanted to come along." He shifted in his chair, nervously crossing and uncrossing his legs. "There might even be other things we find we'd enjoy doing together."

"We'd be the same as housemates." She couldn't believe she was sitting here so outwardly calm, discussing this outrageous proposition. A bargain, he'd said.

"Yes." He actually smiled. "Housemates. A good description. You'd have your own room. Your entire focus would be on the child." He shifted his gaze away. "Of course, there'd be no expectation of intimacy."

Intimacy. The word brought her up short. If she said yes to this, they'd be living together. No going home at five o'clock. How on earth would she share a house with a man she lusted after without ever letting it show?

And what did he plan to do about sex? He wasn't the kind to cheat on his wife, real or otherwise, with a series of discreet affairs. But he also was a man known for his strong sexuality. How would that factor into things?

She looked at him and saw the sexy man as he appeared to the rest of the world—dangerous, dark and edgy. Eyes so black you could fall into them, framed by thick lashes. A square, masculine jaw set off his sensuous lips. The six-foot-four lean, muscular body was topped by a head of thick black hair that framed a rugged-looking face. He had a powerful presence that dominated every room he entered. His graceful movements belied the coiled energy that lay just below the surface. He was like a panther, always poised to leap. Even dressed in his usual outfit of jeans and work shirt he lost none of the power of his presence. "I'll take care of the bills," she heard him say, "but you'll be in charge of everything else—the running of the house, normal chores and activities — those kinds of things. And the child. Especially the child. She'd be your primary focus."

"I see."

"We'd have an agreement so that if it happened not to work out you'd suffer no financial hardship." He looked down at his hands. "I had my attorney draw one up just in case you agreed."

She looked at him for a long time. Finally, she said in a flat tone, "You want to hire a wife."

He gave a short laugh. "It sounds so cold when you put it that way, but yeah, I guess that's what I'm asking."

"And how many others have you interviewed?"

"No one else." His voice was stiff. "Tara, I didn't mean to offend you in any way. I..."

"It's all right." She smiled tightly. "I'm just...stunned and not quite sure what to say." She took a sip of water, trying to collect her thoughts. "Cole, if you're so concerned about your daughter, why do you refer to her as 'the child'? Why don't you ever use her name? And why don't you want to play any role in her care?"Lines of misery were etched on his face. "Please believe me when I say I can't tell you that. Tara, you've only known me for two years, but I think we can take the measure of each other. Can I just ask you to trust me on this when I say there's a real need here and not ask any questions?"

Tara was shocked at the amount of pain in his words. What kind of tragedy had he faced that he couldn't deal with a tiny child? She spread her hands.

"How can I make such a life-changing decision without all the facts in place? And why me?" That was the real question. "Surely there must be others you'd consider. I'd think you could have your pick of a dozen women. A hundred."

"You overestimate my present market value." A tight smile twisted his lips. "Especially these days. In any event, they would demand a commitment from me that I'm unwilling to make."

"Ah." Understanding dawned. "The intimacy issue."

"Among other things." He thought about where his libido had gotten him before. In his present state of mind, he was sure he could live without sex for the rest of his life.

"I just find it strange," she interrupted, "that you're willing to live in a celibate relationship."

"Believe me." Now his voice was bitter. "Celibacy has its virtues. I want a situation that won't be complicated by sex."

Tara's eyes widened and her hands tightened on her napkin. "I beg your pardon?"

"Tara, please don't take this the wrong way, but that's one of the reason's you're the ideal candidate. Sex is something we won't have to deal with."

She didn't know whether to be angry or laugh at him. "Have I just been insulted?"

"No." He shook his head. "Not at all. In fact, you might consider it a compliment."

"If you say so." How ironic, she thought.

"I have to have someone I trust to do this. And I trust you, Tara. Implicitly. I'm convinced you're the person who could make this work."

She was still trying to decide how to react to the offer. Little fingers of warning danced on her neck, but she swallowed hard and banished them. Whatever the problem was, she'd find a way around it. Who could turn away from a child? "I admit you've caught me off guard. I don't know what to say."

"Tara, I'm sorry if this has upset you. I never meant..."

"No, please, it's all right. I think I'm just feeling a bit hysterical at the moment." She sipped at her water again, buying time to think. "You said I'd have full control in all matters where your child is concerned, right?" That was the key here. The heart of the matter. Whatever his problem with his daughter, she wanted to have no misunderstanding about her role.

"Totally." He was emphatic.

"And how much time do I have to think about this?"

"I wish I could give you as much time as possible to make your decision," he said, shifting in his chair, "but I have...let's say...a certain sense of urgency here." He took a deep breath. "I hate to push you this way, but do you think you could give me an answer by tomorrow?"

Tara thought she would faint. Tomorrow! She didn't know if she'd be able to answer him by next month or even next year. Her mind reeled. "Tomorrow. Well. I'll do my best to manage that. Could we leave now, please?"

"Of course. I understand." He signaled for the check. "I'm sure you have a lot of sorting out to do."

She was silent on the drive from the restaurant, very aware of Cole's presence next to her, his scent that filled the air in the car, his strong, lean fingers on the steering wheel. She kept stealing sideways glances at him, trying not to stare at this man whose entire meaning in her life had changed in seconds. What would it be like sitting across the table from him every day, watching the flex of muscles in his jaw and throat as he ate? Trying not to fall into the black pools of his eyes. Feeling the lingering traces of his presence when he left a room.

She was so preoccupied she barely noticed when the motion of the car stopped.

"We're here, Tara." His voice held a trace of amusement under the tension.

She blinked. They were parked in the driveway of her small house in northwest San Antonio. A two-story adobe structure with lots of wide windows, it was set back from the sidewalk on a tiny manicured lawn. A swing hung invitingly on the porch. She loved her tiny refuge, a little gem that she'd bought with Mike's insurance money. It gave her a sense of permanence. Would she have to give it up?

"Sorry." She shook herself. "What would I do about my house? I really don't want to let go of it." Her safety valve, she told herself, if this whole absurd situation blew up in their faces.

"Your decision. You can rent it out or just leave it empty. I'll pay the taxes on it, and we'll hire help to maintain it for you on a regular basis."

"I'll factor it in with everything else," she said, a touch of irony in her voice. "I understand this is a big responsibility you'd be handing me, and in fact, I'm flattered you think of me as the ideal candidate. But I have a lot to consider right now."

"I understand."

She stopped him as he unfastened his seat belt and started to open his door. "Please don't walk me to the door. I'll see you in the morning. I will try to have an answer for you then."

"Thank you."

Tara unlocked her door and stepped inside, turning to wave to Cole before closing it again. She waited until she heard Cole pull out of the driveway. Then she locked the door and leaned against it, heart racing, head throbbing. How could Cole put her in this position? What was he thinking? That she could give him an answer by tomorrow?

But she closed her eyes and thought, not only of Cole but the unknown child that no one seemed to want.

* * * *

Driving away from Tara's house, Cole cursed himself steadily. Jake and Sean were right. He was an ignorant fool. Whatever had possessed him to bumble ahead with this stupid idea? He'd thought it so sensible until he looked at it through Tara's eyes. She was right. He was hiring a wife.

But worse than that was his unexpected physical reaction to her, that unfamiliar tightening in his groin when he'd suddenly looked at her for the first time. He hadn't had sex in so long he'd almost forgotten how it felt, but he certainly hadn't thought of it in the same breath with Tara. He'd better not do it now, or he'd be in worse trouble than he already was. And Tara would certainly run as fast as she could in the opposite direction.

Sweat ran down his spine in rivulets and covered his face with a fine sheen, the aftereffects of nervous tension, and he suddenly felt as if he were choking. Yanking his tie loose and opening his collar, he drew in a deep breath and let it out slowly. Did Tara think he was a damned idiot? What if she turned him down? He hadn't even allowed for that possibility.

Come on, Tara. Say yes. You're my only hope.

Chapter Three

The ringing of her phone brought Tara back to reality. She pushed herself away from the door and rushed to catch it, her "Hello" coming out slightly breathless.

"Tara?"

Oh, God, her mother. Just what she needed right now.

"Honey, are you all right?" Ellen McKee voice had a touch of concern.

Tara looked at the clock. Twelve-thirty. "Mother, what are you doing up this late? You never make it past the news." A terrible thought struck her. "Is it Daddy? Is he okay?"

"Yes, he's fine. I'm sorry. I didn't mean to scare you."

"Then what *are* you doing up so late?"

"I was worried about you. I tried you earlier several times but didn't get any answer."

Of course, Tara thought. *I'm so predictable that the one night I'm out late, my parents push the panic button. You'd think I was eighteen years old.* She hoped her father wasn't worrying himself into another heart attack. His condition was bad enough as it was.

"I'm fine. I was just out for the evening."

"Oh?" She could hear the curiosity in her mother's voice. "Anything special?"

"Not really. Just dinner with my boss."

Please let her leave it at that.

"You had dinner with Cole? How nice. A real night out. I'm sure you had a great time."

Yes, Tara the bore actually went out on a date. And Mother, you wouldn't believe what happened.

"Yes, I did. We had a lot of...business to discuss." *That's the understatement of the year*, she thought. "How's Dad?"

Was that hesitation in her mother's voice? "He's doing okay, honey. Everything's fine."

But the underlying worry about health insurance and further treatments was always there. Tara could sense it. And she had it in her power now to put that worry to sleep.

That's good, Mom. But now I'm very tired. How about if I call you back tomorrow. Okay?" Without waiting for an answer, she said, "Night, Mom," and disconnected the call. Tomorrow would be soon enough to open this particular Pandora's Box.

She popped two aspirins to ward off a threatening headache and crawled into bed, but sleep eluded her. No matter what she tried, she couldn't make her mind a blank. The evening repeated itself over and over in her head, like a television rerun she couldn't turn off.

The proposal tonight had rocked her, the offer coming from so far out in left field she had trouble coming to terms with it. And the terms of the marriage. A hired wife and mother. How trite! If the idea weren't so unsettling, she'd be laughing out loud.

If only she knew what secrets he hid. There had been a problem with his sudden marriage to Maggie, but neither Jake nor Sean had ever discussed it. The only time Cole had smiled in more than a year was when Molly was born. Then Maggie had died and Cole hadn't mentioned either her or the child since. It was more than the grieving process. A hardness and bitterness had settled over him that hadn't been there before.

Too often, she caught a glimpse of such pain it made her want to weep. Tonight was the most outgoing she'd seen him since his marriage. But of course, he had a reason for it. A plot.

She had an insane desire to giggle when she thought of yesterday's conversation with her mother.

"I do wish you'd get out once in a while," Ellen had said. "Solitude is only good for so long."

"I'm fine," Tara had assured her. "I don't need anyone. I don't want anyone."

"Well, it's just not natural. It makes me sad to see what's happened to you. You're still young and beautiful, and you're wasting your life."

Okay, mother. Wait until I tell you about tonight's dinner.

I must be insane even to consider his proposal, she thought, after the tragedy of her first marriage. Could she enter into another marriage, even one of convenience, when she hadn't yet put to rest the last one?

Again she wondered what it would be like living with Cole Cassidy? What did he eat? Watch on television? Read? Did he stay up late or go to bed early? Did he roam the house and would she run into him if she made any nocturnal forays? Her mind drifted as she fell into a half-sleep.

* * * *

He was standing beside the bed, wet from a shower, wearing only the towel wrapped around his lean hips...

The bedside lamp was on low, casting a golden glow on his toned body but shadowing his face. The glow in his eyes had nothing to do with artificial light, however.

"I want you." His voice was rough with desire. "I've wanted you from the first time I set eyes on you. You don't know how many times you came into my office and I couldn't get up from my desk because my cock was so hard.""I want you, too," she whispered. "You don't know how many times I dreamed about you, just like this."

"I had my own dreams. But now we have the reality."

He tossed the towel aside, revealing an impressive erection and the sac with his balls resting heavy against his thighs. The muscles of her pussy quivered and moisture slid out onto her inner thighs. The ache inside her grew until she felt it in every throb of her pulse.

Cole pulled back the sheet covering her and lifted her to a sitting position, deftly sliding the thin nightgown over her head. His gaze raked over her, the heat in his eyes flaring brighter.

"Gorgeous," he breathed."Absolutely gorgeous, just as I knew you'd be."

He lay down beside her, propping his head with one hand as he ran the other lightly over her body. His fingers traced a pattern along her cheek, down her neck and between the valley of her breasts. They glided across her puckered nipples, pausing to pinch each one lightly. Shards of heat streaked directly to her cunt and spread throughout her body.

As he explored her, his mouth found hers, taking her in a predatory kiss that roused her senses. He tasted every inch of her mouth, her own small tongue dueling with his for possession. When he gently bit the tip of her tongue, she reached up to clutch at his head, trying to pull him even closer. When he broke the kiss, she was gasping for breath.

His palm rested a moment on her tummy, then his fingers trailed into the nests of curls covering her mound, finally probing the wetness of her slit. Her legs parted, giving him greater access to her and the tip of one finger circled the entrance to her cunt. He inserted it barely past the first knuckle, and her inner muscles clenched in response. He shifted slightly beside her, and the full length of his cock pressed against her thigh.

She tried to urge him farther inside her with her hips, but he was intent on teasing. As his finger moved slowly in and out of her, never pushing all the way in, he bent his head and captured one tight nipple into his mouth and sucked. Hard.

Tara moaned harder, the coil of need inside her winding tighter and tighter.

"Please," she murmured. "Oh, please."

"Please what?" he asked, lifting his mouth from her breast. "Please kiss you? Lick you? Fuck you?"

"Yes. Everything. All of it." She pressed one hand against the taut muscles of his back, feeling the play of sinews beneath the skin.

He pushed his finger all the way inside her then added a second.

"You are so damn tight," he rasped, scissoring his fingers. "I can't wait to feel my dick inside you."

He moved his thumb to find the hot bud of her clitoris, rubbing it back and forth. Moisture flooded his fingers, and she clenched around them.

"That's it," he encouraged. "I want that wetness so I can slide into you."

She moved her hand from his back and tried to slide it between them, but he pulled it away.

"I want to touch you," she insisted.

"Not yet. If you do, I'm afraid we'll be finished before we barely get started. I've wanted to fuck you for so long I can barely control myself."

Those words, as much as what he was doing to her body, ratcheted up her pleasure even more. When he shifted again to move between her legs, she shivered in anticipation. But instead of positioning himself to enter her, he slid down, opened the lips of her pussy as if they were petals on a flower and licked the length of her with one long swipe of his tongue.

Tara raised her knees, threaded her fingers through the black silk of his hair and pulled his head tight against her.

"Yes," she moaned. "Oh, yes."

His tongue was like a flame heating her flesh. His hands slid beneath her buttocks, lifting her higher to his mouth as he licked and thrust and plundered. She felt the orgasm gathering deep inside her, muscles tightening, pulses throbbing. When it broke over her, she clutched at his head, lifting her hips to him and digging her heels into the bed. She shook with the spasms, her inner muscles trying to draw his tongue in deeper.

As she was still clenching, he withdrew his tongue, rose to his knees pressed the head of his cock against her opening.

"Now you can touch me," he whispered roughly. "Guide me home, Tara."

Still in the throes of orgasm, she somehow managed to reach down for his shaft, widened her thighs and guided him into her body. He rolled his hip, and with one powerful thrust, he was inside her, stretching her, filling her until she couldn't breathe. One movement and she was plunged into another climax, this one even more powerful.

He held himself steady as she convulsed around him, bathing him with her liquid, wrapping her legs around him and digging her heels into the base of his spine. When she was gasping, nails digging into his shoulders, he began to move, powerful strokes in and out in a steady rhythm.

"I can't," she told him in a breathless voice.

"Yes, you can. Ride with me."

He drove into her faster. Beneath the grip of her legs, she felt his muscles tighten as his own climax gathered. His tempo increased as he pounded into her harder and harder. Finally he stopped, his entire body stiffening, and as he began to spurt inside her, another orgasm gripped her, this one the most intense yet.

Her pussy convulsed around his cock, her legs tightened around him, her entire body shuddered in the rhythm of the shared climax. She was spinning into space, rockets exploding in the black velvet that surrounded her. The spasms seemed to go on forever until she wondered how she would survive it.

And finally, finally, the intensity subsided, leaving her breathless and gasping for air. Her heart beat against her ribs so hard she was afraid it would shatter. With great effort, she unwound her legs from him and lowered them to the bed.

Cole collapsed forward, catching himself on his forearms, his breath washing over her as he brushed her lips. *His cock was still inside her, still filling her. He touched his forehead to hers and—*

Tara roused with a start. She was covered in perspiration, her covers tossed aside, nightgown rucked up, her hand between her legs, stroking her still pulsing cunt.

Ohmigod!

She squeezed her thighs together and withdrew her hand guiltily. Another erotic dream about Cole. Her body was weak, nearly boneless, as if she'd actually had multiple orgasms. She was truly losing her mind.

On shaky legs, she stumbled into the bathroom where she dampened a washcloth with cold water and ran it over her face, her neck and he arms. But it was going to take more than that to cool her still feverish body. She drank two glasses of water, hoping that would help, but it barely took the edge off the arousal still coursing through her. Filling the glass again, she wandered back into the bedroom.

She was standing by the bedroom window, rubbing the glass against her forehead, when the telephone rang, jerking her out of her thoughts.

She looked at the bedside clock. One-thirty! Who could be calling at that hour? Nothing good came of calls after midnight. Again, her first thought was of her father. Her stomach knotted in fear as she picked up the receiver.

"Tara?"

"Yes?" Her disoriented mind didn't recognize the raspy voice at first.

"It's Cole." There was a slight pause. "I apologize for the late hour. I hope I didn't wake you."

Cole? Oh, God, now what? And why did his voice sound so strange? Maybe he'd decided he wanted his answer right away. That he couldn't wait until morning. Her stomach churned at the thought.

"No, I was awake." *After an unbelievable dream about you so hot I'm still shaking.* "Is something wrong?"

"No. Yes. That is..."

"That is?" she prompted. She couldn't imagine this man ever fumbling for words.

"I was just thinking maybe I came across too strong tonight." His voice was slightly hoarse, and she caught the edge of anxiety. This must really be damn important o him. "I wanted to make sure I hadn't scared you away."

Too strong? She swallowed a hysterical laugh. A bulldozer would have been softer.

"I'm fine," she assured him. "Just turning a lot of things over in my mind."

"I'm sure you are." He cleared his throat. "Actually, I'm feeling kind of guilty. I don't think I realized I'd be asking you to turn your life upside down quite so much."

"Please don't worry. But I think we'd better hang up now. I'm still trying to sort through everything, and the night isn't getting any longer."

And I need to go to sleep and not dream about you.

"Of course. I'm sorry," he apologized. "I shouldn't have called this late in the first place."

"No, it's all right. Really."

Another pause. "To tell the truth, I think I was afraid you might decide I was totally crazy, pack up and leave."

"Not a chance." Though, after the dream, the idea had occurred to her. How could she agree to a sexless marriage with a man she wanted inside her every time she saw him? "I'm not going anywhere."

"Thank you for that. And Tara? Whatever you decide, I want you to know it won't cost you your job."

Now she really did want to laugh. If she turned him down, how on earth could she go back to their everyday work arrangement—and keep dreaming at night—as if nothing had changed?

"We can discuss it if that turns out to be the case."

"Well, then." He seemed reluctant to break the connection. Again, silence stretched across the line. "See you in the morning."

"Good night."

More restless now than ever, she went to the kitchen and made herself a cup of tea, sipping at it and staring out the window as if the answer waited for her out there somewhere.

She could only hope.

* * * *

At six in the morning, Cole finally gave up trying to sleep, showered and dressed. The child was still asleep, as was the dreadful housekeeper the last agency he'd called had sent him. If he didn't get her out of the house soon, he might have to shoot her.

Entering his office, he was surprised to find Jake already waiting for him.

He grinned at Cole. "Figure to dodge me by being an early bird? Not a chance. So. How did it go last night?"

"Please." Cole shook his head. "I've already had the speech from Sean. I woke him up in the middle of the night to tell him you're both right. I'm a fool."

And what a conversation that had been, prompting that incredibly stupid phone call to Tara.

Jake frowned at him. "Does this mean she turned you down?"

"It means she said she'd give me an answer today." He sat down beside his desk and pretended to busy himself with a stack of change orders.

"You look as if you haven't slept in a year."

"That's how I feel."

Especially after the fantasies that popped into my head when I tried to sleep and now won't get out of my mind. Tara naked in my bed. Tara with her legs spread wide and her swollen, pink cunt—

"Cole?" Jake's voice cut into his mental wanderings. "Did you hear me? I asked how she reacted to the 'No Sex' clause?"

Cole frowned, remembering a mixture of relief and disappointment. "Actually, I think she was relieved." "Well." Jake ambled toward the door. "I'd wish you good luck, but if Tara says yes, she's the one who'll need it."

Cole said nothing. He was too edgy to argue and so uptight he was afraid he'd crack if he bent over. Although he tried, it was impossible to concentrate on the work orders in front of him. He brewed himself at least six cups of coffee from his handy Keurig coffeemaker. Within half an hour, his stomach had a sour feel and his head was buzzing from a caffeine high. His looked through the open doorway to Tara's desk at least every two minutes, although she always got there on the dot of eight.

When she finally arrived, his entire body cramped. What if she said no? What were his choices? What if she said yes? Could he marry a woman his body suddenly craved with desperation and commit to a no-sex future?

She was dressed in her usual jeans and a blouse, clothes he had found decidedly unsexy where she was concerned. But today his mind imagined the satiny skin beneath it, and he wondered what her breasts would be like free of their restraining bra. If her nipple were large or small and how they would taste. How it would feel to be inside her. Was she tight? Would she be so wet for him it didn't matter?

Jesus! What the hell is wrong with me?

He watched her stow her purse in a bottom desk drawer, boot up her computer and call the answering service for messages. Finally, she just sat there with her hands folded, not moving.

She wasn't making a move to come into his office. His head ached, and his stomach churned with anxiety. Was she trying to find a way to let him down easy? Had his stupid phone call in the middle of the night killed any possibility of the bargain he'd presented? Frustrated, he tore off the sheet of paper he'd been writing on, crumpled it into a ball and threw it hard against the office wall.

"Is it safe to come in?"

He looked up. Tara stood at the office door, a tentative smile on her face.

"Of course." He blew out a breath.

"You look as if you're chewing steel," she told him.

"I probably could right now." He motioned her forward. "Please. Come in."

She closed the door, probably to give them privacy in case anyone wandered in, then leaned back against it. Had she slept at all after he'd called? Or had she spent the night as he had, confounded by the whole situation? He gritted his teeth with the tension.

At last, she took a deep breath and let it out. "Before I give you my answer, it would help to go out to your house and see Molly. If I'm going to be her...mother, I don't think that's an unreasonable request."

Cole's body tightened. Of course. She'd want to see what she was getting into. Maybe that would be the last nail in his coffin, but he nodded. "No problem. When do you want to go?"

"I think the sooner the better. Mornings are usually the quietest around here. I can forward the calls to the answering service and, of course, let Jake and Sean know we'll be leaving."

Cole could well imagine what those two would think.

"All right. Let me know as soon as you're ready."

Before nine o'clock, they were heading out I-10 in a tension-filled silence. Whatever sexual overtones might have popped up unexpectedly were certainly absent now.

Cole's house was located in Alamo Heights, a suburb of old money and executive wealth, He'd fallen in love with the architecture of the Georgian colonial and enjoyed living there until his life fell apart. Now, despite the oleanders and bougainvillea blooming in colorful profusion and two large crepe myrtles covered in soft lilac blossoms, everything looked cold and lifeless to him.

"It's beautiful," she commented, turning toward him.

If you only knew.

Cole felt as if Armageddon was just beyond the doors. He had deliberately not called to give the housekeeper any warning, wanting Tara to understand completely what she was walking into.

"Don't think the outside is an indication of the inside. I have an excellent lawn service." His voice was taut as a rubber band. "You may be in for more of a surprise than you thought. The housekeepers haven't done as good a job as the yardmen. This one can't seem to walk and chew gum at the same time."

"Where do you get them?" She raised one eyebrow in curiosity. "The housekeepers, I mean."

"An agency. And this isn't the first one I've tried. I've gone through six in as many weeks." Did that make him sound like an impossible perfectionist to work for? But surely she knew from the office how he was. And if anyone could make order out of chaos, it was Tara.

He took a deep breath, feeling as if he were about to plunge off a cliff. "All right. Let's go on in."

Tara had been prepared for a sterile environment, with a little girl tended to by robots on an orderly schedule. Robots who had no idea how to relate to a child. What greeted her was beyond anything she'd imagined.

A sharp voice drifted out from the kitchen. "Take this bottle. Open your mouth now or I'll throw this away."

Tara couldn't believe the animosity in the tone. But the room they stepped into was worse than any irritable voice. All around them was total disorder, the accumulation of neglect evident. The housekeeper sat in one of the kitchen chairs, a bottle in one hand, a screaming child in the other.

Tara was stunned. Had Cole even noticed what was going on here? She looked at the distressed baby and felt her heart lurch. At the center of the maelstrom was the most adorable infant she had ever seen. A fuzz of dark hair framed a pixie face with round cheeks, now more red than pink. Thick lashes fringed warm dark eyes and dimples flashed at the corners of her mouth. She was dressed in a onesie that was stained in the front and from the odor in the kitchen none to clean.

She spied Tara and Cole and began to scream even louder.

The housekeeper turned, startled. "Oh! I'm sorry. I wasn't expecting you, Mr. Cassidy."

Tara could believe that.

Cole cleared his throat. "Mrs. Randall, this is Tara McKee."

"Hello." She got up from her chair, juggling the baby and sighed. "I've been trying to get this bottle into her for ages without any success."

Cole made no acknowledgement of anything, simply stepped back as if removing himself from the scene.

Tara's mind processed everything. So this was the reason for the urgent proposal. This woman obviously didn't like children, at least not this one. And her housekeeping skills wouldn't win any awards. Why on earth would she take a job caring for a house and child if she hated doing it? And why didn't Cole at least get a cleaning crew in here once in a while? Had he just washed his hands of everything to do with his personal life?

This is a nightmare. But the baby. Oh, that heartwarming child so badly needs someone to love her.

What on earth had happened in this house to bring it to the brink of such destruction? She looked at Cole, hoping for some kind of explanation, but he simply stood near the wall, his posture stiff and unyielding. Every line of his body shouted aversion to the whole thing. She would have thought him cold and unfeeling if not for the torment in his eyes. His gaze begged her, *Please don't judge me so quickly.*

So many emotions bubbled up inside Tara that for a moment she had trouble maintaining her composure. It included a pain that had never left her heart, a secret she hadn't felt the need to share with Cole. This was a disaster, and sooner or later, she had to get to the bottom of this. But not right now, when there were more urgent matters.

Suddenly, Molly hiccupped, stopped crying and reached her tiny arms out to Tara. And Tara's world turned upside down. Gone in an instant were her fears and misgivings at sharing a house with Cole and her dismay at what faced her. With one gesture, Molly Cassidy had become the focus of Tara's world, and an unusual feeling of calm settled over her.

She was getting something she'd never thought to have, and that alone would help her do this. She could make it work. All she needed was to get past the emotional landmines she knew awaited her. She stepped over to the chair.

"May I?" Without waiting for an answer, she dropped her purse on the counter and lifted the baby from the housekeeper's arms. As she nestled her cheek against the soft skin of the baby's face, she felt a painful hitch in her heart. Tears pricked the inside of her eyelids, threatening to run down her cheeks and she blinked hard to contain them.

"She needs cleaning up," Mrs. Randall said nervously.

No kidding!

"That's all right." Tara smiled. "Why don't I take her upstairs and change her?"

The housekeeper looked at Cole for answers.

He just nodded, looking like a caged eagle desperate to take flight. The message was clear to Tara—do whatever needs to be done, but leave him out of it. If she'd had her car with her, she'd have told him to go on back to the office at once. She had never seen him this uptight.

"I'll take care of her." She spoke in a quiet tone to the housekeeper. She turned to Cole. "Which way is upstairs?"

"This way." He led her out of the kitchen, into the hall then to the sweeping arc of the stairway.

Tara stopped at the bottom step. "We have a lot to discuss, but I'll give you my answer now. Yes. I'll agree to this bizarre marriage arrangement. The sooner the better."

Cole visibly sagged with relief. "Tara, I promise you I'll make sure you won't regret this. A bargain is a bargain, and I'll keep my end."

"Don't make promises you might not be able to keep," she said tautly. "Meanwhile, we have some immediate problems to resolve. Get rid of that dreadful woman. Pay her and send her on her way. This seems to be way beyond her capability, and I don't particularly care for her attitude toward Molly."

"Tara, I—"

"It's all right. And call Jake. Ask him to look in my Rolodex for the number for the cleaning service we use for new construction." She stopped, suddenly worried. "I'm not presuming too much, am I? Overstepping my bounds?"

"You're kidding, right? This is more than I hoped for. But what about..."

She shook her head. "When I come back down."

Cole tried once again to say something, but Tara hurried up the stairs with Molly in her arms. The upper floor had the same depressing air of neglect as the kitchen and a musty odor hung over everything.

What's wrong here? I can't understand why Cole would tolerate this kind of existence.

She located the nursery at the end of the hall. Not wanting to take the time for a tub bath, she stripped off the little girl's clothes, carried her into the adjoining bathroom and ran a sink of warm water. While she bathed Molly gently with a washcloth, she talked to her and sang songs she dredged up from her childhood.

I have to be the dumbest person in the world to agree to this. But it's criminal what's happening with this adorable little girl. How could Cole ignore his child this way? He acts as if she's contagious. I would have expected a lot more from him.

But it was what it was, and without hesitation, she decided her next move.

Her mind raced, and her stomach did flip-flops at the thought of the very unTara-like thing she was about to do. She worried that this *really* was pushing it, but the minute she'd seen Molly, everything else ceased to exist. This—a child to love who obviously needed her —was the only thing that mattered right now. And she would do whatever she had to where Molly's welfare was concerned. Even if it meant suppressing those flames of desire that consumed her whenever she was in Cole's presence.

She opened a drawer and pulled out the first onesie she came to, thinking *inventory later*. In a few minutes, she carried a clean and freshly dressed Molly downstairs and went to find Cole. He stood in the kitchen, leaning against the wall, arms crossed, face set in granite.

"She's gone." He paused, his voice and posture indicating his discomfort. "Tara, I know what you must be thinking..."

"One of these days you'll have to tell me what's going on here, but right now this child needs attention."

"Shall I call the agency to send someone else?" he asked, his voice hesitant.

Tara sat down with Molly in her lap, cuddling the infant against her. "No, I think not. You said I could make decisions, so I'm taking you at your word."

"Anything." His relief was evident. "Whatever you want, as long as you don't change your mind."

Okay, she thought, *here goes.* "I think I should move into the house right away." She held her breath, waiting for him to say something, but he was silent. "Does that shock you? The situation with Molly is the most important thing right now. You said to do what's best for her. And we're going to be married quickly, right?"

Breath whooshed out of him in the biggest sigh of relief Tara had ever heard. A smile, the first his mouth had formed in ages, tugged at his lips. "You really are full of surprises, aren't you? I was hoping that was what you'd do. Tackle it the way you do every project in the office."

For a moment, his reminder of the business-like nature of the situation chilled her, but she quickly brushed away the feeling. "I don't suppose that will cause any more gossip among your friends than the wedding itself.""The hell with my friends. They were never there when I needed them anyway. I just want to be sensitive about appearances for your sake."

"I think appearances are the least of the problem here. The only people I'm concerned about are my parents, and I'll deal with that. Somehow." She paused. "But that presents another problem. This means I won't be coming back to the office. That will cause some problems for you." She nibbled at her lower lip, rocking the baby gently in her arms. "I'll call the temp agency we used when I took vacation. I'll tell them we're looking for a permanent replacement and to send us someone qualified who's looking for that."

"I can make the call if that would help," Cole ventured.

Tara shook her head. "No. Not to step on your toes but I know better what's needed in that job so I'll take care of it. But I'll need to get my car, go by my house, put together a schedule to get everything done." She got up and looked in the pantry and the refrigerator. More disaster. "And grocery shop."

"I think we should take care of the license and the rings today. I'll call Judge Harrison about performing the ceremony, unless you have a preference of some kind." The lines in his face deepened. What about the child? Can you do something with her? I don't want to haul her around with us."

Tara bit back the retort that jumped to her lips. "Do you think Lindsey might know of a babysitter we can trust?"

"I suppose. Jake has a big family, lots of nieces. Maybe one of them would do." He tore a sheet of paper from a pad on the counter. "Here's the number of the cleaning service." "Fine. I'll talk to them while you call Lindsey. Then I think we should get going."

And just like that, Tara's life turned upside down.

Chapter Four

While Tara arranged for a cleaning crew, Cole called Jake to ask him if he thought his wife might be able to help them.

"Lindsey came through for us," Cole told Tara, snapping his cell phone shut. "She's making the calls for us, but everyone's in school until two o'clock. She'll have someone here by three. That will give us enough time to take care of business. We can do it right here in Alamo Heights."

"Good. The cleaning crew will be here at noon, so I'd better hustle. I asked for the biggest one they had and offered them double. I hope that's okay. We'll need it."

They had a couple of sticky moments making the rest of their arrangements.

"Do you know where the carrier is?" Tara asked, holding Molly as they prepared to leave the house.

"I think Mrs. Randall put it in the garage."

Tara looked at him. "You mean to tell me this baby has never been out of the house?"

His discomfort was obvious. "I'll go get it."

He brought it to her, holding it as if it would bite him, perplexed as to what to do with it. Tara gritted her teeth and settled Molly in it. "Can you watch her for a minute? I need to run upstairs and get a light blanket to wrap her in and pack a diaper bag."

"Watch her?" Cole looked as if he'd bolt out the door.

Tara fought back her impatience. "She won't get up and run away. Please. I'll be quick." Without giving him a chance to object, she raced up the stairs, dug in the chest of drawers in the nursery for some kind of light wrap, found the diaper bag in the closet and pulled things from the changing table, stuffing them in as fast as she could. She literally ran back down the stairs.

Cole was standing exactly where she'd left him, staring at Molly who stared back at him, sucking on her tiny fist.

She picked up the carrier. "I think we're ready now. Do you want me to come in when we get to the office and get the temp settled?"

He shook his head. "We'll take care of it. We've done it before. Worst comes to worst, if she's a washout, I can forward the main line to the answering service and get one of the payroll clerks to file and help with other things."

And those were the last words spoken until they reached the office parking lot. Tara didn't even go inside, just shifted Molly, the diaper bag and her purse to her own car.

"I'll pick you up at three," Cole said.

Was it her place to ask if he'd be home for dinner? She realized how much about him was still a mystery to her.

"I don't know what time you usually prefer to eat."

"I don't expect you to cook tonight, with everything that's going on today. I'll just pick something up."

"No, please. I really want to fix dinner. I think I've overdosed on takeout and frozen dinners. Would eight be all right?"

"Whatever's convenient for you. I have some things to take care of when we're through with the license and rings. I'll probably be home by seven."

"I'll see you this afternoon, then."

She slid into her car and backed out of her space. Glancing in the rear view mirror as she shifted into Drive, she saw Cole still standing where her car had been, watching her retreating taillights. Her heart pinched painfully when she thought about the look of torment he wore whenever he looked at his child.

Well, kiddo, she told herself, *fasten your seatbelt. You're probably in for a bumpy ride.*

* * * *

Cole sat in his office, staring at the folder in front of him. He'd gotten as far as opening it, but then his mind had shut down. He knew the decision he'd made was logical, a perfect solution to his dilemma. So why was he having such conflicting feelings about it?

It's the 'No Sex' rule, dummy.

The last person he'd expected to make his cock sit up and take notice was Tara McKee. But last night at dinner, he'd had to keep his napkin on his lap and direct his brain elsewhere, because every time he looked at her, every bit of blood rushed from his big head to his small one. After the disaster with Maggie, sex hadn't even appealed to him—strange for a man with such a greedy appetite.

Then he'd taken a really good look at Tara. Suddenly, his cock swelled and his balls ached. He began to imagine her naked in his bed, hair spread out on the pillow, rosy-tipped breasts pointing at him, begging for his mouth. He could almost feel his lips around a plump nipple or his tongue busy between her legs lapping at her slit and tasting the juices in her cunt.

He shuddered inwardly as he thought of that idiotic phone call last night. It was just a good thing he didn't drink, or he'd have blurted out the real reason. He wanted to change the 'No Sex' rule. He could just imagine how she would have reacted to that. So he'd made up a lame excuse, hung up and taken a cold shower, hoping that would help.

No such luck. When he'd gotten into bed, nude—a big mistake—and closed his eyes, his head had filled with images of Tara under him, over him. In frustration, he'd grabbed his demanding cock, trying to squeeze it into submission, but instead, he'd imagined Tara's slim fingers wrapped around it. Or that mouth that suddenly fascinated him so much. Or the tight muscles of her pussy clenching around him, pulsing with her climax, bathing him in liquid heat.

Before he realized it, his spine tingled, his balls drew up and cum spilled over his fingers.

Great, just great.

He hadn't done that since he'd been sixteen years old. At least another cold shower had helped settle him for the night. He wished he had something to settle himself now.

A knock on the doorframe made him look up to see Jake and Sean standing there. He grimaced, then motioned to them.

The Bargain

"Come in. you might as well hear all the gory details or you'll pester me to death."

* * * *

Tara's the morning went by in a blur. She felt like a marathon runner, her mind still in turmoil and moving as fast as her feet. God only knew what Cole thought about her stepping into his life as if she'd always been there. Well, he'd told her to take charge, and that's just what she'd done.

First, she'd gone to her house for some clothes. She'd hurried in with Molly in her carrier in one hand and the diaper bag in the other. But once there, she realized with a sinking feeling she hadn't bothered to get Molly's feeding schedule. She'd smiled down at the baby who sucked happily on her fists.

"Oh, well. We'll just wing it."

Packing two suitcases, she lugged them out to the car. Whatever else she needed she could come back for when she was better organized. Based on what time she'd arrived at Cole's and seen the housekeeper struggling with breakfast, she figured she had at least until noon before the baby was hungry again. That would give her time for grocery shopping and anything else she needed to do right away. Taking one last look around the house, she locked the door with a strange feeling. Tonight, she would be sleeping somewhere else.

Thanking her good luck that the grocery wasn't crowded, she filled the basket with staples and items for the meals she was planning. She had no idea what Cole's food preferences were except for steak, so tonight they'd have spaghetti and meatballs, a dish she figured was a safe choice. She stashed the groceries in the car and hurried back to Cole's, arriving just as the cleaning crew was pulling up in the driveway.

"Top to bottom," she told the crew chief, a man she'd worked with many times. "Dump everything in the refrigerator and pantry and leave all the windows open. And let me know when I can get into the kitchen to put the groceries away."

He nodded. "Leave it to us."

She changed Molly, heated a bottle for her and rocked her to sleep in the nursery. It felt good to hold the baby in her arms, to sing to her and watch her cherub face as she sucked on the nipple and watched Tara with intense concentration. By the time she put Molly in her crib, the kitchen was ready for her. She unloaded groceries and put away things in the cheerful, yellow and white kitchen, now sparkling clean. Sun slanted in through the two huge windows that looked out on a wide backyard and patio.

She found vases for the flowers she'd bought on impulse, putting the largest bunch in the center of the kitchen table. Already the air was sweetened with their gentle fragrance.

Finally, taking a deep breath, she called her mother.

"Well," Irene McKee said, after Tara had laid brought her up to date. "That must have been some dinner."

Tara fielded questions, giving out minimal information. No, they hadn't been dating each other exactly, but the relationship had developed since she'd been working. Yes, his wife had died two months ago, but she understood the marriage was really over long before the baby was born.

"A baby!" her mother said. "Oh! No wonder he wants to move things along."

There was something in Irene's voice now that Tara didn't want to think about. Time to end the conversation.

"I've got to run, Mom, but I'll call you later tonight, and we'll have more time to talk. Okay. Bye."

Her last chore was to unpack her suitcases in the room adjoining the nursery and make up her bed with the sheets she'd found in the linen closet. There. At least, she had a place for herself, whatever that place turned out to be.

She glanced at her watch. Two-thirty. Cole would be there at three on the dot. Time to get ready. Too bad she wasn't looking forward to what should be the beginning of a happy chapter in her life.

* * * *

Pulling into his garage, Cole felt every muscle in his body knot in tension. He had no idea what he'd find—Tara gone in panicked flight, the babysitter watching the child? Or would he find Tara inside, still dashing around in an attempt to make order out of the chaos?

When he entered the house, he stopped short, his senses jarred. He felt as if he'd walked into someone else's house. Everything was different. He heard James Taylor, a favorite of his, playing softly in the background, the soothing notes drifting out into the air. A delicious aroma, drifting from the kitchen, tantalized his nose and blended with the delicate hint of something floral. His nose twitched at the pleasant but unfamiliar fragrance.

In the kitchen, he saw the verticals on the glass door and the window over the sink had been pulled wide, exposing the lawn and shrubs bathed in early evening diffused light. Funny, he'd never taken a good look at the well-manicured, well-tended area, even though he paid a fortune for its upkeep.

Tara was just coming down the stairs with a young, ponytailed girl.

"Cole, this is Nicki, Jake's niece. She's going to watch Molly for us."

"She's just so adorable," the teenager enthused.

Cole simply nodded. "Ready, Tara?"

"Yes." She turned back to Nicki. "We should be back by five o'clock. Are you sure you're comfortable giving her the bottle and everything?"

Nicki grinned. "I've done it for two sisters and a brother when I was a lot younger. You can trust me. Besides, Uncle Jake wouldn't be too happy if I screwed up."

"Well, thank you for doing this on such short notice." She noticed Cole jingling his keys impatiently. "I'm coming."

* * * *

As they pulled away from the house, he announced, "Judge Harrison can marry us next Friday at five. That's a week from tomorrow. Will that work for you?."

"Yes. Fine. That would be good."

"I've asked Sean to be my best man. You'll need to decide on who you want to stand up with you. I know it's short notice, but is there someone you're close to?" He suddenly realized how little he actually knew about her personal life.

"Oh."

He glanced sideways at her and noticed her discomfort. Didn't she have any close friends? What had she done with herself since her husband died, lived like a hermit? And now he was consigning her to another kind of isolation. He needed to find a way to make this more comfortable for her. "Let me make a suggestion? You know Jake's wife, Lindsey. You've had lunch with her and talked to her when she's come into the office. If there's no one special you want to ask, I know she'd be happy to do this."

"Cole, she's your partner's wife, not really a personal friend." Tara's voice was strained. "I'm sure she'd think that's a terrible imposition."

"I don't believe she'd see it that way." He softened his voice. "Call her. I'm sure she'd be honored."

"If you say so."She shrugged. "I'll call her when we get home. Thank you."

By four-thirty, they had applied for and received their license, and stopped at a jewelry store to buy rings.

"Pick whatever appeals to you," Cole told her. "You don't need to worry about the price."

Red stained her cheeks, and she turned her head away. "I don't need anything expensive. It should be something that represents our...bargain."

Cole didn't know what to say after that, so he simply kept quiet while she chose a plain gold band. Her eyes held a shocked look when he purchased one for himself.

"Good protection," he said matter-of-factly.

He dropped her back at the house, his parting words brief. "See you about seven."

As he backed out of the driveway, he couldn't help but spare a glance for her slim figure climbing the steps to the front door, back straight, determination in every line of her body. Somehow, he had to find a way to make this pleasant for her. Make this work. But he'd be damned if he knew how.

He would have stayed at the office much later. Finding busy work, if Jake hadn't chased him out at six-thirty.

"You're about to get married," he pointed out. "You got Tara to agree to the bargain. At least, behave with common courtesy.

Reluctantly, not knowing what kind of reception to expect when he got home, he put away the bid he was working on and went home. He held his breath as he walked into the house, hoping the earlier scene hadn't just been a dream. But the air was still fresh and a delicious aroma wafted from the kitchen.

Tara was stirring something on the stove and humming along with the little under-the-counter stereo, her body moving to the music. She'd changed back into her jeans and pulled her hair back into a ponytail. The shiny mane swung in time to her movements. The soft denim of the jeans molded to her hips and the T-shirt emphasized the fullness of her breasts. This was a Tara he'd never seen before. She looked softer, more relaxed. Less businesslike. Certainly less tense than she'd been last night and earlier in the day.

He wanted to pinch himself because he still had trouble believing this warm, inviting atmosphere was his house. And this very sexy woman was about to become his wife.

Then he froze in place. What the hell was this? Shocked at the way his eyes roamed her body, at the hardening of his penis the minute he looked at her, he reminded himself this was an arrangement of convenience, nothing more. He couldn't let this assault on his mind and senses shove him off track. No good could come of that.

He moved, making a slight noise, and Tara looked up, flushed from the heat of cooking. "Sorry. I guess I didn't hear you come in."

"Am I in the right place?' he asked. "This doesn't look or feel as if it's the same house."

"Thanks." Her smile was tentative. "Dinner will be in just a minute. It's really nothing special, just spaghetti and meatballs. I hope that's okay."

"It's fine. More than fine." He stood there stiffly, as if trying to figure out what to do with himself. "Well, I'll get rid of this jacket and tie and be right back. Tara, I want to thank you again..."

"I told you. No thanks necessary." She turned her gaze back to the stove.

"You know," he said, "both times I came home today, I worried all day that you'd decided it was more than you wanted to handle. That you wanted to run back to your desk as fast as possible."

"Not when I see how much Molly needs me," she told him firmly.

"Speaking of the child, where is she?"

"Molly," she stressed the name, "has been fed and bathed and is sound asleep."

Cole just shook his head, completely amazed.

* * * *

The atmosphere at the table was stilted, each of them trying to adjust to the idea that from now on they would be sitting down to meals together. *What should we talk about?* Tara wondered. *How does he expect me to act?* Lord, all the little things she hadn't thought about. Did Cole feel as out of place as she did? By the time the meal was finished, they hadn't gotten much past the basics.

How did things go at the office?

Fine. The temp is very bright. I'll keep her a couple of weeks in the hope that she works out.

Would you like me to come by and go over anything with her?

No, I can handle it.

Fine. More iced tea?

When the dishes were cleared, Cole stood and filled his coffee mug from the freshly brewed pot. "I want to get out of these clothes. Can you meet me in my den in a few minutes? It's just past the stairs. I have some papers to go over with you."

Tara tensed. "Is everything all right?"

"More than all right. I just want to make sure everything is in order before I ask you to sign anything."

Of course. The bargain.

She relaxed. "Okay."

But her nervousness returned as she waited for him. She wiped her sweating palms on her jeans and fiddled with her ponytail. The den was very much him. Wood paneling on the walls, thick carpeting, a heavy oak desk, with a credenza that held enough electronic equipment that Tara was sure they could have launched a NASA expedition. The desk chair, the couch and the large armchair were upholstered in the soft leather she knew he preferred. The only pieces of artwork in the room were a Russell painting she knew he'd paid the earth for at a charity auction and a copy of the Remington bronze statue, *Broncobuster.* He'd tried and failed to get his hands on the original.

When Cole came in wearing sweat pants and a University of Texas T-shirt, her eyes widened. Oh, lord. How was she supposed to remain neutral, keep her mind on the reason she was there, when he dressed this way. She couldn't help noticing the way the soft material clung to his narrow hips and emphasized the leanness of his body. Or the outline of a semi-erect cock pushing against the fabric. Dark, curling hair just peeked over the neck of the shirt, the same masculine hair that dusted his corded arms and the backs of his strong-looking hands. His hair, wet from what was obviously a quick shower, looked even darker than usual and curled slightly at the nape of his neck. Delicious.

Get yourself under control before you make a mess of everything!

She swallowed, hard. This was not good.

"Sorry," he said stiffly, noticing her reaction. "I guess I dressed down a little too much. This is just what I'm used to throwing on when I get home."

"No, no, that's fine. This is your house. You should wear whatever you want. I'm...just not used to seeing you so...casual."

For a moment, his eyes darkened even more. "Same here." Then he sat down at his desk, indicating Tara should take the armchair and handed her a folder and an envelope in front of him.

In the next few minutes, she was alternately stunned and amazed. The amount of money stated in the agreement was completely absurd. More than she could need, even with the financial demands of her father's illness. She knew exactly how much money Alamo Construction took in and that Cole could well afford this, but it still bothered her.

Her eyes widened when she opened the envelope to find a thick wad of cash with a rubber band around it and bank signature cards.

"This is ridiculous," she said, when she could find her voice again. "I can't possibly sign this."

"Too little?" he asked, frowning.

"Too much," she insisted.

He picked up a pen from the desk and rolled it in his fingers. "You've agreed to turn your life upside down and enter into this crazy agreement with me. There isn't enough money to express my gratitude. And you can't know at this point what financial assistance your parents will need. So please don't argue with me about the one thing I can provide in this arrangement, okay?"

Her pulse jumping at the enormity of what he was offering her, she finished the short document, reached for a pen and signed it.

"The signature cards, too," he prompted. "I opened an account, but it will have your new, that is, your married name. The cash is to tide you over until then."

"It could probably tide me over until next year!"

"Please, Tara, just allow me this," he pleaded.

"I guess this will work out okay," she told him. "I need to shop for Molly, anyway."

He frowned. "I also thought you might want to buy something new for the wedding." But he sounded as if the words were dredged up from six feet under.

She didn't know what to say so she just nodded.

"Well, then."

Silence dropped like a cement wall.

"I spoke to my mother today. Needless to say, this was a shock to her. I thought I'd take Molly by in the morning and see if I can talk my mother into going to the mall with us."

"Whatever you think best."

Whatever I think best? Don't you ever think about this?

"I grocery shopped today, but I really don't know the kinds of things you eat. If you'll give me a list I'll make sure we have them."

"I'm not fussy. Anything is fine."

"Fine."

Something simmered between them that neither of them wanted to acknowledge.

Cole cleared his throat. "I'm sure you must be exhausted and ready for bed."

"Yes. I guess I am." She rose on legs not quite steady and pushed back her chair.

When he handed her the folder with her copies of everything, their hands brushed, and she almost jumped at the spark that passed between them. She saw him pull his hand back and realized he'd felt it, too.

They stared at each other, the look a mixture of surprise, bewilderment and panic.

Oh, this is so not good. This stupid agreement isn't twenty-four hours old and already I can feel trouble.

"G-Goodnight," she stammered, backing out of the room. She literally ran for the stairs and up to her room, dropping onto her bed and throwing her arm over her eyes. Her heart raced and her whole body felt flushed. Pulses she didn't even know she had throbbed as if they were some animated neon sign.

Was this what happened when you didn't have sex for years? Hadn't even wanted it? She'd better get control of herself, or her business arrangement would turn into a disaster. The fact that Cole had reacted, too, only made things worse. How had she gotten herself into this?

Forcing herself to sit up, she dug her cell phone out of her purse and called her parents to give them the details of the wedding ceremony. *That* ought to get her heated urges under control, she thought.

* * * *

Cole sat at his desk with his head in his hands.

You stupid shit.

He was batting a thousand in his "How To Fuck Up My Life" program. Hadn't he learned a thing with Maggie? Of course, comparing her to Tara was like comparing Hell's Kitchen to Park Avenue, but the end result was still the same. His dick kept getting him in trouble.

Sex had been the farthest thing from his mind when he'd concocted this crazy scheme. It was one good reason why Tara had seemed the logical choice. Efficient well-groomed, sexless Tara.

Sexless? Bull!

Damn Sean anyway. Ever since he'd rearranged Cole's thinking about the woman, Cole couldn't make his body behave. Definitely not his cock. Well, he'd better figure out how, or he'd be in deeper shit than he already was.

* * * *

Tara opened her laptop and surfed the Internet, looking for information on the care and feeding of five-month-olds, but it seemed no two babies were alike. She'd have to wing it, at least until she could throw herself on her mother's mercy and get some advice. She called Lindsey, who put Tara at ease at once. And her mother agreed at once to go shopping, but Tara knew she had an ulterior motive and prepared herself for what she knew would be a not-so-subtle interrogation. Finally she showered and pulled a robe on over her nightgown. Molly was sure to wake soon for a bottle, and she didn't want to traipse around the house in a way that sent the wrong signals to Cole.

Actually, they're the right signals, but I'd better shut them down. Fast.

At eleven, Molly woke, making little noises in her crib. Tara managed to get down to the kitchen, heat a bottle and be back in her room without running into Cole. She peeked down the hall and saw the den was dark, and when she passed his room, heading back to hers, the door was shut with a faint beam of light shining out beneath it. Was he in there reading? Thinking? Regretting the bargain? Pushing the thoughts from her mind, she fed Molly, rocking her to sleep before slipping back into her own bed.

Even as tired as she was, she had trouble falling asleep. The major changes in her life had her mind in turmoil. Applying for the license and buying the rings felt as if they'd happened to someone else. And of course, overriding everything was this unexpected and increasing sexual attraction to Cole. She closed her eyes, and immediately Cole's face swam before her.

"You're so beautiful." In her dream, he was lying beside her, his hand mapping her body with gentle strokes. "I love your nipples, the way they feel when I put my lips around them."

She felt the familiar flutters in her pussy, the surge of liquid inside the swollen, pink folds. His fingers danced through the curls surrounding her sex then dipped into her slit, finally probing at the entrance to her wet channel.

"Spread your legs for me." His voice was hoarse, thick with lust.

She complied, but at the same time reached for his shaft, its thickness burning against her thigh. When she wrapped her fingers around its length, his breath hissed through his teeth.

"Do that too much, and we'll be over before we start."

She slowly slid her fingers from root to tip then raised her hand and moved it across his chest. She loved the soft feel of the fine hair covering his hard muscles, and she twisted her fingers through it.

"You feel so good," she murmured, heat building inside her like a fire spiraling out of control.

"So do you. And you taste good, too."

He shifted his position and dipped his head between her thighs, his tongue lapping the trail his fingers had traced on her slit. When he reached her clit and rasped back and forth across the tip, her body began to shake with need. He teased her with his tongue, tormented her, while one hand reached for a breast and fingers lightly pinched a nipple.

Her orgasm gathered deep inside her, and she pushed at his head.

"Inside me," she whispered. "I want you inside me."

He gave her cunt one last lick then reached for the condom on the bedside table. Sheathing himself, he moved into position, lifted her with his hands and plunged inside her with a swift stroke. The first flutters of orgasm clutched at him, drawing him deeper inside her. Tara wound her legs around him, locking them at the base of his spine and arching herself to ride his pulsing cock.

"I can't last." His breathing was harsh, uneven.

"I'm there." She moaned his name.

His eyes, dark with lust, bored into hers. "Now, Tara. Now."

He thrust one last time, a powerful movement, and they exploded together, shudders racking her as his body stiffened. She felt him spurt through the thin latex sheath and pressed his rigid body harder against her.

He rode her through the aftershocks, gasping for breath himself and...

Tara sat up in bed, heart racing. Once again she'd fallen into an erotic dream. Her body was covered with perspiration, her hand again between her legs. Panicked, she leaped out of bed and raced for the bathroom, turning the shower on and stepping into it. As she let the cool spray beat down on her body, she was thankful she'd closed her door. In her own home, she slept with it open, but here, she wanted the privacy. She could just imagine Cole's reaction if he stumbled on her little performance. The bargain would be ended before it even began.

Chapter Five

Cole was gone when Molly's cooing noises drifting in from the nursery to wake Tara the next morning. Even though it was only six, she worried about running into him in the kitchen, but he must have been up at dawn and left the house. There was no sound of anyone in the house, his bedroom door was slightly ajar, and when she checked the garage, his car was gone.

Was he running away, escaping the confines of their situation? Did he have buyer's remorse? In any event, she felt relief, unsure if she could face him without the remnants of last night's dream showing on her face.

Back upstairs, she lifted the little girl from her crib.

"Oh, sweetheart, you are such a love," she said, nuzzling her cheek against the baby's soft skin. The pain she'd lived with for so long shifted, fading in the warmth of the tiny child she cradled.

Molly blinked at her and gave her a drooling smile.

Tara hugged her tightly. Already she felt a sense of possession. After she'd changed and fed Molly then put her back in her crib, she called her mother.

"I need help," she confessed. "I have absolutely no idea what Molly's schedule is, and I have to shop for her, too. There seems to have been some...miscommunication about what she needs."

And isn't that an interesting way to put it. "I'm kind of winging it," she went on. "But she just had a bottle so she'll probably sleep for a couple of hours."

"You can figure she'll be up by ten," Irene said. "I'm more than happy to help with the shopping."

"Thank you," Tara breathed, relieved.

"Feed her then come pick me up. Bring another bottle for backup, just in case. If you leave as soon as she's fed, we should be able to get enough done before she has to go down for her afternoon nap."

After she hung up, Tara wandered through the house, exploring the place that was now her home. Although well designed and beautifully decorated, the atmosphere had a sterile quality with no personal objects of any kind anywhere, no hint that a child lived within its walls, or even a memory of Maggie. The house was wiped clean of her existence.

Tara frowned, wondering if she could find a way to ask Cole about this. She had no idea yet what topic was forbidden and what wasn't.

Back upstairs, she peeked into Cole's room, noting the bed hadn't been made and she chastised herself for it. Of course, she should have checked this morning. Tomorrow, she would remember to take care of it.

While Molly napped, she made her own bed, showered and dressed in slacks and a short-sleeved sweater and fixed herself a cup of coffee. Sitting at the kitchen table, sipping from the mug, she stared through one of the big windows at the peaceful scene outside and wondered for the thousandth time if she'd just made the biggest mistake of her life. A week from today, she'd Mrs. Cole Cassidy. She would be able to ease some of the financial strain on her parents and, for once in her life, have no worries on that score herself.

And she'd have a child to love and care for, to watch grow into a young woman. Was it a fair enough trade? And could she fulfill her role for what seemed like an endless stretch of years? What about the growing attraction to Cole? Would she be able to hide her feelings indefinitely?

Her stomach cramping as tension rolled over her, she dumped the rest of her coffee and rinsed the mug. Time to put all of that out of her mind. She could do this. She could. And she would.

* * * *

"I have to say, Tara, your father and I are completely stunned by this whole thing."

Irene McKee sipped at her hot tea, watching her daughter over the rim of her cup.

They'd decided against the mall for a number of reasons, first and foremost being there didn't seem to be a stroller or carriage anywhere that she could use for Molly. In the end, they chose a huge baby store that had everything she needed. Dipping into the cash Cole had given her, and with her mother's guidance, she'd purchased everything she needed, including some adorable new clothes and what looked as if it were a year's supply of diapers.

Molly now sat in her carrier on a chair between Tara and Irene, batting at a tiny mobile Tara had fastened to the handle, while the two women treated themselves at an exquisite French bakery and coffee shop.

"Yes, I'm sure you are." No more than she was, Tara thought. "But sometimes things happen that just seem so right you can't say no."

Irene sighed. "I just hope you know what you're doing." She looked over at Molly. "And this child. She's absolutely adorable, but what's the story here? Cole's wife has only been dead for a couple of months. Is he just looking for someone to raise his child?"

Tara concentrated on pulling a tiny piece from her croissant. She didn't want to look directly at her mother, afraid her face would give too much away.

"Of course, he wants someone who'd be good for Molly," she finally answered. "But that's not the primary reason. We're good together, we know each other well. We fit."

She could feel her mother's eyes on her.

"I haven't heard you say yet that the two of you are in love with each other," Irene pointed out.

"Of course, we are." Tara concentrated harder on her pastry. "That goes without saying."

Irene sighed. "It's your life, honey. I just don't want you to make another mistake."

"I'm fine, Mom. Honestly." Now, she looked up then glanced at Molly and back at her mother. "And you get a grandchild without having to wait any longer."

At that moment, Molly gurgled, and the two women laughed.

"I guess, I'll just have to trust you know what you're doing." Irene squeezed Tara's hand. "In any event, your father and I would like to have dinner with the two of you. We hardly know Cole."

She means, except as someone I work for. If I were in her place, I'd have the same reservations.

"Why don't you come to the house Saturday night, and I'll cook. That way you can see where I'm living too."

"Yes, where you're living..."

Tara leaned across the table. "Please don't judge me. I want to do this, and I need your support."

"Oh, honey." Irene sighed. "You know you've got it."

* * * *

She was in the kitchen putting the finishing touches on dinner when she heard Cole come in through the utility room.

He stopped to survey the scene, much as he had done the night before. "I guess I wanted to make sure I wasn't imagining things." He smiled. "Everything seems so...organized."

Tara flushed with pleasure at his words. "Having a routine is nice," she agreed. "But you still haven't told me what you like to eat. I want to be sure to fix foods that appeal to you."

"I'll eat just about anything that I can chew," he told her. "Please, just fix whatever you want to."

"Why don't you go and change. Molly's down for the evening, and dinner is just about ready."

"All right."

She breathed an inward sigh of relief when he reappeared in a polo shirt and jeans rather than the too-revealing sweat pants. She filled their glasses with iced tea and served their food from the stove. When everything was in place, she sat down opposite Cole. The tension between them was almost visible, certainly obvious in their posture. Was she wrong, or was it more than just the climate of the situation? Was that heat she saw in his eyes as they swept over her or just wishful thinking on her part?

Tara shook out her napkin and placed it in her lap, took a sip of iced tea and set down her glass. Might as well get this over with now.

"I saw my mother today," she began.

Cole's features tightened. "How did that go?"

"Fine, fine." She sipped more tea. "She and my father have asked us to have dinner with them, if that's all right with you."

He put his fork down. "Tara, they're your parents. They know you're getting married. It's reasonable they would want to get to know me better."

A soft puff of breath whooshed from her in relief. One hurdle down. "I invited them here for dinner tomorrow night. Saturday. If we eat at eight," she continued in a hurry, "Molly will be down for the evening. If they want to see her, I'll take them up to the nursery. She won't be part of the...festivities."

A muscle jumped in Cole's jaw line. "Fine. If that's what you think would be best."

She'd hoped for a little more enthusiasm, but at least, he hadn't said no. "Thank you." She picked up her fork then went on in a casual tone. "I was taking inventory for tomorrow night and noticed that your liquor cabinet is empty. Would you like me to restock it?"

"No." He bit off the word, his tone vicious. "No liquor in this house. Wine for dinner, but that's it."

Tara was shocked. She wanted to ask him why, but at the look on his face, she kept her mouth shut. She was walking through a minefield here and would need to step very carefully. Then she almost stepped on one more.

"I apologize for not straightening your room today. I guess I was just too busy with everything else. I'll do it tomorrow, though."

Cole put his fork down carefully and squared his glass with his plate. "You do not need to do anything with my bedroom. There's no reason for you to go in there. You don't need to clean house, anyway. Set up a regular day with the service. They can change the sheets and towels when they're here."

What was wrong with her going into his room? Was there some secret she wasn't allowed to know? Sighing internally, she switched to a different topic, trying to diffuse the situation.

"All right. Thank you. I had a chance to really look at the house today. It's beautiful. Your wife had excellent taste." The moment the words were out, she could have bitten her tongue. Maggie was a closed subject—one of the rigid rules set down.

"My wife had nothing to do with it," he said, the edge of bitterness back in his voice. "It was done before we were married."

Things were getting more complicated by the minute. Tara wondered if she would ever know the whole story, or if she'd just keep falling into black holes. They finished dinner in silence then he headed for his den. Tara didn't know if he expected her to stay downstairs and talk to him or just make herself scarce. She was still struggling to adjust to a Cole completely unfamiliar to her.

In twenty-four hours, she'd discovered she was living with a man who was uncomfortable in his own house, who couldn't interact with his own daughter, and who hid painful secrets that laid traps she seemed to keep falling into.

But there was a need here so great there was no way she could turn away from it. She paused tentatively in the doorway to the den. "If there's nothing else, I'll go upstairs now."

He looked up, forcing a smile, then leaned back in his chair. "I'm sorry, Tara. This is still very new for both of us. Don't worry. We'll figure it out as we go along."

"All right." What else could she say?

"I'll be leaving early in the morning again," he told her. If you need anything just call me at the office or on my cell."

"Thank you." She backed away headed upstairs.

* * * *

Cole stayed in the den long after Tara went to her room, disconnected thoughts bouncing around in his brain. In just two days, things here had improved beyond his wildest expectations. For the first time in months, he felt better about life, not so absorbed in his own misery.

When he finally felt tired enough to go upstairs, the nursery door stood open as well as the door to Tara's room. Knowing he was making a big mistake, he walked silently down the hall to stand just beyond her door. She was just turning back the covers on her bed. Backlit by the bedside lamp, the curves of her body were visible through the sheer fabric of her gown. At once, his rebellious cock hardened to almost painful rigidity.

Why couldn't he have married someone like her to begin with? But he knew the answer to that. He'd been down that road and had no one but himself to blame. The problem was what did he do with his body that refused to obey commands anymore?

She turned, startled at seeing him. "Oh!" She grabbed for the robe at the end of the bed. "I...didn't expect to see you."

Nor had he expected to be standing here. But he couldn't stop staring at her, at the body the robe couldn't hide very well or the cloud of dark sable hair floating to her shoulders. His hands itched to reach out and run his fingers through it, but thankfully, his feet were rooted to the floor.

"I'm sorry," he finally managed. "I was just checking to make sure you were all right."

"I'm fine. Thank you." Hugging her robe around herself, she walked to the door and put her hand on it to close it.

For a moment, she stood there. Her eyes met his and the heat that flared between them was hotter than any fire he'd ever lit. Hell! This was a problem he didn't need. He was no doubt the world's biggest fool. One of them had to be sensible until the feeling went away. This whole situation was precarious enough without introducing sex into it.

"Goodnight," he finally managed.

"Goodnight." She closed the door firmly, clicking it shut with a definite finality.

Cole trudged back to his room, four walls that held some of the most unpleasant memories in the world. A prison of his own making. Would this torture never end?

At last, he got into bed, but he lay staring into the dark for a long time.

Chapter Six

"I'm in town, and I'm coming by for lunch, if that's okay."

Lindsey Varner's voice was bubbling and just the tonic Tara needed as she fretted over the coming evening.

"Great." Tara smiled. Lindsey was obviously making an effort to smooth over an awkward situation. "I'll throw together a salad."

"I'll bring a fattening dessert."

Even though it was Saturday, Cole had been up early, just leaving for the office when she came downstairs to heat Molly's bottle. His way of avoiding things, Tara was certain, so she was glad to have some company.

Lindsey arrived at twelve-thirty sharp, carrying a small bakery box and grinning broadly. "I never can resist Charlotte's goodies. They make the most wonderful French pastries."

"I've set us up in the kitchen."

Lindsey looked around as she walked down the hall to the big sunny room. "God, I can't believe the difference in this house in just two days. It even *smells* fresh."

"I raided a lilac bush I found in the back." Tara pulled a big salad bowl from the fridge. "I haven't even had time to see what all is planted. I want to look at everything before the yard service comes next week."

"It's a real transformation, but I guess you know that."

Tara busied herself pouring their iced tea.

"I know we don't know each other all that well," Lindsey said, sipping the cold liquid, "so please tell me if I'm overstepping here. I just have to say, you have more guts than I think I would. This is quite an arrangement you've agreed to."

Tara picked at her salad. "I figured Jake had told you all the details."

"Please don't be upset with him." Lindsey reached over and put a hand on Tara's arm. "We have no secrets from each other, and Cole is a very close friend."

"I know, and it's all right." She sighed. "I guess I'm just glad he has someone to talk to."

"And you need someone, too." Lindsey fixed her with her clear blue eyes. "We don't know each other that well yet, but I'm hoping that will change. I want to be your friend, Tara. You've taken on an enormous job here."

"Molly is well worth it," Tara said, forking a piece of lettuce into her mouth.

"This past year almost completely destroyed Cole, or I might have killed him for putting you in this position. It's just that, well, I know what he's been through so I can excuse a lot of things."

Tara wanted to ask Lindsey what she was referring to and why things were so weird in the house, but she wasn't sure how to approach the subject. "Do you know the whole story of his marriage?" she asked finally.

Lindsey hesitated for just a fraction of a second. "I think that has to be Cole's story to tell. And he will, when he's ready. All I can tell you is he's one of the finest men I've ever met. He was a rock for Jake and me when everything came down for us."

Tara nodded. She knew that the Varners had run into some rocky times before they'd married, and Cole had been there for both of them. "I wouldn't have accepted this if I didn't admire and trust him a lot. Right now, everything is very fresh, though, and I think we're still feeling our way."

"'Each day in its own way,' my mother used to tell me, and I have to say I believe it. I just want you to know I'm here for you."

Tara looked at the woman across from her, so calm and serene and warm. She was suddenly grateful to Cole for suggesting the phone call.

"Do you think Nicki could babysit for us next Friday? The wedding's at five, and it's a bad time to be juggling her schedule. Not to mention the fact that Cole will freak if he has to be anywhere near Molly."

"I'm sure she'd love to. I'll call her tonight and give her a heads up."

The situation with the baby was another thing she wanted to ask about, but she was sure Lindsey would punt this back to Cole, also. Would he ever get around to telling her the whole story?

Cole still hadn't returned by late afternoon, and Tara began to wonder if he as just going to hide out until dinner was over. Dinner was in the oven, the dining room table set and she was just getting ready to go upstairs to feed and bathe Molly when Lindsey called to tell her she'd spoken to Nicki.

"She's happy to do it. And she only has a half day of school next Friday, so she'll come early if you want. She can watch Molly while you and Cole dress for the wedding."

"That would be perfect. Thank you again." She hung up the phone.

"Who are you thanking for what?"

She'd been so engrossed in her conversation she hadn't even heard the garage door go up or Cole come into the house.

"That was Lindsey. Nicki's going to babysit Molly next Friday. She's going to come here a little early so we have time to dress."

"Good." Relief flashed across his face for a brief moment. "And I'm glad you and Lindsey connected. I think the two of you could become good friends."

"So do I." *And heaven knows I'll need one.*

Despite her misgivings, the evening went even better than she hoped. Of course, she shouldn't have been surprised. She'd seen Cole at work, talking, smiling, using the famous Cassidy charm. She knew how well he could play a part. In the role of the perfect host, he was on solid footing.

Her father kept squeezing her arm and whispering, "Smart move, Tara. Very smart move."

"Thank you for tonight," she told Cole as they waved goodbye to her parents.

He frowned. "Tara, you must have a very low opinion of me to think I wouldn't want your parents to feel comfortable with this situation."

"I'm sorry." She felt herself tense up. "I just didn't want to put you in an awkward situation."

He sighed. "I know, and I'm sorry you have to worry about it. I want to make things as easy for you as I can."

"They think Molly is adorable."

"Fine. That will make life a lot easier for you." His face was lined with pain, his eyes filled with such anguish, Tara didn't know what to make of it.

"Don't you like children?" The words were out before she could stop herself and she wished she'd bitten her tongue.

A muscle jumped in his cheek.

"More than you know," he said in a harsh whisper. There was no mistaking the heartbreak in his voice. He turned on his heel and headed toward his den.

Tara bit back her tears and slowly climbed the stairs to her room. Whatever was eating at his soul, she hoped they could fix it before it destroyed him. Or both of them.

* * * *

The next week was a blur for Tara. She moved her clothes and personal things from her house and shopped with her mother for a wedding outfit. She checked daily with Cole to make sure the temp was working out. And Friday moved closer and closer. She was glad for all the activity. It kept their problems at bay and her hormones from getting out of hand. Living in the same house with Cole was proving more of a challenge than she'd expected. If they accidentally touched, that same current sparked through them, like a miniature thunderbolt, startling them both. By unspoken agreement, they carefully avoided mentioning it, but it didn't seem to be going away. At least, she hadn't had any erotic dreams for a few nights.

Thursday night when Cole came home, he startled her with the news he'd made reservations for dinner after the ceremony.

"I thought we should do a little something to celebrate," he said.

"That's very nice of you." She hadn't expected a celebration of any kind.

"I want this to be a nice evening for you, Tara. It may not be the most standard marriage in the world, but we should treat it as something special, don't you think?"

She was touched by his thoughtfulness and felt the tension begin to ease. She smiled her thanks at him.

Promptly at one-thirty on Friday, Nicki Varner rang the doorbell. Once Tara had given her instructions, she hurried upstairs to get ready. She expected Cole home in a little while. He'd said they needed to leave at four.

Upstairs, Tara organized everything she needed. Her treat for the day was going to be a long, relaxing soak before she dressed, something to soothe and relax her. She was determined to approach the ceremony and dinner with the right attitude, although she wasn't exactly sure what that would be. She closed the door from that bathroom to the nursery and locked it, giving herself complete privacy. Submerged in the hot water and bubbles, she closed her eyes and just let her thoughts drift.

He stood at the door to the bathroom studying her in the tub, that same heat flaring in his eyes...

"That looks good. Is there room in there for me?"

Tara felt her body respond immediately. "It's a big tub. Come on in."

In seconds, his clothes were piled on the floor and he was lowering himself into the water behind Tara. His legs bracketed her on either side, and she felt the thick hardness of his cock pushing against her buttocks. His hands slid up the soapy slickness of her ribs and cupped her breasts, thumbs rasping against the already hardened nipples.

"I love to touch you everywhere." Cole's breath was warm against her skin as he pressed his lips to the sensitive spot beneath her ear. "Your body is so responsive."

"Only with you," she murmured.

He pressed his thighs against her, gripping her, pushing himself more tightly against her. "You have no idea how much I love to fuck you. Your cunt is so tight it's all I can do not to come the minute I'm inside you." He nipped at her earlobe. "Is it the same for you?"

"Yes. Nothing's better than having you inside me."

"Nothing?" he teased. "What about this?" One hand slipped down to cover her mound and press against her folds. "And this?" His finger dipped into her flesh and rubbed up and down. "Or this?" He slid the finger inside her, curling it to scrape the sensitive nerves.

"*Yes*," she hissed, shifting to impale herself on the finger. "Oh, yes."

"And what about this?" The finger moved upward to touch her clit, lightly rubbing back and forth across the tip.

She felt the familiar flutters in her pussy, the clenching of the walls and wriggled against him.

"I'd fuck you now, but I don't have a condom."

For a heart-stopping moment, she thought he'd leave her in this state of suspended arousal. Then he moved his hand back down to her opening, and this time he thrust three fingers inside her. With the fingers of his other hand, he pinched her nipple, hard, then shifted it downward so his thumb and forefinger could grasp her clit. As his fingers moved in and out of her cunt, he stroked her clit with the same rhythm. His voice was almost harsh in her ear as he described to her over and over what he was doing to her and what he wanted to do.

Tara had to clutch the edges of the tub to hold herself steady, leaning back against the solid wall of Cole's chest. The orgasm rose up and grabbed her so suddenly it took her breath away. She convulsed around his fingers over and over again, pushing down on them, needing to get them as deep into her as possible.

"That's it." His voice was heavy with lust. "Come like that for me, Tara. More. Yes. Like that."

She was barely conscious of the water splashing over the side of the tub, rolling in little waves. *For some strange reason, it was making a loud, banging sound. Like a knock...*

"Tara?" Cole's deep voice. "Are you okay? I heard some strange noises and got worried about you."

Her eyes flew open.

Oh, shit.

That *was* a loud banging, Cole's knuckles n the door. She sat up, sloshing more water over the side, trying desperately to compose herself. She certainly didn't need him breaking in here because he thought she was in distress. Oh, it was distress, all right, but of a different kind.

"I-I'm fine," she called. "Doing great. Thanks."

There was a slight pause. "Okay. If you're sure. Remember, we need to leave at four."

"I'll be ready," she assured him.

The tub water soothed her body, but her face was steaming hot, not just from the dream but because she'd nearly been caught. What was she going to do? She couldn't keep doing this. Maybe she could take some kind of pill.

Yeah, right. She snickered at that. She'd need a lot more than a pill.

Sighing, she used her toes to release the plug, pulled herself out of the water and stepped onto the bathmat. Every inch of her body still tingled, especially her now-sensitive nipples and the walls of her cunt. She definitely needed to pull herself together before facing Cole again.

She looked at the little clock on the vanity. Three o'clock. Time to get busy. Wrapping herself in an oversized towel, she seated herself at the vanity and began to work on her hair and makeup.

* * * *

What had she been doing in the bathroom that caused the noises he'd heard? Cole imagined her in the tub, and immediately, his cock hardened. That naked body under a froth of bubbles, maybe with her dark hair piled on top of her head, leaving her neck bare for him to...

Stop it! You'll ruin everything.

In his room, he stripped off his clothes, headed for the shower and turned it on full force. Maybe the water could beat whatever this out of him.

Whatever this is? It's pure lust, damn it all to hell. Remember the trouble you got in last time? And this woman is going to be living in the house with you, so get over it.

But his body and his brain didn't seem to be in sync. He closed his eyes and his stupid brain took off on its own again.

The spray from four showerheads danced on the satin skin of her naked body...
God, he didn't think he'd ever get tired of looking at it. High breasts with dusky rose, pointed nipples. Slender waist. Slightly rounded tummy, just enough to give it a sensuous curve. Hips curving down to her thighs, with the soft thatch of dark curls between them, covering her delicious cunt.

"Let me bathe you," he murmured, working the shower gel into a lather with his hands.

"All right," she whispered in a husky voice.

"Close your eyes."

When she did, he began sliding his hands down her body, from shoulder to hip, from neck to navel, pausing along the way to knead her breasts and tease her nipples until she was moaning softly. The moan turned into a hum when he smoothed the lather over her hips, her thighs and down the length of her legs. He circled her ankles with his fingers then trailed those same fingers up to the inside of her thighs.

She was trembling under his touch now. When he probed her slit, finding the entrance to her pussy, the humming sound grew louder and she flexed her hips at him. But before he could impale her on his fingers, she jerked away from him.

"What..."

She shook her head, smiling and reached for his iron-hard shaft. The feel of her fingers around him shattered every ounce of self-control. He had wanted this to be for her, but as always, she refused to take pleasure without giving. In his entire adult life, he had never had this kind of off-the-charts sex with a woman who gave as much as she took. It pierced him emotionally as well as physically.

"Lean back and enjoy," she murmured to him.

And so he did, propping himself against the tile wall of the shower, closing his eyes and giving himself over to the carnal enjoyment. One hand reached down to cup his balls while the other set up a steady rhythm, stroking his cock from root to tip, moving faster and faster.

Then he was there, hips rocking as he jerked in her hands, spilling over her fingers.

He opened his eyes, wanting to see the heat in her eyes as he came for her and...

Shit! Damn it all to hell.

The shower was empty except for him. It was his hands pumping his cock and squeezing his balls. He'd fucking done it again. He was angry, aroused and panicked, all at the same time. Angry at his lack of control, aroused by the erotic images and panicky because he had an underlying feeling that something was going on here that was more than just jerking himself off.

In disgust, he turned the shower to freezing cold and let it pound at him, hoping to beat the lust from his body and jumpstart his brain. If he didn't stop having these dreams, he was going to be so totally screwed.

For a fleeting moment, he wondered if, by some rare chance, the same thing was happening to Tara. Was she having the same scorching fantasies about him? Ridiculous as it seemed, if she was and they ever actually did this for real, they would probably set the house on fire.

Meanwhile, he had to stuff himself back behind the walls he'd erected and get on with today's activities. And hope that what was going on in his mind didn't show on his face. Or worse, on his body.

* * * *

Finished in the bathroom, Tara took out the silk lingerie she'd bought and slipped it on. The feel of the smooth material against her skin was almost sensuous.

Why am I doing this? No one will ever see it.

It made her feel good, and she really needed that. Dressed in an ivory suit and matching heels, she took a look at herself in the mirror. It had been a long time since she'd dressed in anything but jeans and a blouse or T-shirt. That's what she wore to work, and that's what she wore at home. Her meager social life didn't demand anything else. She looked at the new dressed-up Tara with a mixture of anxiety and pleasure. All she needed to add to her outfit was her jewelry and she'd be all set. She hoped.

She was just tucking a pearl comb into the back of her hair when someone tapped on her bedroom door.

"It Cole. May I come in?"

Cole? What now? "Yes, of course."

He came to stand behind her. Reflected in the mirror, he looked incredibly handsome in his dark suit and snow-white shirt. The cloth hung impeccably on his large body, the shirt setting off his dark, good looks. She knew his feet would be encased in his familiar trademark boots, polished to a high gloss.

He cleared his throat. "You're an extraordinary woman, Tara. I appreciate the fact that you've agreed to do this. It appears to be working out well with the child. I want you to know I'm very grateful."

The stilted words weren't the romantic speech she'd hoped for in the unlikely event she ever remarried, but they certainly weren't words to take lightly. If gratitude was what she got, she'd take comfort from that.

"I appreciate that."

With great care, he reached around in front of her and handed her a small box.

She frowned at it. "What's this?"

"Just a little wedding gift from the groom to the bride." There was a stiffness, both to his posture and his voice. "I believe it's appropriate."

She opened the box with fingers that shook a little then gasped. Nestled on blue velvet were a pair of exquisite pearl and diamond teardrop earrings. "Oh, Cole they're gorgeous. How did you know I love pearls?"

"You're mother is a great source of information." He smiled in relief at her reaction, obviously pleased with himself. "She was only too happy to make a suggestion. I see she was right. They're perfect."

He reached to take them out of the box for her, and their fingers touched for the briefest instant. They stared at each other in the mirror, wrapped in the heat they generated. All Tara could think was, *How I wish we were going to have a real wedding night.* Mentally shaking herself, she broke the spell.

"This is very thoughtful of you," she breathed. "I'll treasure them."

His eyes never left her while she fastened the earrings in place. "You're a beautiful woman, Tara. Today you're absolutely radiant. I'm proud that you'll be taking my name."

Tara wanted to cry. It was the most personal thing he had said to her since that momentous dinner. "Thank you," was all she could manage.

He took a slim leather portfolio from his pocket, all business again. "Here's your checkbook, with money already in the account. I'll put money in every month for your personal everyday needs and for the child's. Spend it, save it, do whatever you wish with it."

Tara looked at the checkbook and stifled a gasp. "This is so much," she protested. "And I still have a great deal of the cash you gave me."

He went on, as if she hadn't spoken. "There are also two credit cards in your name. You don't need to worry about a spending limit. Use those whenever you can and save your cash for when you need it. Oh and I'm adding your parents to the company health insurance policy. This..." he indicated what he'd just given her, "should help you take care of any other needs they have that might arise. I think that should take care of everything."

She didn't know what to say. It wasn't as if he were bankrupting himself to do this. No one knew better than she did that he didn't have to pinch pennies. Alamo Construction was booming. Jake was even bidding on out of state projects. Well, Cole had done what he'd said he would and now she would do her part.

"I think I'm ready," she finally managed. "Let me check on Nicki and the baby, and we can leave."

Molly had just awakened and Nicki was in the process of changing her. Tara bent over and planted a soft kiss on the tiny forehead. The baby gurgled at her.

"She's so sweet," Nicki said, deftly taping the diaper in place.

"Yes, she is." And Tara's heart turned over. No matter that the baby's father didn't seem to want her. She would make sure Molly was loved and cherished.

The Bargain

The teenager hefted the baby to her shoulder and smiled. "Don't worry, we'll have a great time, won't we, cutie pie?"

Cole waited by the front door when Tara came downstairs. "I left the car in the driveway. I didn't think the bride should exit through the garage."

She appreciated how hard he was trying to make the day as pleasant for her as possible. It had to be twice as difficult for him. "I guess we're set then."

Everyone else was waiting for them at Judge Hoffman's office when they arrived. The judge shook hands with Cole and kissed Tara on the cheek when they were introduced.

"I always kiss the bride," he twinkled.

Tara's mother hugged her, as did Lindsey, and her father kissed her forehead.

Even Sean gave her a brotherly peck. "You've got guts, girl," he whispered. "If he gives you a rough time, just give me a call. I'll straighten him out."

"We're always here for you, Tara," Jake said in a quiet voice when it was his turn. "Don't forget that."

She was so grateful for their support she almost wept.

Then they were standing before Judge Hoffman, Lindsey to one side and Sean to the other, and the judge delivered the words that would bind them together. For better or worse. That covered a lot of territory for them. Sean handed them the rings to exchange, and they became man and wife.

Tara was dazed. There was an awkward moment when it was time for the bride and groom to kiss, but Cole never faltered, touching his lips to hers. For a moment, that spark hovering around them threatened to explode, but they quickly broke apart. Everyone hugged and kissed again, and she felt Cole's firm hand at her elbow.

"We have reservations at the restaurant for six o'clock," he told everyone, "so we should get going. We'll meet you all there." He shook hands again with Judge Hoffman then led Tara from the chambers, his hand still firmly on her elbow.

Unexpectedly, the dinner turned into a festive occasion, and it was well after ten before everyone said their goodnights and headed for home.

At the house, Tara paid Nicki and saw the young girl off to her car. Then she and Cole both headed upstairs. She had checked on Molly and was sitting on her bed in her robe and gown, her hair down and curling softly below her shoulders, when she looked up and saw Cole in the doorway.

"I just wanted to say goodnight." His eyes scanned the room. "I didn't think to ask. Are you comfortable in here? Is this room all right for you? Do you have everything you need?"

"Yes, I'm fine. Everything worked out very well." When he showed no sign of moving, she asked, "Did you need something else?"

Before she could react, he walked to the bed, pulled her gently to her feet and brought his lips down to hers. They were pressed together from shoulder to knee, her breasts against the heated wall of his chest, his erection outlined against the softness of her abdomen. Skyrockets went off in her body. Her nipples hardened into sharp points, and she felt wetness flooding her pussy. When Cole moved his tongue against the seam of her lips, she opened for him without protest. Oh so slowly, his tongue slipped into her mouth. She felt the texture of it as he danced through her warm, wet recess, the softness of his lips pressed against hers. The hands holding her were like burning fingers of flame, and his spicy cologne surrounded her. Her senses were on overload.

She couldn't pull herself away, and the kiss seemed to last forever. At last, Cole lifted his head, but his face was still only inches from hers. He cupped her cheeks in his large, gentle hands.

"I've wanted to do that every day since our first dinner. God, Tara, you taste like heaven."

She stared at him, heat rising in her face and her legs shaking. She didn't know which affected her more—the kiss or the fact that she'd responded. Cole looked as if he was about to say something else, then turned on his heel and strode from the room, leaving Tara more confused than ever.

* * * *

Shutting himself in his room, Cole fell across the bed still fully clothed, his cock still harder than steel, his balls aching. Two more seconds and he would have yanked Tara's robe and gown from her body and carried her down to the bed. Just the feel of her against him spiked his desire to an almost unmanageable level. What the hell had he been thinking?

The answer was simple. He hadn't been. His little head was leading his big head around with a chokehold. It wanted to be inside Tara McKee so badly it was driving him crazy.

What a stupid thing he'd done, but he'd been drawn to Tara like a magnet. She was beautiful, desirable, and not in the cheap way Maggie had been. Tara was a woman who deserved to be possessed with dignity, and he'd attacked her as if he were a horny teenager. The feel of her body when he'd given into impulse and pulled her into that kiss was still imprinted on him, and he could still taste her mouth.

Another minute and he'd have had her out of the robe and gown, naked on the bed, plunging himself into her.

God, wouldn't that have just taken the cake. But he'd felt her respond to him, heard her breathy little moans as his tongue plundered her mouth. She had to have been as turned on as he was.

So much for his emphasis on celibacy. She must think him either the most arrogant jerk or an insufferable ass. Had he ruined a perfectly good arrangement because he couldn't keep his hands to himself? Was she insulted because he wanted her or hurt because he thrust her away before he lost his head completely? Now what did he do? Could they wake up tomorrow and act as if nothing had changed? But it, had and it would take superhuman effort from both of them to pretend otherwise.

His fingers curled as the memory of the feel of her breasts and the hard buds of her nipples shot through him. He'd been a nanosecond away from sliding his hand beneath her nightgown to feel just how wet her cunt was. To dip his finger into that delicious liquid... At least, he was sure it was delicious. He was dying for a chance to taste it, to slide his tongue through her swollen pink flesh and probe at the entrance to her pussy. To take her clit between his lips and draw on it until she was ready to explode.

Her hand closed around his shaft and she could feel the pulsing of his blood through the thick veins. The feeling was so sensual, like velvet stretched over a rod of steel.

Somehow, her nightgown was gone, tossed to the floor, exposing her flesh to him from head to toe. He lowered himself to the bed beside her, his hands going again to her breasts even as his mouth sought hers once more. Her hardened nipples pressed against his heated palms, and he bent to take them in his mouth, one then the other. The skin of her breasts tightened as she felt the hot, moist heat of his mouth, and she bowed her body, giving him greater access.

She lay almost in a stupor as he suckled her, caressed her and nibbled the pebbled tips gently with his teeth. The hard, thick shaft of his cock pressed against her thigh, the moisture at the slit dropping onto her skin, and she rubbed herself against him. He groaned, and his hands began a further exploration of her body, drifting down the softness of her stomach, brushing the soft curls covering her mound, until he found her labia, already damp from stimulation.

Slowly, slowly, he separated the lips, his thumb rasping back and forth against her engorged clitoris. Gently, he nudged her thighs farther apart, spreading her opening and inserting one of his long, lean fingers. When a second slid in beside it, he began a slow, stroking motion, her body nearly jackknifed. She reached for him, anchoring her hands in the crisp, curling hair on the hard plane of his chest. *He felt the heavy thud of his heartbeat...*

Shit!

He was doing it again.

He pushed himself off the bed, stripped of his clothes and went into the bathroom. He turned the shower on to icy cold. It helped but only marginally. Toweling himself off, he crawled into bed, wondering how he was going to face his brand new wife in the morning, knowing he had already violated one of the bargain rules he'd set himself.

Chapter Seven

Needed to do some things with Sean. Be back in time for dinner. Don't cook. I'll bring home food. Call me on my cell if you need anything. C.

Tara read the note propped up on the kitchen counter. Just before she and Cole had returned home from the dinner, Nicki had given Molly a bottle. Wonder of wonders, the baby actually slept until quarter to seven this morning. Tara walked softly into the kitchen, wondering if Cole was wandering around at that hour, only to find the note he'd left. Apparently, he'd had the same thoughts she had. She sighed. Saturday morning, the day after the wedding and her brand new husband had made himself scarce.

In a way, she was glad. She needed the space to deal with their encounter last night and get her own raging hormones under control. Not to mention the fact that another erotic dream had consumed her last night and was still vivid in her mind. She shivered just remembering images of the hot coupling of their bodies. She couldn't seem to shut them away. Somehow, by the time Cole came home, she had to put distance between them, find a place where they could get past this little bump in the road, be cool, reserved Tara again and stay that way, without making him uncomfortable that they'd nearly violated their 'No Sex' rule.

She looked around the house before going back upstairs to get the baby. The cleaning crew had been back twice, and the windows sparkled and the wood cabinets shone. Everything had a fresh, new garden smell to it. The blinds in all the rooms were open now and sunlight flooded everywhere, casting a golden angel's kiss glow.

She had yet to venture into Cole's room, mindful of his orders. But her room was filled with her personal knick-knacks, and she'd hung some prints on the walls. The nursery was now a zoo of stuffed animals in every conceivable color, the same animals marching across the wall in prints she'd found in the children's store. Instead of the depressing environment, she'd seen that first day, the room was now lively, cheerful and smelled of the strawberry-scented lotion she used on Molly after every bath.

"Okay, sugar," she told the little girl, plucking her from her crib.

Molly sucked on her fist and stared at her with huge blue eyes.

Tara smiled, hugged the child to her heart and kissed her soft cheek.

"Looks as if it's just you and me today, kiddo. How about if after we eat, we get out the stroller and take a look around the neighborhood."

Feeding Molly was accomplished with a minimum of fuss and a lot of giggles. Once she'd washed the chubby little face and hands, she pulled out the stroller and placed Molly in the seat.

Spring in central Texas was always balmy, just on the verge of being sultry. This beautiful late spring morning was a perfect example, warm but not hot. The scent of fresh cut grass mingled with the perfume of freshly blooming flowers, swirled together on the fingers of a gentle breeze. The air had the heady feel of approaching summer.

"Guaranteed to put us in a good mood, right, sweetheart?" Tara said, fastening the safety straps.

They walked up one street and down another, letting the warmth of the day wash over them, the faint breeze kissing Molly's skin. If Tara hadn't known better, she'd have thought the infant actually smiled. It was just after ten when they got made it back to the house. The phone was ringing, and she rushed to answer it, Molly in her arms.

"Where have you been?"

She almost didn't recognize the harsh voice. "Cole? What's wrong? I just took the baby for a walk."

"Where's your cell phone? Why don't you have it with you?"

She couldn't believe how angry he sounded. "I guess I just forgot to take it. We weren't going very far. It's probably still in my purse."

"Well, take it with you, damn it. I thought something had happened to you. I've been calling every half hour."

She looked and saw the answering machine light blinking furiously. "I'm sorry," she apologized. "I guess I just didn't think. I've lived by myself for so long I'm still not used to checking in with someone. It won't happen again. Is something wrong?"

"No." She could hear him suck in a deep breath. "Lindsey's trying to get hold of you."

"What did she want?"

"She and Jake want us to come out to the ranch tomorrow for lunch." He paused for a moment. "And bring the child, I suppose."

Or what? Lock her in a closet for the day?

"That sounds terrific. Shall I call her back myself?"

"Yes," he said, his voice still abrupt but not quite so tight. "I'll be home about six. I'll pick up Chinese take-out. And don't go anywhere without that phone."

A loud click told Tara he'd hung up. She stood staring at the receiver in amazement. Apparently, he was still confronting last night, too.

After lunch, she called Lindsey.

"My God, Tara, what's wrong with your brand new husband today?" Lindsey asked. "When I told him I couldn't get hold of you, he went ballistic."

"You've got me. I just took Molly for a little walk."

"Maybe he thought you'd had second thoughts, run off and left him," she laughed. "It would serve him right."

After last night, Tara could believe it. "No such luck. I'm still here."

"Anyway, he may have already told you, but I just wanted to invite you to the ranch tomorrow. Jake wants to barbecue ribs, and he's got enough to feed a regiment of Marines. What do you say, about one o'clock? We'll eat around four."

"That sounds great. Can I bring anything?"

"Just yourselves. See you tomorrow. We'll have fun."

* * * *

Across town, in his brother's condo, Cole Cassidy snapped shut his cell phone and shoved it into his pocket, feeling like a fool and an idiot.

Sean scowled at him, having heard one side of the phone conversation. "Well, that went well," he commented. "I thought you were going to bite her head off. That should endear you to her. Don't you think you should go home? You've been pacing and fidgeting all morning."

This morning, climbing out of the bed he'd grown to hate, Cole had felt suffocated even as his body experienced an unfamiliar emptiness. Unnerved by his actions the night before and fighting a new assault of thoughts and emotions, he'd pounded on Sean's door when the sun was barely in the sky.

Now Sean pretended to read the paper, watching his brother but keeping his mouth shut while Cole alternately paced and threw himself into an easy chair.

"I had to get out of the house."

"You just got married, and you're spending the day with me?" Sean stared, incredulous. "Are you nuts?"

"This is going to be harder than I thought." He rested his elbows on his knees and dropped his head into his hands.

"Especially if you keep running away from home," Sean pointed out.

"Can it, will you? This morning I felt I'd choke if I didn't get away."

Sean quirked an eyebrow. "Is there something going on here I don't understand?"

"I don't know. I'm trying to make this work, Sean. Everything's just...weird. I can't explain it."

"So you're hiding here with me?" He shook his head, a grin teasing his mouth. "God, you do have a problem."

"People tell me that a lot lately." He leaned his head back in his chair and rubbed his eyes. "I didn't mean to yell at her. I just didn't know where she was. I thought...she'd left."

"With or without Molly?" Sean put the paper down. "Did you do something to piss her off?"

Cole was silent, staring out across the balcony.

Sean snapped his fingers. "You want to have sex with her, don't you. That's it. Ha! I knew that ball of ice where your dick is would melt sooner or later."

"Just shut up, okay?"

"Jesus, it's not a sin to fuck your own wife. Maybe she'd even be willing."

Cole glared at him. "I said shut up."

"Fine. Tell me. Don't tell me. But whatever it is you'll have to deal with it sooner or later."

After a while, Sean made sandwiches, and they ate them on the balcony, Cole still brooding and Sean watchful.

"You think I'm a real jerk, don't you?" Cole said after a long time.

"Sometimes," Sean said, with irritation. "Listen, nobody knows more than I do what you've been through. But you can't keep running away from your life."

He let out a whoosh of air. "It doesn't seem to do much good, does it?"

"Nope. And you married a woman most men would snap up in a hot minute. You need to go home and figure out what you're going to do. So why don't you see if you can make this a real marriage?"

That was exactly what he wanted to do. Run home and carry Tara off to his bedroom. But he was sure he'd really screw himself over if he did that. He couldn't figure out where all this was coming from when he'd been prepared to live like a monk for the rest of his life. He was afraid to acknowledge the undercurrent of desire that swelled every time he looked at Tara. Or

The Bargain

the dreams that plagued him. What the hell was he going to do about it?

He sat out on the balcony, long after Sean had gone inside. His mind was such a jumble he wondered if he'd ever get it straightened out.

Sean was watching a baseball game when Cole went back into the living room.

"I guess I need to go home," he ventured.

"No kidding. Don't forget, you promised Tara you'd bring dinner."

* * * *

Tara was upstairs bathing Molly when she heard the garage door open and close. In a few minutes, Cole was standing in the door to the bathroom, watching her, not quite knowing what to do with himself. After a moment, he walked to the other side of the bathroom where the sink was out of his line of sight.

He cleared his throat. "I owe you an apology, Tara."

"Yes, you do," she said, not turning to look at him, her voice very calm. "Which particular thing are you apologizing for—running off for the day or shouting at me on the telephone? I'll take either one." She carefully avoided mentioning the scene from the night before.

"Both, as a matter of fact." He leaned against the wall. "I was stupid and thoughtless today. I'm sorry. I'll try not to do it again."

"Fine." She ignored him while she diapered Molly and dressed her for the night. "I need to give her a bottle then she might sleep through the night again."

"I've got food downstairs," Cole said. "I'll get it ready to heat in the microwave."

Molly's eyelids were drooping by the time the bottle was finished. After laying the little girl down in the crib, Tara turned on the mobile. Turning out all the lights except the night-light, she forced herself to go downstairs. In the kitchen, she poured herself a glass of water, leaned against the counter and eyed her husband. The air between them crackled.

"Everything's heated," he said, indicating the array of white cartons on the table. He'd also gotten out plates and silverware.

Good. Apparently, he wasn't going to mention last night either.

"Then why don't we eat? I don't know about you, but I'm starved."

They ate in a silence filled with electricity and tension. At last, Tara put down her fork and looked at him.

"I don't know what's going on here, Cole. There's a lot you haven't bothered to tell me. Of course, that's your choice."

He watched her through narrowed eyes, saying nothing.

She hoped he couldn't see the slight trembling in her hands. "But you might as well accept the fact that everything's got to come out sooner or later. The appropriate time will make itself known, but I wouldn't wait too long if I were you."

Panic flashed across his face. "Tara, please, I—"

"Not now. I'm really tired. I think I'll just go on upstairs."

She walked out of the room with dignity, leaving a frustrated Cole behind. But no more frustrated than she was. Secrets were going to kill them if she couldn't find a way to break down the wall he'd built. And she'd better do it before it collapsed on them, destroying everything.

* * * *

The Bargain

Sunday morning heralded another bright and beautiful day. With Cole hiding in his den, Tara took advantage of the early morning cool to push Molly around the neighborhood in her stroller again. She fixed sandwiches for lunch, but when Cole didn't emerge from his self-imposed exile, she left his food on the counter and went upstairs to dress herself and the baby for the afternoon.

The said very little to each other on the drive to the Varner ranch. Molly was wide awake, for which Tara gave thanks. That meant the baby would nap during the afternoon. Tara felt as if the trip was thirty hours long instead of thirty minutes and sighed with relief when they drove down the narrow road and pulled up before the ranch house.

"My God, Lindsey, this is gorgeous," Tara said, when the Varners came out to meet them. She sniffed the air, a heady mix of prairie grass, hay, horseflesh and leather.

Lindsey grinned. "We love it here. Jake was a city boy all his life, but now he wouldn't live anywhere else."

The afternoon proved a respite for Tara. She and Lindsey sat on the porch drinking lemonade and eating sugar cookies baked by Luisa, the Varners' housekeeper. Jason, the Varner's year-old child, sat in the playpen burbling to himself and playing with his toys; Molly napped in the portable crib Lindsey had set up. Jake and Cole headed for the back patio. Tara sat up in surprise when she saw Emilio, Luisa's husband, lead two horses from the stable and Jake and Cole approaching.

"I didn't know he could ride," she commented.

"Cole rides a lot when he comes out here. Says it works out the cobwebs."

Tara eyed her husband carefully as he and Jake swung into their saddles. In his faded jeans, denim shirt and scuffed boots, he looked every inch the cowboy, sitting on the horse as if he'd been doing it for years. Her breath caught in her throat, and she forced herself to swallow hard. No sex, they'd agreed, and after last night, she needed to make sure she didn't give him the wrong signals. Why had her body chosen this particular time to decide to come out of the deep freeze?

She tried to focus on conversation with Lindsey, but her mind kept drifting. She was glad when the men returned and Mary announced it was time to eat.

They had dinner at a picnic table under a huge oak tree, the heat of the day fading and the huge oaks providing a leafy canopy against the sun. Despite the fact they had Molly with them, Cole seemed more relaxed, more at ease, sprawled in a chair as he laughed and joked. His enjoyment was evident in his body language and his easy conversation. Tara almost regretted when it was time to leave.

By the time she'd settled the baby, Cole had once again gone directly to his den. Avoiding the issue, she told herself, but she was grateful not to have to deal with the awkwardness tonight. Sighing as she climbed into bed herself, she wondered what was going to happen to this relationship that seemed to be turning itself upside down.

He still hadn't taken down the invisible walls around his bedroom, seeming to be much more comfortable in her room. And bed...

By now, she was more familiar with his body as he was with hers. Foreplay didn't require testing and experimentation any more. Now they remembered which touches elicited the sounds of pleasure, which ones brought forth the most heated response.

Tara loved when he took her nipples in his mouth as he was doing now, sucking on them and biting them gently until they were aching and swollen, each touch sending darts of pleasure through her body. His warm hands cradled each plump breast, kneading them while he drew on her nipples, knowing the effect it had on her and chuckling softly against her flesh.

His mouth moved farther down her body, trailing wet kisses to her navel where he circled the indentation with the tip of his tongue. But when she tried to urge him lower, he moved his head completely and placed soft kisses at the crook of each elbow and the soft inner side of each wrists. Not until Cole had she realized how many erogenous zones lurked on her body.

"Cole." His name rolled from her lips on an urgent sigh.

"Tell me what you want," he commanded, his mouth now just above the curls on her mound.

"You know," she whispered. "You always know."

"Tell me," he repeated.

Tara licked her lips. He always liked to hear her say it aloud. "Suck my pussy. Lick me with your tongue. Please." This last a little more frantic.

His low chuckle had a hoarse sound to it. "Right now."

He opened her labia as if he were unwrapping a present and lapped at her flesh as if he were a man dying of thirst. Darting inside her quivering channel, then out, then in, then tracing the entire length of her slit. Her hands fisted in the sheet as pleasure raced through her in a rush of heat. Her hips automatically lifted to urge him on more and more. When he slid two then three fingers into her waiting cunt and closed his lips around her clit, it took barely one or two movements before her orgasm crested and rippled through her like waves crashing on a shore.

Tara bucked against his mouth and hands, barely recognizing the keening sound low in her throat as spasm after spasm rocked her. The more she convulsed, the more rapidly Cole moved his fingers in and out and the harder he sucked on her clit, until he'd wrung the last drop of liquid and the last spasm of response from her convulsing body.

When he moved, she was sure he was reaching for the condom on the nightstand but instead he straddled her body. His mouth came down on hers in a greedy kiss, his tongue thrusting inside the hot well and dueling with hers. He slanted his head this way and that to give himself better angles. When at last he lifted his head, he bent to the valley between her breasts and licked the skin until it was slick and wet with her juices and his.

She watched him, wondering what came next.

Cole pressed his cock so it lay in that same valley, used both hands to compress her breasts until they gripped his cock and began moving slowly back and forth.

He was fucking her breasts! Holy hell!

"Do you like that?" he asked, his words uneven, his hips jolting back and forth.

"Yes. I-I do." And unexpectedly she did. The rasp of his cock against her skin was more arousing and carnal than she would have imagined. That was if she'd thought about it at all.

"Keep watching me," he told her. "Watch my cock. That's it. Lick your lips, Tara, as if you're tasting me."

He kept up the same motion, the same speed, until she saw his cock jerk, felt his body go rigid, and in a moment, his hot liquid splashed on her in hot spurts. She stared, fascinated, as he came again and again. When the tension finally left him and his muscles relaxed, his cock softening, he rubbed the thick liquid onto her cheeks and across her lips.

"Now you are truly mine." His voice was ragged as he labored to breathe, but his words were firm. "Mine."

"Yes. I am." She reached her arms up to him and...

The sensation of falling woke Tara. When she could brush the cobwebs from her brain, she realized the dream had been so real she'd reached for Cole and nearly rolled herself out of bed. She rolled back onto the tangled bedclothes and pressed her hands to her hot cheeks.

Hell!

This was really getting out of hand, but what could she do? How was she supposed to stop it?

* * * *

She woke in the morning more tired than when she went to bed. This time the erotic dream was even more graphic than previous ones. She swore she could feel the imprint of Cole's hands on her breasts and thighs, feel his semen on her skin, but when she looked at herself in the mirror, there were no visible marks. Nothing there. Only an insistent throbbing that demanded release.

She stared at herself in the bathroom mirror.

What's happening to me? I never had dreams like this about Mike.

Or this kind of sex with Mike, if she were honest. She shivered, hoping cold showers would work as well for her as she heard it did for men.

For the rest of the week, Cole made it a point to avoid her. He left early each morning before she was up, calling during the day to check on her in a very formal voice and telling her he would work late and eat dinner out. Well, he'd hired her to be a single mother, and it seemed that was exactly what she'd turned out to be.

Tara longed to use Lindsey as a sounding board, but the situation was too intimate to discuss. She would have felt uncomfortable sharing the details, so she kept everything locked inside and wondered how she and Cole were ever going to find some kind of even footing.

* * * *

Cole threw himself into the routine at the office. If he'd worked with a frenzy before, now he was in overdrive. No one had any idea the agony he was suffering, sitting in his office long after others had left, staring out the window into the darkened night, wondering what he was going to do.

At odd moments, in the office or in meetings, he would find his thoughts drifting and images of Tara would flit across his mind. She moved with such a graceful economy of movement, always in control, the light scent of her perfume an aura around her. He didn't trust himself to go home to her, to be alone with her.

His original idea seemed to be working, because it was obvious Molly adored her. He heard "Mama! Mama! Mama!" until he wanted to scream. It just wasn't fair. He had what most men dream about—a gorgeous wife and an adorable child—and he couldn't bear to be around one or trust himself with the other. Now, in addition to the child, he had to stay away from his wife.

Sometimes when he climbed the stairs late at night, he'd pause at the door of Tara's room, the way he had that first time and watch her sleeping. He gave thanks she couldn't see the enormous erection that sprang to life just by looking at her. How had he gotten himself into this mess?

When he couldn't stand there any more, he would go to his room, lie in the bed that he hated and stay awake until dawn, anguishing over his stupidity and his mistakes and his raw hunger for what might have been.

* * * *

Friday afternoon, while Molly was napping, Tara poured herself a glass of iced tea and took a new book out to the patio. She was so engrossed in reading, she didn't hear Cole come out of the house.

"Good book?" he asked.

She was startled. He never came home early in the day.

"Yes, it is. Thank you for asking." She frowned up at him. "Is something wrong? You're home early."

"Wrong? No, not at all. Can you call Nicki Varner and ask her to sit for a couple of hours?"

"I'll call her." Tara tried to keep the surprise out of her voice. This was the first conversation they'd had all week, and she wasn't about to break the mood. "What did you have in mind?"

"We're going to pick up your new car."

She blinked. "Excuse me?"

"That tin can you run around in isn't safe for you and the child. I ordered a new SUV for you. They called and said it was ready."

She wasn't sure if she should laugh, cry or throw something. "Cole, you can't just make this kind of decision for me. We need to discuss things first."

He looked as if he wanted to swallow his tongue. "Tara, I've been a real jerk since the wedding. I need to apologize to you."

Her jaw dropped. "By buying me a car?"

"You need one, anyway. Please. Just let me do this."

She wanted to put her foot down and tell him what he could do with his car, but he looked so unhappy she didn't have the heart.

"All right. I'll call her."

Cole leaned against the counter, hands in his pocket, watching her in frustration. He couldn't seem to do anything right, and he was afraid he was losing the battle in his desire for her. Tonight, they would pick up her car, maybe have a quiet dinner someplace, and he'd try to get his libido under control before Tara washed her hands of him.

"She'll be here in thirty minutes," Tara told him, hanging up the phone. "Molly's still asleep, and when she gets up, Nicki can feed her supper. How long will we be gone?"

"I thought maybe we'd road test the new car and grab a quick bite while we're out. Does that sound okay?"

"Oh. Of course. Just let me put myself together."

He wanted to tell her she looked totally together, but he was afraid a compliment would give her the wrong message. God, he'd made such a mess of things he was afraid to even tell his wife she looked nice.

* * * *

The Bargain

Tara had to admit Cole had chosen well with the vehicle. The Chevy Blazer wasn't so large she felt overwhelmed by it, and the silver color made it look less threatening. He made her get behind the wheel and drive it herself as they left the dealership.

"No time like the present to get used to it," he said.

They stopped for an early meal at a small, little-known Italian restaurant that Cole had discovered years ago. The place was jammed, but the owner greeted them as if they were long lost family and set up a corner table for them.

"I found this place by accident one night," he explained as they were seated. "The food is excellent, and the atmosphere's casual and relaxing."

And that it was. The aroma of garlic teased at their nostrils and stimulated their hunger. They shared an antipasto, savoring the sharp taste of their food and sipped on a bold, red wine. For the first time since the night of their wedding, the atmosphere between them eased. Over the main course, they chatted about common subjects—books they enjoyed, movies they'd seen, things that they liked and things they didn't. It amazed them both that they agreed in so many areas.

By the time they finished the meal, they were both feeling loose, without the tension that had gripped them. Cole took the keys to drive home, and when they pulled out of the parking lot, he took a CD from his pocket and slipped it into the player.

"New music for a new car," he told her. "I heard you listening to Springsteen one night when you were cooking dinner. This is his latest."

She was touched that he'd remembered and that he would take the time to do something so thoughtful. Maybe there was hope for them after all.

* * * *

Their social life, with the exception of one or two business dinners when Tara acted as hostess, consisted for the most part of time spent with Lindsey and Jake, but Tara was content with that. She felt comfortable with them, they knew the truth about the marriage so she didn't have to pretend, and she and Lindsey had become close friends.

And they spent more time with her parents than she had since Mike died. The Colsons adored Cole, and he seemed to genuinely like them. But it made it harder to hide the reality of their situation from her mother.

"You look, I don't know, contented but not completely, Tara," Ellen said one day when she dropped by. "Sometimes you seem as if you're living in limbo. Is everything all right with you and Cole?"

"Yes, Mother. I'm doing fine. It's a good marriage, and he makes me happy."

"I hope so, darling. You deserve to be happy. Not that we don't like Cole. We're crazy about him. I'm just concerned about you."

"Please don't worry. Everything's great."

"You're sure?"

"Yes. Positive. I have a wonderful life." She made a mental note to act less distracted when they were together. "By the way, did someone call you about information on you and Dad? Cole's adding you to the company health insurance policy."

"Yes. I meant to ask you about that." Ellen's voice sounded puzzled. "Why on earth is he doing that?"

"It's very common in situations like this." Tara had rehearsed her answer. "A lot of companies include extended families."

"Well, you be sure and thank him for us. It certainly makes things a lot easier."

And it means he's kept his part of the bargain.

She and Cole were finally at a point where they were more comfortable with each other, but only concentrated effort tamped down the sexual tension both felt bubbling beneath the surface. They dealt with it by avoiding physical contact and by going up to bed at different times.

The other problem wasn't going away, either. Weekends, Cole locked himself in his den so he wouldn't have to deal with Molly. Tara wanted to weep with frustration. She had no idea how to break down the wall he'd built around himself, and every time she tried to bring up the subject, he shut her down at once.

"I don't know what to do," she told Lindsey. "If I could just find out what's behind it, maybe I could come up with a solution. I've just never seen a man reject his own child this way, especially one so affectionate and lovable."

"He's fighting a lot of demons," Lindsey told her. "I keep hoping he'll pull himself out of it before it destroys him."

"Can you at least give me a hint?"

Lindsey's sigh was so heavy Tara heard it through the phone wires. "If it were my story to tell, I would. Cole has to realize he can't keep secrets forever and tell you himself."

Once again, he avoided both her and Molly on the weekend except for the stilted dinners when they averted their eyes and made stilted conversation. The following Monday, he came home and told her he had to go to Colorado to meet with a new client.

"I should be able to wrap this up in a day or two, but it may take a little longer," he told her, his voice uninflected. He might have been giving her a report. "There's a major developer who's interested in contracting with us to do the construction work."

"We'll be fine," Tara assured him. "Just go and do what you have to."

She found she was actually glad to have him gone for a few days. It gave her a little breathing space and, at least temporarily, took care of the problem of two strangers living in the same house.

A larger problem was the erotic dreams that just wouldn't go away. She awoke every morning feeling as if she'd spent the entire night in heated lovemaking. Her nipples would be hard, and she could feel fluid between her legs. She tried staying up late and reading, watching documentaries on television, exercising before bedtime—nothing worked. She was thankful Cole was gone for a few days. At least, she didn't always have to be on her guard.

He said little about the trip when he returned except that it was successful, and he'd tell her more about it when he had all the details together. He knew she was still interested in what went on at the office, and it was a safe area of conversation for them. The one night of easy camaraderie didn't seem about to repeat itself.

A week later, Cole came home to tell her the Colorado people were coming to town to look at some other projects Alamo had done and two of the executives were bringing their wives.

"I'll be taking them to dinner on the Riverwalk. Will you arrange for Nicki to sit so you can join us? I think having you there would make their wives more comfortable.

"Of course. I'll call her right away."

The Bargain

She made all the arrangements at the restaurant, and Cole came home from work to change and pick her up.

"Thank you for doing this," he told her.

"It's part of the bargain," she assured him and turned away. She didn't need his impersonal thanks. She'd rather have nothing. But she'd walked into this bargain with her eyes wide open so she certainly couldn't shut them now.

Sitting in the restaurant, she glanced at Cole seated at the opposite end of the table. He was looking at her with an unreadable expression in his eyes, almost as if he were seeing her for the first time. A sudden shiver ran through her body as she remembered that brief scene in her bedroom. She smiled at him, and he returned the smile, raising his glass to her in a silent toast.

God, she's beautiful, Cole thought to himself, not for the first time. He watched his clients falling under her charm, as did nearly everyone. She had taken to wearing her hair clipped back with a barrette or in a loose braid at home, but tonight she wore it loose around her shoulders, a look that reminded him of clouds of soft, brown silk. The earrings he'd given her on their wedding day glistened and shimmered in the muted light whenever she moved her head. He'd been doing well keeping his feelings under control, but he felt a sudden surge of possessiveness that came at him out of nowhere.

He was shocked to realize how much he wanted his stamp on her. He'd loved to see that coffee-colored hair with its warm golden highlights hanging loose, the way it was when she got ready for bed, and run his fingers through it. He wanted to touch that skin with its honeyed glow and make her eyes blaze with passion. He wanted the world to know this exquisite creature was his wife. That she belonged to him.

What could he say to her? *Tara, I'm sorry I was so clumsy about this before, but I want you?* Yes, in a way he'd never wanted any of the other women in his life. *I love you?* He wasn't sure he even knew what love was any more, except it led to vulnerability and pain. All he had to do was think of Molly to know how right he was.

Damn. He'd made a bargain and, if nothing else, he was a man of his word. Now, he was choking on it.

Chapter Eight

Cole and Tara arrived at a somewhat easier pattern to their existence. Dinners were not quite so uncomfortable, and she could tell Cole was making a real effort at conversation. He still avoided Molly except when it was totally unavoidable, but at least, Tara told herself, he was making an effort to make her feel more comfortable. The dreams came in intervals now, giving her some nights completely free of them. But she knew whatever she felt was still there.

She saw it in Cole's eyes, too, this unspoken sexual desire. But he'd made it plain from the very first night. No sex. They were so careful not to let whatever this was break free, but secretly they both knew it couldn't go on forever.

Fall arrived and with it the football season. Often on Sundays, the three of them would troop out to the Varner ranch to barbecue and watch the games. The visits eased the weekend tension, allowing Cole to be part of the activities and still retain his remoteness from Molly.

* * * *

Sometimes when he watched her, Cole had the urge to tell her how much she'd come to mean to him, but he was afraid to open that Pandora's Box. He had enough trouble dealing with the threads of desire lurking in his subconscious. No Sex. What a stupid rule he'd established. At the time, he'd been so sure no woman would ever tempt him again. Maggie had destroyed his normal sexual desires, perverting them and degrading them, and he wasn't about to make himself vulnerable again. Even if the situation was different.

Now, of course, he was hung by his own rules.

"I wonder what she was like before her husband was killed," he mused one day when Sean asked how things were going. "I only know how she's been since she came to work for us."

"I would guess a lot like she is now," Sean told him. "You don't get to be that self-possessed and composed overnight." He looked at his brother, searching his face for something. "Still fighting those feelings about your wife, huh?"

Cole shrugged. The last person he wanted to admit anything to was his brother. "Just curious, is all. She's stepped into this whole thing so naturally."

How could he tell anyone what was really in his mind? That he didn't think he could any longer avoid that fact he was falling in love with her? That he wanted to change the rules of this ridiculous marriage?

* * * *

In November, Tara took a chance and told Cole she'd like to have a big Thanksgiving dinner at the house. Invite her parents, the Varners and Sean.

"I need to do something," she pleaded when he frowned. "We've been to the ranch so many times I'm beginning to feel as if I'm a hospitality hog. I don't want to impose on my mother by adding extra people, and I'd like to have a good holiday for Sean, too."

"Fine," he bit off. "We'll have Thanksgiving. Just keep the child out of my way."

Oh, goody, what a swell holiday we'll have. Maybe, he can hang around and be the Grinch for Christmas, too.

Tara shopped and cooked for three days, choosing the menu with care and refusing all offers of help. By the time the day arrived, she was in too good a humor even to be annoyed when Cole shut himself in his den for the morning. She knocked on his door when she went to get Molly from her nap.

"Everyone will be here in an hour," she hollered at him.

"I'll be ready," came the muffled answer.

Tara shrugged and went on upstairs.

She bathed and fed Molly then dressed herself in a long hostess skirt and silk blouse she'd bought just for the occasion. Molly, no longer an infant, was adorable in ruffled pink and white. As Tara came down the stairs, her nose caught the tantalizing scents of the roasting turkey, sweet potatoes, pumpkin and apple pies and the spicy aroma of her special hot punch—all the Thanksgiving smells filling the house. They always gave her such a good feeling.

She had very high hopes for this holiday. The heat between her and Cole had been increasing in its intensity, no matter how carefully they tiptoed their way around it. Many nights Cole hid in his den while she headed for her bedroom right after dinner, and she knew it was just to avoid their being alone together.

She had finally admitted to herself that the erotic dreams weren't going to go away, and she had feelings for this man with whom she'd entered into this strange marriage, feelings it might be time to explore—if she could find a way that didn't bring them a tipping. She'd expected nothing out of this arrangement in the beginning except a child to lavish her love on. Now, it seemed Fate had taken a hand and turned things upside down for her.

Maybe this would be the night to heal whatever was wrong between Cole and Molly. The holiday spirit could open a lot of doors. Tonight, after everyone was gone, she'd find a way to test the waters.

Her parents arrived first, bringing wine and fall flowers, then Sean with more wine.

Lindsey and Jake arrived a few minutes later, both of them wearing an air of barely controlled excitement and bringing a box of their housekeeper's special cookies. They insisted on seeing Molly and playing with her for a few minutes. Cole excused himself, announcing that he needed to carve the turkey and taking the sting out of what was turning into an awkward moment. When the little girl's eyes began to droop, Tara carried her upstairs, followed by Lindsey and Ellen. They all talked nonsense to Molly while Tara put on her sleeper and settled her in her crib.

When everyone was seated at the dining room table, Jake lifted his wine glass.

"I want to make a toast. Here's to the newest Varner, who will be joining us sometime in June." His eyes sparkled, and he reached for his wife's hand.

"Do you mean what I think you do?" Tara gasped.

"Yup. Lindsey's pregnant. We saw the doctor yesterday afternoon."

Tara watched Cole, and his reaction to Jake's announcement stunned her. His eyes were filled with such despair and longing she didn't know what to do. She quickly jumped up from the table and hugged Jake and Lindsey in turn.

"I am so glad for you," she told them. "That's such great news. Does the doctor say everything's okay?"

"Yes," Lindsey told her. "I have to take it very easy again, and this is my last glass of wine for a while. But the doctor said he doesn't foresee any more problems than before. This one might even be a little easier."

"How wonderful for you. Isn't that great, Cole?" She turned to her husband, who was trying hard to rearrange the expression on his face.

"Yes, it is. That's terrific." He managed a stiff smile. "Congratulations to both of you." He shook Jake's hand and kissed Lindsey on the cheek. "It will be nice for Jason to have a little brother or sister."

The turkey was roasted to perfection, the sweet potato casserole fluffy and light, the yeast rolls hot and crusty. Compliments flew across the table. Everyone seemed immersed in the holiday spirit, and Tara's sense of expectation rose.

She kept an eye on Cole, and as the meal progressed, he visibly relaxed, although the amount of wine he consumed might have had a lot to do with it. She didn't remember ever seeing him drink more than a glass or two except for the night of his strange proposal. She tried not to stare at him, wondering what he was thinking. But the flex of the muscles in his throat as he swallow, the movement of his strong jaw as he talked, the deft way his long, lean fingers handled the wine goblet fascinated her.

Lindsey and Jake were the first to leave.

"Gotta get Mama home," Jake winked, ushering his wife out the door.

Sean and the McKees were the next to go. Tara stood in the doorway, waving and smiling until the last car had pulled away, then she turned back to Cole.

"Well, I thought everything went well, didn't you?"

"Yes. You did a great job. Everyone enjoyed themselves." He cleared his throat. "It was a wonderful evening."

"Molly was good as gold when we had her downstairs," Tara pointed out. "Don't you just want to give her the warmest hug?"

As soon as she looked at Cole's face, she knew she'd made a mistake.

"Don't presume beyond your job description." His voice was harsh, his tone cutting.

Tara's heart shifted painfully, but she reached out and touched his arm, not willing to give up. If anything were to happen between the two of them, Molly would have to be a part of it.

"Just try holding her." She made her voice soft rather than demanding. "Just once. Please. You'll see. You'll fall right in love with her. I just know it."

Cole froze then slammed the front door so hard the walls echoed with it. He nearly knocked both of them down in his haste to move away.

"You run this house," he shouted, "you run the child, you run the basic structure of my existence, all with frightening efficiency. Which I appreciate. That's what you're paid to do." His eyes blazed with fury. "Leave it at that. Do not attempt to run this one tiny corner of my life. Can you not learn to mind your own business?"

As soon as the words left his mouth, Cole wanted to take them back. Tara looked as if he'd slapped her. Her face was paper white and her hands trembled.

She turned away with more grace than he had any right to expect. "I think I'll go upstairs now. Good night."

Cole felt sick to his stomach. Well, he'd done it now. What the hell was the matter with him? How could he say something like that to Tara who deserved so much better?

Nice going, jerk.

That was the price he paid for drinking too much wine. Or anything. His mouth got ahead of his brain. Hadn't he learned his lesson yet?

"Tara, please." He turned to follow her. "I'm so sorry. I didn't mean...."

But she was already gone. An intense pain captured his heart, worse than the night he'd found out about Molly's parentage.

Tara, Tara, Tara. Oh, God, how I want you. I didn't even have the chance to tell you. Please come back and let me put my arms around you, apologize, try to tell you how I feel. For a man who's such a raging success in business, I certainly manage to keep screwing up my private life big time.

Cursing himself for his stupidity, he slammed out of the house, not even bothering with a jacket. He opened the garage door and stood for a moment breathing in the unseasonably cold evening, letting it shock the effects of the wine from his system. He leaned against the car for a long time, waiting to make sure he was competent to drive. The last thing he needed was to be arrested for drunk driving. Secretly, he hoped Tara would come looking for him, but after a long time, it was painfully obvious that wasn't going to happen. Finally, when his head had cleared and his hands were steady, he started the car and backed out into the street.

* * * *

Tara made it to the rocking chair in the nursery before she collapsed, forcing back the tears that threatened. All she could do for a long time was sit in the chair, shaking like a leaf, staring at Molly sleeping so peacefully.

Well, now what?

All day, her growing feelings for Cole had kept bubbling to the surface. Every time she sensed his eyes on her and raised her own, there was no mistaking the heat that flashed between them. Little shivers of anticipation had chased themselves along her spine as she'd thought of what tonight might bring. Would her erotic dreams finally come true?

The confrontation had destroyed all of that and wiped it away as if it had never happened. The harsh words lay there like unexploded bombs. She was as angry as Cole but wounded that he could say the things he did. Why had she forced the situation? She knew better. Clearly, after all these months, his head was still in the same place. He was a long way from dealing with whatever pain he carried. Trying to ease him into interacting with Molly hadn't been a raging success. Even today, he'd found a way to leave the room when the little girl was downstairs.

Tara had just been so sure, with everyone wrapped in the holiday spirit, that this was the time to try moving forward. Instead, she feared she'd only made things worse. What dreadful thing had happened to turn him against his adorable daughter? What tragedy in his life had closed him off from a child who was so easy to love? The hidden hope that their feelings for each other might be something real was swallowed up by the bitterness of the words he'd flung at her like so many sharp knives.

I knew better. That was a stupid thing for me to do. Now he'll hate both of us, and any hope for the future is down the drain.

Whatever drove him might just end up destroying them all.

She kept listening for his car to start, wondering if she should go out there and make sure he was all right to drive. But she knew she couldn't face him at the moment. Her pain was too intense, too sharp. She was barely holding herself together as it was.

What was he waiting for out there? Was he planning to come back inside?

Then she realized, knowing Cole, he was waiting until he was sure it was safe for him to drive.

After a long time she finally heard the growl of the engine turning over and the squeal of tires as he backed out of the garage. She managed to rouse herself and, assured that Molly was still sound asleep, went into her own room and took off her clothes. Throwing them on the chair, she pulled on the first nightgown she found in the drawer. Tired to the bone, she crawled into bed, resisting the urge to pull the covers over her head. She closed her eyes, willing herself to sleep, praying that tonight the erotic dreams wouldn't plague her. But her restless subconscious sought the pleasures she was denied when she was awake.

* * * *

Well, that was a great performance, asshole.

Cole banged his fist against the steering wheel.

You finally figure out you're in love with the woman, so you show it by insulting her. Big time. Way to go, jerk-off.

He'd give anything if he could take back the words he'd flung at her. What Tara had done was the most natural thing in the world, connecting father and child on a holiday. Her intentions came from the heart. Unfortunately, she had no idea why he felt the way he did.

It was all that damn wine he'd drunk, way past his two-glass limit. Still, the pain was so sharp a drink seemed the only logical choice to blunt his pain. And he knew right where he could get one. Jake's office where he kept liquor for celebratory drinks.

For everyone but me and rightfully so.

They had keys to each other's offices, so access there wasn't a problem, but the cabinet with the liquor was also locked.

Shit. Paranoid son of a bitch.

In his own office, he dug through a junk drawer, looking for anything to help him, finally coming up with a screwdriver. Jake would kill him for sure, he thought, as he worked to pry open the lock, but this was an emergency. At last, the cabinet was open, the door hanging lopsided. Pulling out a bottle of bourbon, he poured a shot straight and raised the glass.

"To the world's greatest screw-up," he toasted himself and gulped down the liquid. Then he refilled the glass, took it and the bottle back to his office and sprawled on the couch.

But one drink followed another and soon all he could think of was Tara. He still remembered that clumsy scene in her bedroom the night of the wedding ceremony, felt the softness of her mouth when he'd touched it, the silkiness of her skin against his palms. The heady scent of her perfume still lingered in his nostrils. He knew he couldn't run from the truth any longer. All those nights he'd lain awake in his bedroom craving her, all those erotic dreams when he'd fucked her every way possible. His body had been sending him messages. So had his heart, but he was too bitter to recognize it

Desire had grown within him all day today. He'd been impatient for everyone to leave so they could be alone, and he could try to tell her how he felt. He was filled with an almost overpowering need to make love to her and tell her how she'd made a place for herself in his heart. Then in seconds, with a few thoughtless words, he'd killed that chance.

So Maggie had made a fool of him, played a cruel joke on him. He was the one who'd gotten into the mess to begin with, and he was the one who refused to deal with its aftermath. Everyone was right. He'd turned into a self-pitying wreck that no one even wanted to be around anymore, including himself.

He wanted what Jake and Lindsey had—a loving marriage, children—and he wanted it all with Tara. He was gripped with a fierce desire to hold her naked in his arms, her breasts warmly covered by his hands, her body arched against him. He couldn't stand the thought he might lose her, and he might not ever have that opportunity. Right then, he wanted her more than he'd ever thought it possible to want a woman. But what could he do about it now?

He had no idea how long he sat there, drinking steadily. The more he drank, the more depressed he became. *What if she leaves me?* he thought. Panic coursed through him, chilling his blood. He didn't think he could stand it without her. He could not lose her. Somehow, he had to make her understand, let her know how he felt.

Afterward, he blamed what happened on the alcohol. It was easier than blaming himself. If he hadn't gotten drunk, none of it would have happened. In his right mind, he'd have slept it off and waited for the sober light of day to plead his case. But the liquor had wiped away all sense of sanity, urging him to yet greater folly. He swallowed the last of the bourbon and headed for his car.

His alcohol-fogged brain had lost all ability to reason. He had no idea how he managed to get home without running the car off the road or into a tree. He hoped Tara had not come back downstairs and set the alarm because he didn't think he could remember the code tonight.

Chapter Nine

Tara stirred restlessly in her sleep, twisting her body. The dream had engulfed her again.

A naked Cole stood beside her bed, holding his pulsating erection in his hand, staring down at her...
"I can't wait." His voice was thick with desire.

He didn't bothering stripping off her nightgown. He pressed her back against the pillows and pushed it up to her neck. She felt his heavy, naked presence as he lay down in her bed, caressing her, murmuring to her. Her hands, reaching up, touched hot, naked flesh covered with the now-familiar mat of chest hair.

His hands caressed her breasts, tugging at the sensitive nipples, laving them with a hot, wet tongue the way she loved. She pressed against his body, sliding back and forth against the hair on his chest until her skin felt stretched to bursting. He swept his tongue across them, nipping with little bites then soothing with the warm moisture. Bite them, she wanted to scream.

He moved to her mouth then down the slender column of her neck, pausing to bite nip at the tender spot on her shoulder. His breath whispered against her ear as he described in detail how he wanted to possess her, to open her up like a flower and drink of her female juices, to suck on her clitoris until she begged for mercy.

She could feel the familiar touch of his rock-hard penis prodding against her cunt, rubbing sensuously against her. He roused her body to fever pitch, and an erotic fog clouded her mind.

His mouth ravaged hers once more as his hands continue to roam over her body, touching the wetness between her legs and slipping two strong fingers into her waiting pussy. Quickening breath blew puffs of air on her skin as he followed his fingers with his mouth. His lips captured her clitoris and sucked until she tried to push his head away, the arousal was so intense. But when he slipped his tongue into her inner wetness, she could only wrap her legs around his head and hang on for dear life. She felt him all the way to her womb, lapping and tasting, as her juices poured into his mouth. Just as she thought she'd reached the crest, he backed off and moved up her body again.

Come back! she wanted to scream.

"Tara, Tara, don't leave me. I need you, Tara." His mouth slanted over hers again, his tongue probing insistently, giving her a taste of herself. "I want you, Tara. I'm so sorry. I never meant to hurt you. I love you. Don't leave me. Please. I love you. I want you."

The words she had wanted so desperately to hear.

Hot hands trailed over her soft skin, caressing the insides of her thighs, just brushing the soft, damp curls at her pussy. She was writhing and twisting under him as his fingers probed and teased, driving her mad with desire. Her body quivered at the touch. Instinctively, she opened her legs wider for him.

More, more, voice screamed in her head. Then the thick, hot length of him entered her with slow, demanding thrusts. Hands grasped her buttocks, pulling her up to him, driving deeper, harder.

Long past any semblance of control, she moved with him, matching him stroke for stroke. Consumed with an urgent need, wanting to capture him as deep inside her as she could. The top of the roller coaster ride tantalized just beyond her reach.

He was relentless, holding her hips in place, using his mouth on her breasts, sliding his hand between their bodies to rub her clit and push her beyond endurance. The roller coaster crested and plunged, taking her down into a black abyss while her world shattered around her. As her whole body clenched, she felt him thrust with his hips one last time and explode inside her, his penis throbbing, his heart thundering against her.

Then it was over, and he collapsed on top of her, spent.

A feeling of joy swept through her. Somehow tonight was different, more intense. Did that mean Cole was ready to make a real commitment to her? *She wrapped her arms around his neck and pulled him closer...*

Warm breath against her ear jarred Tara to sudden wakefulness, and she gasped with shock. Cole's naked body, slick with the sweat of exertion, lay heavy on her, his breathing labored. No! Her mind recoiled. Not a dream! Not her imagination. Reality. Slamming into her like a train wreck. Jolting her with its painful impact. Far from the reality she'd expected. All those dreams should have been the forerunner to the most explosive sex of her life, building to a climax beyond proportions. She felt somehow cheated. Unfinished.

Then the sharp, unexpected scent of bourbon assaulted her, bringing her fully awake. He was drunk. Drunk! She was stunned. Cole never drank anything stronger than wine or beer. What was going on here?

They'd certainly violated the 'No Sex' rule and not the way she'd planned or hoped for. Her husband had come home drunk and taken her as she'd dreamed about every night. And she'd let him, in a way so wanton she shuddered at the memory. Never mind she'd thought she was dreaming. It had happened and she'd let it.

Nausea rose at the back of her throat. How much worse could things get? This was not the way it was supposed to be. How could this happen with so much pain still lying between them? God, what would he think of her now? Would he hate her for accepting him? Would he apologize for being drunk, but tell her he'd needed the courage and could she please forgive him? And do it again cold sober?

Gathering what strength she had left, she pushed at his shoulders while she tried to twist her body from beneath him.

"Cole. Please. You have to move." He still lay there pressed heavily against her, and she wondered if he'd fallen asleep. Or even worse, passed out. She gritted her teeth and pushed harder at him. She didn't want to raise her voice too loud and wake Molly. That's all this god-awful nightmare needed.

"Cole. Come on. Help me here."

At last, he lifted his head, a glazed look on his face, as her words cut through the cotton in his brain. He looked down at her in bewilderment, blinking his eyes, trying to focus on the scene. She knew the moment awareness struck him. His body recoiled as if struck by ice water. Just like that, the effects of the alcohol were banished, and the truth struck him. Shaking, he climbed off the bed.

Shock replaced bewilderment on his face as his eyes raked over Tara, lying in a rumpled bed, clutching her gown as if it were a shield. He took in his own nakedness, and all the color drained from his face. For a minute, he looked as if he would be ill.

"Oh, god. What have I done? Please tell me I'm imagining this. I didn't mean..." He shoved his fingers through his hair. "Tara, I'm so sorry. So very sorry. Oh, god. I just wanted..." His voice cracked. He throat muscles worked with his effort to swallow. "This isn't the way I wanted it. Not the way at all. I don't even..."

Even what?

He turned and stumbled out of her room without finishing his sentence, head down. In a few minutes, the sound of the front door slamming reverberated through the house.

Tara lay in her bed a long time after that, trying to gather the tattered remnants of her mind. She struggled to find a shred of self-respect and reason.

Why didn't I stop him, push him away until we could deal with what was between us?

She didn't even want to think about how *he'd* feel when everything was exposed in the light of day. Would he ever want to look at her again? Could *she* face *him*?

Finally the tears she'd been forcing back all night flooded her eyes and cascaded down her cheeks. She made no effort to wipe them away, just let them keep flowing. She wanted to scream, to rage, but she could only lie there, crying silently.

At last, she pulled herself out of bed and went to the shower, standing under it for a long time, as if she could wash away the searing memory of the night. She dried herself off, pulled a fresh nightgown from the drawer and crawled back into her bed. She had no idea how she would face the next day.

* * * *

There was no sign of Cole in the morning and no note, but Tara wasn't expecting any. In fact, his absence was a relief. She felt as if she'd been in a prolonged battle, her senses and pride battered and bruised. She had no idea how they were going to get past all this. The memory of last night was burned into her mind—the brief but terrible argument, the deep, exhausted sleep she'd fallen into and the dream that wasn't a dream after all. She could still feel the imprint of his body on hers, the slide of their skin together and his touch that had drawn her up the spiral into explosive ecstasy. As much time as they'd spent dancing around it, last night should have been wonderful, not the unbelievable disaster it really was.

Why hadn't she turned him away? That was the question she kept asking herself. He must have wanted her very badly to do this, but why had he gotten so drunk? What demons pushed him to lash out at her then claim her as his own? And what had he thought when she'd accepted him so willingly into her bed and her body? Every time she thought of it, her face burned with shame. The why didn't matter. She'd done it. That was all.

"I love you, Cole," she whispered, saying it aloud for the first time. And despite what had happened, she knew it was true. "Why can't you tell me the awful secret that keeps that haunted look in your eyes? Why

The Bargain

can't we love each other the way I know we both want?"

Well, it was all blown to hell now. Any chance they might have had was certainly wrecked by what had happened. A sickness and despair settled in her heart. She didn't think it would ever go away. If not for Molly needing her, she would have gone back to bed and hoped she didn't wake up until next year.

"Oh, sweetie," she whispered to Molly as she dressed her, "I think your mama has finally run into a problem she can't solve. Whatever's got your daddy hurting so bad is more than I can handle." She pressed her lips to Molly's baby-soft skin. "If it weren't for you, I'd be gone in a flash. But don't you worry. Mama will never, ever leave you. I just wish you were old enough to give me some answers."

Molly cooed and reached up a chubby little hand, patting Tara's cheeks.

Tears pricked Tara's eyelids. No, there was no way she'd leave this child. But how could she and Cole get past this nightmare? Could they even talk to each other? What would she say to him, for God's sake?

"I want you, Tara," he'd murmured in his drunken haze. "Please. We'll be so good together."

I want you, too, Cole.

She made a pot of coffee then burned her lip drinking it while it was too hot. But the strong, black liquid seemed to shock her brain into motion and allowed her to perform her necessary tasks. She had a child to care for. A self-indulgent collapse would have to wait.

The phone rang several times while she fed Molly breakfast. She ignored it, letting the machine pick up. There was no way she could talk to Cole right now, or anyone else, so she just listened numbly as the messages played.

"Tara?" Her mother's voice. "Darling, are you there? Can you pick up? I just want to tell you what a great time we had yesterday. Well, all right. Call me when you get back from wherever you are."

I'm in hell, Mother. I don't know if I'll ever be back.

Four or five hang-up calls. Cole? What could he possibly say to her? Or she to him?

Then Jake. "Tara? Can you please answer? I just want to talk to you for a minute."

Not on your life.

"Please? Tara?"

Two more calls from Jake, the message the same. Then a call from the ranch.

"Tara? It's Lindsey. I guess you must be busy with Molly. Please give me a call."

Lindsey was the one person she even thought about talking to, but what would she say? *My husband hurt me last night with words that still sting. Then he got drunk, climbed into my bed, and I welcomed him with open arms.* That would make for great conversation.

She turned the volume down on the answering machine, but the ringing still drove her nuts, so she unplugged the phones. For a long time, she sat in the nursery with Molly, rocking in the chair while the little girl lay in her playpen and played with her toys. She wondered if her heart could possibly ache more than it did. Finally, needing the closeness, she picked Molly up and snuggled her in her lap, laying her cheek against the warm skin.

"Mama's having a bad day, sweetheart. Maybe a bad year."

Maybe a bad life.

The Bargain

* * * *

Jake had driven into town to pick up a file he needed to work on at home and get some things Lindsey needed. He was surprised to see Cole's car parked in the lot, even more surprised when he entered his office, saw the cabinet door jimmied open and the bourbon missing. When he knocked on his partner's locked office door, he got no answer so he knocked again more loudly.

"Go away." The voice was like that of a wounded bear.

"Cole. Damn it, let me in, or I'll let myself in."

"Just go away. Leave me alone."

Using his key, he unlocked the door and pushed it open then stopped, hardly able to believe what he saw. Cole was sitting hunched over on the couch, his head in his hands. His clothes were a wreck, his hair unkempt, and it was obvious he hadn't shaved. The entire office reeked of bourbon and stale sweat.

When Cole looked up, his bloodshot eyes were full of unbelievable pain. His red-rimmed eyes were those of a man not just drunk, but one who'd been crying.

Jake felt a stab of panic. "Jesus, Cole. What the hell happened? You didn't look this bad during the Maggie crisis. Why aren't you home with your wife and child? "

"It isn't my child. And my wife should pack up and leave me if she has any sense."

Jake shoved his hands in his pockets. "You want to tell me what's going on?"

Cole scrubbed at his face. "I'm a miserable bastard. That's what's going on."

"I'll agree to that if you want, but I still want to know what the hell put you in this shape. You haven't had anything but a glass or two of wine in two years." He frowned. "Did you do something stupid again?"

"Stupid. Yeah, that's a good word." He leaned against the back of the couch, his eyes closed. "First, I blew up at Tara, insulted her, said things she'll never forgive. Then I got drunk, went home and climbed into bed with her, naked. How's that for a happy holiday?"

Jake silently counted to ten. Surely, he hadn't heard right. "Is that why you broke into my cabinet and stole my liquor like some teenager? I'm sure there's a saner explanation than that."

"I wish I hadn't had so much bourbon. I could probably use another drink to blot everything out. Maybe I wouldn't hate myself so much."

"Yeah, right. That's a wonderful remedy. Go wash your face and pull yourself together while I make coffee."

When Cole returned to the office, he looked only marginally better. Jake handed a fresh mug of coffee to him.

"Don't spill it, please."

Cole sat down at his desk, his hands wrapped around the mug. "Thanks. But you better go home to your wife and child. It's a holiday, remember?"

"I'm not leaving here until you tell me what's happened," Jake said. "Or do you want me to call Tara?"

"God, no." Cole took another sip of coffee. "That's the last thing I want."

"Then start talking."

And so he did, laying out every sordid detail. He didn't know how long he talked, but he managed to get it all out. When he was finished, he looked up, his face filled with such self-loathing that Jake was appalled. In all the years, they'd known each other, he'd had never seen his friend falling apart this way.

"Jesus, Cole," he said, at a complete loss. "What the hell got into you? And to get drunk the way you did? What did you think that would accomplish? Remember what happened the last time you got into the booze. You're supposed to be an adult. It's time to start acting like one again."

"I know, I know." Cole shook his head. "The worst part is, I can't even remember everything that happened."

"What?" Jake stared at his partner. "You mean you don't know if anything happened or not? If she kicked you out of bed or..."

"That's right." Cole held his head in his hands.

"For God's sake, how drunk were you?"

"It seems quite a lot." There was nothing heroic about Cole Cassidy this morning. He was a human being whose mistakes had all come back to haunt him in one big explosion. He'd managed to fall into the hole he'd been digging for himself.

Jake knew he needed more than a pot of coffee to fix this problem. He took out his cell phone, stepped outside the office and tried calling Tara, but the answering machine kept picking up. He was sure she was ducking calls and for good reason. He hoped when she heard his voice she'd answer, but no such luck.

After three tries, he gave up and called Lindsey. "I'm only calling you because Tara's going to need someone." He visualized the stunned look on her face as he told her what had happened. "I'm sure she feels as if a truck ran over her. I don't have a clue as to how you'll handle this, but we can't just leave her alone. Someone has to be around for her, whether she wants it or not."

"Oh, my god, Jake, what a disaster."

"And listen. If you can believe this, Cole doesn't even remember if he...if they...if anything. I mean, you can't exactly ask Tara to give you details. You know?"

"That's the truth. Good lord. What a mess. Don't worry." Her sigh was loud over the phone. "All right. I'll figure out what to do. I won't leave her sitting alone in that house. But don't you dare let him go back there."

Walking back into the office, Jake found Cole sitting just as he had left him, staring out the window. He walked over and took the coffee mug out of his partner's hand.

"You can't stay here," he told him, "and you can't go home. We have to figure out what to do."

Lindsey called back before Cole could say anything.

"Tara's still not answering," she told him.

"Not even for you?"

"No. Emilio's going to drive me into town." Because her pregnancies were high risk, Lindsey's doctor didn't really want her driving and neither did Jake.

"Just take care of yourself."

"I will. Don't worry. You know, she'll be humiliated that I even know about this, but I can't worry about that now. I'm going to pack up her and Molly and bring them out to the ranch for a couple of days. And when you come home, be very gentle and discreet around her."

"You don't have to tell me that, sweetheart," he assured her in a soft tone. "I can't even imagine what she's going through."

"What are you going to do with Cole?" Lindsey wanted to know.

"You mean besides shoot him or throw him off the top of the building? I guess I'll take him to Sean's. I'm going to call there right now."

Cole's brother cursed a steady stream for more than a minute.

"I can't believe this is the same man who kicked my ass growing up and taught me self control and respect for other people." His voice held a mixture of both anger and disappointment. "This Molly thing has left a festering sore on his soul. It needs to be lanced and drained before it becomes terminal."

"Well, if we can't help him patch this up with Tara, it may not make a difference. I think it's time for us to take charge here and make things happen." Jake paused. "Can I dump him on your doorstep?"

Sean snorted. "Do I have a choice?"

"Not much." Jake laughed grimly. "Lindsey's taking Tara and Molly out to the ranch, and I damn sure don't want to leave him to his own devices."

"Sure, bring him on over. When you get done beating on him, I can take my turn."

"I'll call when we're on the way."

They both hung up, and Jake turned back to Cole.

"Okay, your brother took pity on you," he told his partner. "I hope he has some clothes you can change into. You'll probably have to burn these."

"I don't know what to do, Jake." There was a heavier note of depression in Cole's voice than his friend had ever heard. "What the hell got into me?"

"Be nice to know the answer to that." Jake shook his head. "I think you were looking for one more way to punish yourself and took Tara along for the ride."

"You want to know something else?"

Jake widened his eyes. "You mean there's more?"

"Oh, yeah." Cole ran his fingers through his hair again. "I was jealous of you and Lindsey and the new baby coming. How's that for being a good friend? I wanted a baby of my own, a child with Tara. But I didn't know how to change the rules."

Jake studied his partner's face, seeing the deep lines of pain etched into it. "Well, you sure picked the wrong way to do it." He would have said more, but he shut up, seeing the look of despondency on Cole's face.

"Do you think she'll ever talk to me again?"

"Let's hope so."

"I wanted her, Jake, but I sure hadn't meant for it to happen this way."

"Well, here's the plan," Jake told him. "Lindsey's going to take Tara and Molly out to the ranch for a few days. Tara will hate the fact that this dirty little secret is out, but I'm more concerned about leaving her alone at this point than I am about her pride."

"I shouldn't go anywhere near her after what I did." Cole's voice was full of revulsion.

"And we're done with the pity party. You're going to your brother's, where you'll hide out while we try to find a way for both of you to get past this. But first, you have to answer one question for me."

"Hide out? What about the business?"

Jake twisted his lips in disgust. "I sure don't want our staff to see you in this miserable condition. There's nothing on the books I can't handle for a week or so."

"Fine. Okay." Cole rubbed his face then ran his fingers through his hair. "Whatever you want."

"Answer one question for me," Jake repeated, "and tell me the truth or I'm outta here. Are you honest to god in love with her? No bullshit. Say it out loud so we both hear it."

"So much it's killing me," Cole admitted it. "I just couldn't... I didn't know how..."

"All right, all right." Jake cut him off. "Will you do whatever we tell you to get her back?"

"Anything. I'll do whatever it takes. I can't lose her, Jake." His voice was raw with need and hunger, the pain in his heart coloring his words.

"Okay. We're heading to Sean's. We'll just leave your car here. I'll have whoever's around deliver it to Sean's tomorrow."

He called Sean and told him they were on the way.

Chapter Ten

Tara had no idea what to do next. She could always go back to her house, taking Molly with her. She had kept the place as a backstop in case this stupid bargain came apart. But even in her darkest thoughts, she'd never envisioned anything like this.

The doorbell rang just as she finished feeding Molly her lunch. She tried ignoring it, even when it rang three more times. There wasn't a person in the world she wanted to see right now. The ringing stopped, but heavy pounding on the door replaced it.

Then she heard Lindsey's voice. "Tara, if you don't open this door and let me in, I'm breaking a window and coming in that way. You don't want to do that to a pregnant woman, do you?"

Reluctantly, she opened the front door. Lindsey stood there, her eyes intent on Tara's face. Emilio was just behind her.

"You look like hell," she said. "Come on." She grabbed Tara's arm and marched her into the kitchen, Emilio on her heels.

Molly was banging noisily on her highchair tray. The little girl looked up at everyone and smiled, showing two new teeth. Lindsey sat Tara down in a chair, found a teething cookie in the pantry and handed it to the baby.

"All right." She dropped into a chair. "Don't open your mouth until I'm finished. I know what happened last night and before you start feeling uncomfortable and trying to hide, Jake had to tell me because he was worried about you."

"Jake knows?" Tara's face turned red then white. "Oh, my god. Everything?"

"And Sean," Lindsey added.

"Has Cole told the whole world?" Tara's eyes filled with tears. She covered her face with her hands.

Lindsey tugged gently at her hands, forcing Tara to look at her. "He didn't want to tell anyone, but when Jake found him holed up at the office this morning, Cole was close to suicidal, so Jake got the whole story out of him."

Tara shook her head. "I was thinking of taking Molly to my place for a while. I can't face anyone right now."

"You listen to me." Lindsey leaned forward, forcing Tara to look at her. "I am not going to leave you alone, no matter what you say. You're coming out to the ranch for a few days."

When Tara started to protest again, Lindsey just shook her head. "Everything's already set up. You and Molly will have my old room. You don't have to do anything but sit. Luisa's wonderful about taking care of people with emotional wounds. I should know. She did it for me many times."

"Oh, Lindsey, I can't. Thank you but that's impossible." She covered her face with her hands again. "There are things you don't know."

Lindsey was adamant. "Being alone is the worst thing you can do. Cole is a good, decent man, who suffered a terrible blow, but it's time for him to deal with it. Then the two of you need to talk."

"I can't talk to him." Tara shook her head. "I can't face myself, much less him."

"Honey, when the time is right, you have to. This thing can't just lie between you like the elephant in the room."

"There's so much I don't understand," Tara cried. "What is he hiding? What is so awful that he can't tell me about it? Why does he hate Molly so much? Why did he get so drunk? Why couldn't he just come to me and..." Tara stopped, her voice threatening to crack.

"Stop. Not another word. You need some space to think, and the ranch is just the place for that. So let's get going."

"But Jake will be there and..."

"Tara." Lindsey took Tara's hands and pulled them away from her face. "Jake is one of the gentlest, most sensitive people in the world. He has his own history. I guarantee you he will go out of his way to respect your privacy and make you feel comfortable." She chuckled. "On the other hand, if I don't have any success with you, he's going to come here, throw you over his shoulder and drag you out to the ranch himself."

Tara smiled weakly at the thought.

"All right." Lindsey wiped Molly's face and hands and lifted the little girl out of the highchair, handing her to Tara. "Tell Emilio where the luggage is so he can bring it upstairs. We're going to pack whatever you need for a few days for you and Molly. What we forget we can buy. And don't argue with me. Stress isn't good for a pregnant woman."

Tara had to admit getting away from the house would be a relief. She needed to sort out her feelings.

The ranch was such a soothing place to be, and it would be great for Molly.

"You're right," she said, giving in. "The luggage is in the garage. If you can keep Molly busy, I'll get us packed." She handed Molly back and hugged her friend. "Thanks. I don't...I just..."

"It's all right. You don't need to say anything else."

* * * *

Luisa was waiting for them when Emilio brought the suitcases into the ranch house. She reached at once for Molly, who smiled and gurgled at her. The woman gave the little girl a warm smile.

"She hasn't had her nap today," Tara told her.

"We'll take care of that right now. We'll just get her into bed, and she'll go off like a rock. If you want to come up with us, Mrs. Cassidy, I'll show you how the room is fixed, and you can let me know if you need any changes."

"Tara. Please call me Tara." Formality certainly wouldn't work in this situation. She hugged Luisa. "And thank you so much."

She was touched at the trouble they'd gone to, trying to make her comfortable. Lindsey's old bedroom was huge, with a king-sized bed and a large dresser. The crib was set up close to the bed and even had a mobile attached to it. Jason's old changing table was set up in a corner and Luisa had stocked it with everything she'd need. Fresh flowers stood in a vase on the dresser and a stack of mysteries sat on the bedside table. There was even a rocking chair. Sun poured in through the oversized windows, giving everything a warm glow.

Tara was overwhelmed. She could feel the tears starting again. "I don't know what to say except thank you."

The Bargain

Lindsey took Tara's arm and steered her to the door. "Why don't you let Luisa put Molly down, and we'll go dig into the pot of hot chocolate that's waiting."

Lindsey carried the tray with the mugs and a plate of Mexican wedding cookies into the living room, where Emilio had built a fire that now roared and crackled in the fireplace. Sitting on the big couch, she patted the cushions for Tara to sit next to her.

"Cole is at Sean's under house arrest, which is why you aren't hearing from him. He won't bother you until you're ready to see him. So just kick back, okay?"

Time passed in a blur for Tara. For the next two days, she was like a zombie. She ate, she slept, she washed and she dressed. While Luisa cared for Molly, Tara sat in one of the rockers on the front porch, huddled into her jacket, thinking yet trying not to think. Her mind was as battered as her body. She was so cold on the inside she didn't think she'd ever get warm again, yet she sat by the hour in the chilly weather.

I'm punishing myself for my own part in this fiasco. Maybe, I'll be lucky and freeze to death.

"Something hot for you."

She hadn't even heard Luisa come out.

The woman pressed a cup of hot chocolate into her hands. "You should come inside, though."

Tara shook her head. "I'm fine. Really." But she wasn't, and they all knew it.

Jake tiptoed around her when he was home. He never brought up Cole's name, never asked a question and stayed out of her way except for meals, taking his cue from his wife.

"Is she okay?" Tara overheard him ask Lindsey in a low voice. "She hardly says a word."

"She needs to work this out herself," Lindsey whispered back. "She'll talk when she's ready. I'll make sure of it."

They all left her pretty much alone, watching her wrestle with her feelings. And she said little as she kept to herself. She responded politely when spoken to, but other than that, she said nothing.

After dinner one night near the end of the week, when Jake and Lindsey were sitting in front of the fire and Luisa was getting Jason and Molly ready for bed, Tara pulled on her jacket and went out on the porch again. She'd reached a point at which she could go no further. Her mind was paralyzed with the necessity to make some decisions, but she couldn't focus on what they should be.

In a minute, Emilio came out and sat down in the other rocker. He rocked silently with her for a minute before he started to speak. "You know, Tara, life is full of challenges. Every day, we make decisions that affect us and the people around us. We just hope for the best. My parents lived in a little town in Mexico I'm sure you've never heard of. We were dirt poor, scrabbling out a living. There were seven of us kids to support. We all worked from the minute we were old enough, but our parents still insisted we all go to school and to church every Sunday.

"They loved each other very much. They just weren't very good at saying the words. But we saw it in the way they treated each other and the love they passed along to us." He stopped for a minute, as if gathering his thoughts. "One time, something happened between them. None of us knew what it was, but we heard angry words, long into the night. Then my father stomped out of the house, slamming doors on the way.

The Bargain

"In the morning, when he came back, they acted as if nothing had happened, but we all knew. We never found out what caused the argument, only that it was so bad my mother stopped speaking to him. All those good years together down the drain.

"After that they might as well have been two strangers under the same roof. No matter what he did, she turned him away. You could look into her eyes and see that, whatever it was, it had bruised her soul.

"Then one day, my father came down with the flu, and, bang, just like that he was gone. My mother mourned every minute, not just for his death but also for what she'd wasted by never healing the breach between them. She died a year later. We always believed it was because her heart was broken. Don't let your heart break, Tara. Cole is a good man. I don't know the whole story here, and I don't want to. But if you don't deal with it, you'll never get past it, your life will be gone and maybe you'll have missed something very important."

He stood up, went to her rocker and patted her shoulder.

His touch unlocked the floodgates. She began to cry in huge, rasping sobs, her body shuddering and her cries those of a wounded animal. Emilio just kept his arm on her shoulder and let her weep. She heard Jake come to the door and speak to Emilio, who waved him away.

Finally, when she was totally exhausted, when there were no more tears to cry, she wiped her eyes on her sleeve and sat back. "Emilio, I..."

"That's okay, Tara." He was a solid presence next to her. "I know."

"Would you please ask Lindsey to come out here?" She sniffled and blinked her eyes. "I think I'm ready to talk now."

"Why don't you come inside, and I'll chase Jake upstairs. Luisa and I are going to our own place next door, and he can keep an ear out for the kids. I don't want either of you girls freezing to death in this chill."

So that's what she did. Jake went upstairs to make sure the kids didn't wake up, and Tara sat with Lindsey by the fire, spilling all the wretched details. Molly. What happened the night of the wedding. And what she'd hoped for with the Thanksgiving holiday.

"So you see, it's an impossible situation," Tara finished, hardly able to look at her friend. "I want him, I love him, but we have so many problems lying between us now. I don't know if we can ever face each other again. I don't even know if I can trust him again."

Lindsey put her hand on Tara's arm. "I have to tell you something else that might be hard for you to hear. But you need to know this."

"What? What is there that could make this any worse?"

Lindsey took one of Tara's hands in both of hers. "Cole doesn't exactly remember everything that happened that night."

"What?" Tara felt shock zip through her body. "How can he not remember?"

"I think the alcohol might have had a little something to do with that. Anyway, I don't want any details, that's between you and Cole. But when the time comes, you can decide how to handle it."

"My God, Lindsey. If he doesn't remember if we actually made love, what does that say about the whole thing? How do I even deal with that?" Humiliation crawled over her.

I gave him my body, and he doesn't even remember. We made love for the first time, and he doesn't even know if we completed the act.

For a moment, Tara thought she would throw up.

"Tara, how you play this is up to you. But you've known Cole long enough to know he's a good person." Lindsey put a hand on her arm. "He's just got his life twisted in a knot he can't undo. What happened that night—him blowing up at you, what happened afterwards—is all part of that."

"Why won't he tell me what's wrong?" Tara persisted.

"There are reasons why he didn't, and he needs to tell you those himself. You need to let him explain everything to you."

"I guess you're right," Tara said miserably.

"Well, then." Lindsey let out a breath. "You have to know that he loves you."

"What?" Tara's head jerked up. "What did you say?"

"I said he's desperately in love with you. We've all seen it coming for months, and he admitted as much when Jake asked him. Jake thinks Cole's been in love with you since you came to work for them but was too stupid to recognize it."

"Oh, Lindsey, I don't think so," Tara disagreed. "He married me because he thought I was the best candidate to pick up the pieces of his life."

"Maybe he thought so in the beginning, but not now. That's why he's so busy beating himself up. He's convinced he's destroyed the one good thing in his life."

Tara was stunned.

Lindsey was silent for a long moment. "This is a complicated situation. But I think he's ready to be honest with you now, whatever the consequences. Just listen to him. Then you can decide what you want to do."

"I guess I'm just nervous about facing him." Tara twisted her fingers together. "I'm not sure I'll even know how to act."

"He's scared, too," Lindsey said. "Just talk to him and see what happens. Is that fair enough?"

Tara nodded slowly. "I guess so. I can't hide from this forever. But can I just stay here for another day? I need to get myself ready for this."

"Oh, honey, of course you can. You can stay here as long as you want to."

"No, I think I'll go home day after tomorrow. If you'll ask Emilio to drive me, I'll be ready by then."

* * * *

For Cole, this was one of the worst periods in his life. The giant hangover he nursed only added to his misery. The first day at Sean's, he could hardly look at either his brother or his partner.

"What I don't understand," Sean told him, "is how you thought this kind of marriage could work in the first place. It's the most ridiculous setup I've ever seen, and I told you so. It caused all kinds of complications and look what happened."

How could he explain it when he still didn't understand it himself? Somehow, he'd been stupid enough to think he and Tara could just transfer their working relationship from the office to the house. He certainly hadn't planned on falling in love with her.

"Just so you know," Sean told him, "I'm hiding the liquor."

"Don't worry," Cole muttered. "I don't think I'll ever drink again."

The Bargain

After that, Sean kept him busy every minute, never letting him out of his sight. They worked out in the health club on the top floor and swam in the pool. They drove to Brackenridge Park and jogged until Cole's legs threatened to collapse with the strain. When his muscles wouldn't respond any more, he lay on the bench in the steam room trying to sweat away the remnants of his disgust with himself.

Thank God, Jake was minding the store because business was the last thing he was thinking about. He called his partner several times a day to check on Tara, knowing Lindsey had taken her to the ranch. He was desperate to see how she was.

"Mind your own business," Jake told him. "You'll get a report when there's something to tell."

Anguish and misery were Cole's constant companions. At night, he lay in the bed in Sean's guest room, sleep eluding him, thinking of Tara and how she had changed his life. Unbidden, images came to his mind of her and Molly. Looking at them, at the obvious bond between them, no one would have doubted she was Tara's biological child.

He saw himself standing on the outside, locked out by his own anger and withdrawal, and his heart ached worse than his body did. His entire world had turned gray, and he had no one to blame but himself for washing away all the color she had brought into his life.

By the middle of the following week, he was able to concentrate enough to do some work from the apartment. Jake brought him project files and reports, as well as his laptop and cell phone. And by Friday, he felt ready to face his problems.

"I think I'm ready to enter the world of the living again," he told Sean, "but I'm not sure I know how to face Tara. Jesus, what do I do next? Look at me, the man who can do anything and I don't know how to fix my life."

"Everyone makes mistake," Sean pointed out, "but I think you've used up all the ones you're allowed. Come on. Let's hit the gym then we'll talk."

After their morning workout, while Sean was still in the shower, Cole fixed a late breakfast for the two of them, the one meal he was good at.

"Is this a bribe or what?" Sean walked into the kitchen, pulling on a T-shirt. "What are you softening me up for?"

"Sit down. I need a plan, and you need to help me." He had to find a way to get Tara to at least listen to him. "I love my wife—god, have I ever even called her that? And I've screwed up to the max. I don't deserve a second chance, but you have to help me get one."

Sean just looked at him, waiting.

"You have to help me figure out what to do," Cole insisted. "I just can't think straight."

They ate in silence, Cole wrapped in misery, Sean watching him. When they finished, Cole cleaned up in the kitchen and Sean went out on the balcony and called Jake.

"Tara's much better," Jake told him in answer to his question. "Not great but she'll survive. What's up?"

"He's ready, and he wants me to help him figure out how to do this."

"Tell the truth," Jake said and hung up.

In the kitchen, Sean refilled his coffee mug and studied his brother. "All right. I think I have a plan, but there's a catch. You have to tell Tara about Maggie and Molly."

The Bargain

"I can't." Cole's voice was agonized. "She'll never want anything to do with me after that."

"Cole, you've built this thing up in your mind until it's far bigger than it needs to be. If you really want a relationship with Tara, you have to be honest. You have to tell her what the real problem with Molly is. Otherwise, you can forget about any second chance."

Cole was silent for so long Sean wondered if he'd turned to stone.

"All right," he said at last. "Now, tell me how I'm going to get my wife back."

"Okay," Sean poured himself more coffee. "Here's the plan."

And he told Cole in great detail what he was going to do and how he was going to do it.

* * * *

Tara was glad to be home, even if the house was filled with painful memories that kept prodding at her. She felt, if not refreshed by her stay at the ranch, at least released from the grip of emotional disaster. Regardless of the circumstances, she and Cole had taken a leap into intimacy. Somewhere in all this mess were real feelings propelling both of them. If they could just negotiate the obstacle course, maybe they could examine how they really felt about each other.

She wasn't sure how she would ever sleep in her bed again without thinking about that night. She still had so many unresolved conflicts. Loving Cole was not enough if he didn't love her back. Despite what Lindsey said, she needed him to tell her that himself. She would listen to whatever he had to say then decide what to do next.

She went to her room early, emotionally and physically spent from the previous days. She forced herself to crawl into her bed and, with an effort, banished the Thanksgiving night images from her mind. Unbelievably, she fell into a deep, dreamless sleep and didn't wake until the sun was bright and she heard Molly calling from her crib.

Taking advantage of the beautiful day, Tara decided to walk Molly in the stroller. The weather was gorgeous if you were celebrating the holidays. She wasn't doing much of that, but she could at least enjoy the cool, crisp, sunshine-washed weather.

She remembered to take her cell phone in case Cole called, mindful of what happened the time she'd forgotten it. She actually heard from Jake first.

"Where are you?" he demanded. "I'm cooling my heels on your front steps."

"I'm taking a walk with Molly." She frowned at the phone. "What are you doing at my house?"

"I'll tell you when you get here. How far away are you?"

"Just a few blocks. I'll be right there."

He was standing by the door when she got there, looking at his watch with impatience. He plucked Molly from her stroller and hugged her, planting a kiss on her cheek. "How's my beautiful girl today? Do you know we're hoping for one just like you? Do you think that's possible?"

"Jake." Tara tried to conceal her impatience. "Are you going to tell me what this is all about?"

"Inside the house. Then we'll talk."

She put Molly in her highchair with a cookie and turned to Jake. "All right, what's going on?" she demanded.

"Go pack a bag for Molly," he ordered. "She's coming to the ranch to stay until tomorrow. Don't argue. Luisa's more excited about this than Lindsey. And where's the car seat?"

"What? Not until you tell me what's going on. Have you heard from Cole?"

"More than I ever want to." He blew out a breath. "Tara, you are a wonderful woman and a special friend, but just this once, will you shut up and do as you're told? Where's the car seat?"

"In my car in the garage," she said, dazed.

"I'll get it. Go pack her things."

Realizing she would get no more answers, she handed Molly to Jake and went up to the nursery to gather some of the little girl's things. When she got back downstairs, Jake was standing in the kitchen still holding Molly, a huge gift-wrapped box sitting on the table.

He pointed to it. "This is from Lindsey. You're not supposed to open it until after I leave. She said it's not what she wanted, but I only had time to take her into Cibolo this morning so she had to settle for what she could find in town. And no questions, remember?" he said, as he saw her open her mouth.

"All right. Molly hasn't had lunch yet. I was just going to feed her."

"No problem," Jake grinned. "Luisa is delighted to feed anybody she can."

"Okay." She stared at him. "Are you going to tell me what this is about now?"

"You have a date tonight, Mrs. Cassidy. With your husband. He'll be here at seven, and all you have to do is be ready and waiting." He picked up Molly to take her with him. "Cut him a little slack, will you? Hold onto the thought that he's madly in love with you and shaking in his shoes about seeing you. Okay?"

"But..."

"Just call us in the morning and let us know if you've shot him to death and where we should come to pick up the pieces."

"Wait, I..."

"No more questions." Jake gave her a swift peck on the cheek, shifted Molly in his arms and was gone.

Tara closed the front door and leaned against it, forcing herself to breathe. Cole was coming to the house. He was coming to see her. She was filled both with dread and anticipation.

When she opened the package from Lindsey, she didn't know whether to laugh or cry. Inside were bottles of bath salts and bath oil, a gold and pearl clip for her hair and a long, silk gown in pale yellow. Cut temptingly low both front and back, the material was sensuous and luxuriant, and she knew it would cling to every curve of her body.

Lindsey had enclosed a note with the gown that said, "Knock him dead, Tara. And you can't wear anything under this. It shows every line. If you decide to throw him out, at least, let him see what he'll be missing."

She dropped into one of the kitchen chairs, holding the silk gown and allowed herself one more crying jag. Then she took the box and went upstairs.

Chapter Eleven

A long bath was a luxury Tara didn't indulge in much these days, so it was heaven just to sit in the scented water and close her mind to everything. Her muscles were loose and relaxed when she finally climbed out and turned on the shower to wash her hair. A brand new bottle of scented lotion stood on the vanity. Despite everything, her body tingled at the thought of seeing Cole again, and she felt wanton as she slowly massaged the lotion into every inch of her skin. Then she dried her hair, brushing it until it shone, and pulled it back with the clip Lindsey had sent. Carefully, she sprayed perfume on every one of her pulse points, even dusting some across her triangle of curls. She took extra pains with her makeup, redoing it twice because her hands shook so much.

She was nervous, afraid and aroused. A deadly combination. What if they couldn't stand the sight of each other? What if she wanted him, and he turned away from her? What if that terrible night was an impossible obstacle to climb? Deliberately she banished her morbid thoughts and went back to dressing.

When she slipped on the silk gown, she nearly took it off again. She hadn't put on any lingerie, as Lindsey had instructed and she looked more naked with the gown on than off. She fastened her wedding earrings in place and took a last look at herself. Well, she'd come out firing on all guns.

She had no idea how long he would stay. She didn't know if she should prepare food or if he wanted to go out or what. She'd just have to play it by ear.

In the living room, she noticed that logs and kindling were set in the fireplace. She assumed Emilio must have taken care of that the day he'd brought her home. She had just lit the fire when the doorbell rang. She looked at the mantel clock. Seven on the dot. Trembling like a teenager on a first date, she took a deep breath to steady herself and opened the door.

Cole was elegantly dressed in a gray suit, striped dress shirt and dark tie. Her heart skipped at the sight of him, but she didn't know if it was desire or nervous anticipation of what they might say to each other. His face was so full of tension it accentuated the hard planes and angles. His arms were loaded with packages, and he looked scared to death. He started to say something then looked at her, and his jaw dropped.

"My god, you're gorgeous. Why haven't I told you that before?" He just stood there, gaping at her.

She was flustered by the compliment. "Thank you." Looking over his shoulder, she saw his car in the driveway. "Why didn't you park in the garage?" she asked, curious.

"I needed to be sure you wanted me to come in," he told her. "I didn't know if you'd just slam the door in my face."

"Of course not." She trembled. "Please come in. It's cold out here."

The Bargain

He plucked a huge florist box off the pile in his arms. "I have some flowers here that I think need water."

"*Some* flowers?" she said, incredulous at what she saw as she lifted the cover. Four dozen perfect roses, pink, white, red and yellow glistened against the nest of soft green paper. She touched the petals gently, caressing their velvety softness and inhaling their rich fragrance. She felt as if she were standing in a flower garden.

"Are they all right?" he asked, sounding anxious. "I had no idea what your favorite color is so I took them all."

"Cole, they're beautiful." She was overwhelmed. "You're right. They should be in water. Come into the kitchen while I get a vase. Then we'll bring them into the living room with us."

Cole followed her and put his other packages on the kitchen table while she arranged the roses. "I gave the maitre d' at Le Reve enough money to retire on if he'd squeeze in a reservation for us. I had no idea how tonight would turn out, but I wanted to have a nice place to take you if everything was okay. And if you wanted to go, that is."

"Why don't we just wait and see what happens?" she said.

He held up a long, thin shopping bag. "I brought some of the Merlot you order when we go out." He pulled out a second bottle and grinned like a small boy offering an apple to the teacher. "And some champagne for later, just in case. I've sworn off the hard stuff, for sure. It only gets me into deep trouble. Shall I get out the wine glasses?"

"Yes. If you would." She was afraid her hands were trembling too much to handle them.

He put the rest of his packages on the table. "I'll leave these other things here for the moment."

"Why don't you take the wine and the glasses into the living room while I fix the flowers? I lit the fire, and it's very comfortable in there."

When she joined him, he was standing in front of the fireplace, the light from the flames playing across his face. As she walked, the gown moved over her body and she could see him staring at her, eyes glittering with barely concealed desire. Little jolts of electricity traveled along her nerve endings.

He handed her a filled wine glass and raised his own. "A toast. To the most magnificent woman in the world. And a prayer that you'll have some understanding of what I'm going to tell you."

Her stomach knotted. "Why don't you sit down?" She gestured toward one of the wing chairs.

"I think I'll stand for the moment. I can talk to you better this way. I want to get this all out right now before I lose my nerve." He looked hard at her face, as if searching for some indication of her mood. "Tara, I'm so sorry about Thanksgiving night. There's no justification for any of the things I said or did. You deserve much better than that."

"Yes, I do." She bit her lip, not knowing what else to say.

Cole raked his fingers though his hair. "I've been so terrified of losing you. The things I said that night? I wanted to take them back the minute they were out of my mouth, make them go away, but you were already up the stairs. I felt worse when I finally admitted to myself how much I love you, but I didn't know how to fix things."

"So you decided to get drunk instead." She said the words flatly, watching him.

"No. I was just trying to blunt the pain and find some answers. By the time I realized they weren't in the bottle, I was already wasted."

"Why didn't you let me know how you felt?" she asked. "What did you think would happen? That I'd run away?" She fiddled with her wine glass, forcing herself to be calm. "Surely you had to sense I had feelings for you, too."

"Truthfully? I was afraid."

She stared at him. "Afraid of what?"

"Of my own life, I think." He took a healthy sip of wine. "And in the end, afraid of what you'd say if I came to you sober and gave you the whole story. And told you I loved you."

"What story?" she cried. "What is it that's so hard for you to get out? The real issue here, whether you want to see it or not, isn't what happened the other night. The root of the problem is Molly. Everything leads back to her. If you can't tell me the truth, if you won't let me know what this is all about, then I don't know what we have to talk about."

He drew another deep breath, as if sucking courage from the air. "You're right. I need to tell you things you should have known from the beginning. I was just so sure if I did, you'd turn me down. Then what would I do?" He sucked in a breath. "This is an ugly story that doesn't make me look so good, but you deserve to know it all. Then I guess the rest is up to you."

He turned toward the fireplace, leaned his arm on the mantel and with his head bowed, told her a tale that by turns shocked and saddened her. In short sentences, he told her about the death of his parents when he was still in college, his fight to hang on to

Sean who was four years younger. The decision he and Jake made to open their own company.

In fourteen years, they'd built Alamo Construction into what it was now. But while Jake put a failed marriage behind him and now had Lindsey and a child, with another on the way, Cole had avoided all but the most casual relationships. He reminded her of his vacation two years ago, the first he'd ever taken. He told her about Maggie—voluptuous, exotic and predatory—who'd targeted him that first night. The heady tropical drinks, seductive and treacherous in their sweetness.

He had an inability to properly metabolize alcohol, which was why he seldom drank anything but a glass or two of wine. But he was thousands of miles from home where no one could see if he made a fool of himself. And a week of the basest kind of lust where he never remembered one sober minute. And his haste to get away from her when he finally stopped drinking.

Then the news of her pregnancy and her demand for marriage. He was adamantly opposed to abortion, and he realized he wanted a child very badly. He was able to keep Maggie off the booze while she was pregnant, frightened to death of fetal alcohol syndrome, but the baby wasn't a week old before she was binging again.

And in a tortured voice, he told her how Molly had captured his heart at once, how she'd made it all worthwhile, given his life new purpose. Then Maggie had destroyed it all. He was a rich prize, and she'd baited the trap with someone else's child. He still felt disgust that he'd let himself be trapped by her. Since then, he could hardly bring himself to look at the little girl without being reminded of how he'd gotten himself in this position and how he'd been betrayed.

When he finished, Tara sat rooted to her seat, stunned. She didn't know what she'd expected to hear, but it wasn't this awful tale of greed, deception and betrayal. How could a woman be so uncaring with the lives of a wonderful man and a beautiful child?

"I acted like a fool," he rasped. "Something I try not to do very often, you know. Just," he shrugged, "it happened. I was drunk and thought I was the one taking advantage of her."

Tara sat perfectly still, not saying a word.

He began pacing again. "I don't think Maggie and I even liked each other. What we had was lust of the basest kind. She knew how to punch my buttons and get whatever she wanted. I let her do it. You can't be any more disgusted with me than I am with myself. I deserved what I got."

So here it was at last. She'd known it had to be something this bad to make him behave the way he had. She'd worked with this man for two years and been married to him all these months. She knew him underneath it all—a good, decent person whose only failing was he was human. So much was clear to her now.

"I know you must hate me for the way I've treated the child." He shook his head. "It was very painful admitting to myself that a big part of this was my pride."

He took the poker and stirred the logs in the fireplace, obviously giving himself something to do. "Please try to understand. I only married Maggie because she said she was pregnant with my child. And I wanted that child. When Maggie told me the baby wasn't even mine, I was destroyed. I'd gone through the marriage from hell for nothing."

Tara thought of Molly, the unknowing center of the turmoil, a constant reminder of everything. Her throat tightened with emotion.

"Tara?"

She could hear the edge of fear in his voice as he waited for her to break her silence.

"That's why you'd never let me into your bedroom, isn't it?" she said at last. "Because Maggie had slept in there with you."

He nodded. "I didn't want you touched by her filth."

"And why there are no pictures anywhere in the house."

"Yes."

"I thought it was because you loved her so much you couldn't bear to be reminded of her," she whispered. "I thought you wanted a contract marriage because you were never going to get over the death of your wife."

"God, no." A harsh laugh escaped his lips. "That's so far from the truth it's not even on the same planet." He rubbed his forehead. "When I asked you to marry me, I didn't realize what a selfish thing I was doing. I was concerned with my needs, not yours. I don't know how you've put up with everything. You've been far more than I could have expected."

"What did you expect?" she asked, her voice soft.

"Not nearly what I got." His eyes searched her face again. "And I certainly didn't expect to fall in love with you. Maybe Jake and Sean are right, and I've been in love with you since the day I hired you. My feelings for you kept growing stronger. It got to the point where I could hardly be near you without getting hard."

"But then you ran away from me," she said.

The Bargain

"Because I knew what a jackass I'd been. Everything got so mixed up that night. I reacted without thinking to the situation with the child and figured I'd blown my best chance to tell you how I felt. So, jerk that I am, I went off and got drunk. And the rest, as they say, is history."

"How do you feel now?" Her voice was so soft he almost didn't hear her.

He looked at her with everything he felt in his eyes. "Tara, I want this to be a real marriage, if you'll just give me the chance. I want a life with you more than I've ever wanted anything. I love you so much I can't see straight. I've been terrified that I'd chased you away."

"I had such mixed emotions the night everything happened," she said slowly. "Then, to find out you didn't even remember the details, well, I wasn't sure I ever wanted to see you again."

"I know. I wouldn't blame you." His voice was agonized. "Can we put this behind us and start fresh? Is that possible? Do you care for me at all?"

"And Molly? None of this was her fault. What about her?"

"Yes, what about her." A look of intense sadness crossed his face. "You're right. She's the innocent in all this. The way I've treated her, I think, is the greatest crime of all."

"But can you change that?" she asked quietly.

"I just don't know, Tara." He shook his head again. "I promise I'll do my best. But I know for sure I can't do anything without you."

"Didn't you have a DNA test? That would have been proof."

A muscle jumped in his cheek. "Of course. Jake insisted. The results weren't good. But I'll try to get past that."

The room was filled with tension as thick as fog, the silence broken only by the snapping of sparks in the fireplace and the hissing of logs. Tara looked down at her hands, fighting for composure. She was acutely aware of Cole, face rigid, waiting for her to respond.

"Tara, if you want me to leave, just tell me."

His voice was so ragged she barely recognized it. She knew the next move was up to her. There were still problems, all right, but she saw with sudden clarity just how empty her life would be if she turned him away. Once she admitted this to herself, the rest was easy. Rising from the couch, she put down her wine glass and walked to where he stood.

"Tara?" he said her name again. He raised his eyes to hers, fear of what she might say written in them.

She still wouldn't look at him. "I have no idea what you must think of me, to make love with you the way I did when things were so bad between us. To make love with you at all. Without preamble. Without anything. When we'd never even spoken about it before."

Now he reached for her, forcing her to look at him, pulling her towards him. "Tara, I'm the one who's humiliated. And more disgusted with myself than you can imagine. To insinuate myself in your bed that way?" He shook his head. "And to barely even remember all that happened." He searched her eyes. "Did I...? Did we...?"

"Yes, we did." She bit her lip. "We did."

"Then the thing I regret most is not being sober enough to enjoy it."

"But..."

"No. Listen to me. People make choices in their lives. Mike had an accident that was in no way your fault. You've got to stop blaming yourself for something you had no control over. And I've got to try not to live in the past anymore." He started to reach for her and stopped himself. "Is it all right, then? Will we be okay?"

"It's all right," she told him, and at once, she knew it would be. The major challenges could wait. Right now, being in his arms, feeling his body so close to her was the more important than anything else.

She put her arms around him and pressed her body against his, inhaling the spicy scent of him.

"Oh, God," Cole groaned, the sound a mixture of relief and desire. He wrapped his arms around her tightly, sliding one large hand up to hold her head. His kiss was not a gentle one, filled as he was with desperation. His lips were soft yet bruising and demanding. He thrust his tongue into her mouth, plundering it, devouring it, tasting every inch of it.

Tara slid her tongue against his, returning movement for movement. His taste was heady, intoxicating, the mint of his toothpaste mingled with the bite of the wine. The kiss went on and on until she couldn't breathe.

When they finally broke the kiss, he lifted his head and looked at her, studying her eyes. She could tell he saw something that made him relax just the slightest bit. He took off his jacket and tossed it on the couch, rolling back the sleeves of his shirt.

"Now, I think it's time to stop talking. Tonight, I'm totally sober, and I plan to remember every minute of what happens."

With that, he brought his mouth down to hers again, claiming her with a kiss that seared her soul. His tongue probed the seam of her lips and she opened for him. It was a kiss beyond any she'd ever had before, heating her blood, melting her bones. She wanted him to swallow her whole.

"Let's go upstairs," she said breathlessly, when they separated.

Cole shook his head. "No. I'm a desperate man, Tara. I prayed for this every minute since the other night. I want you right here, right now. In front of the fire. In this room where there are no specters to haunt me." He pulled the soft pillows off the couch and tossed them to the floor. "I want to look at you," he told her, his voice thick in his throat. "I want to see every bit of you. Come here."

He reached behind her and unzipped the gown, the flimsy cloth falling at once in soft folds at her feet.

She was naked before him except for the diamond and pearl earrings reflecting the firelight. The flames cast shadows on her body, giving it a rich, warm glow. He stepped back, his eyes raking her, his breath catching involuntarily. She was more magnificent than he'd imagined. Her breasts sloped proudly upward, the nipples dark against the pale flesh. The firelight cast shadows at the hollows of her hips and at her navel. The nest of curls covering her mound was as rich in color as the thick mane she held back with the clip.

He reached around her and released her hair, letting it fall around her shoulders in shimmering waves. He touched the silky softness with his fingers. "God, you're gorgeous. You should wear your hair this way more often. It makes you look more tempting than any woman has a right to be."

He pulled her naked body against him, feeling warmth of her breasts through the fine cloth of his shirt, his hands exploring the unbelievable softness of her skin. The jasmine scent she favored teased at his nostrils, and he pressed his face to her skin, inhaling her fragrance. They kissed again, tongues exploring mouths, lips pressed hard against lips. The fire snapped and crackled, casting gold and orange colors on them. The delicious scents of spruce and cinnamon and holly heightened their senses.

Tara's hands were at his shirt, opening buttons, yanking at his tie. He felt her fingers at his belt buckle then at his fly, unfastening, unzipping. Her touch was bold, brazen.

"I want to look at you, too," she said against his mouth.

His hands were working with hers to rip away fabric. In seconds, he was as naked as she was. He stood before her, his tall, powerful body outlined in the firelight, his eyes boring into hers.

Tara was transfixed by his nudity. He reminded her of some primitive god, ready for the mating ritual. His cock stood out from his body, the root settled in a thick nest of dark hair, his sac lying heavy against his thighs.

Just like in my dream.

She wet her lips, captivated by the sight of him in the flesh, and pressed her hands against his warm skin. He was so hard and muscular, his chest matted with a thick carpet of dark curls begging for her fingers to touch them. A soft line of down trailed along his abdomen and down into his groin. She nearly fainted when she touched his thick shaft. It was more enormous in real life than in her dream, so large it mesmerized her. She couldn't imagine how she could accommodate it.

"Cole." She bowed her head, catching her lower lip with her teeth. Sudden shyness and uncertainty intruded on the wave of desire sweeping through her.

"I know." He brushed his lips across her forehead. "It's all right, Tara."

He bent his head to hers again, slanting his mouth to capture her lips. When he slipped his tongue into her mouth, she welcomed the taste of him, reveling in the texture of his tongue and its demanding thrusts. He tasted wonderfully of mint toothpaste and the smoky Merlot, reminding her of that first kiss they'd shared.

With a touch that was almost reverent, he skimmed her with his fingertips, running his hands over her breasts, her waist, her flat stomach and the curve of her buttocks. Every place he touched ignited another lick of flame.

"No other woman has ever affected me this way." His voice was hoarse and not quite steady. "You reach into my very soul. I want you, every bit of you, every way I can have you and I never want to stop."

Tara circled his erection with her fingers, but he grabbed her hand.

"Not yet. This is for you, darlin'. Just for you."

Laying her down with great gentleness on the bed he'd made of the pillows, he touched her nipples with fingers that shook, teasing each one until it stood hard and erect against his hand. His fingertips drew a line along her ribcage and back in to her navel, circling it with his thumb.

He let his hand drift lower, until he reached the soft feel of her delicate curls. Placing his palm over her mound, he slid his finger between the folds of her pussy, seeking her opening. With a feathery touch, he stroked up and down her slit in a gliding motion, touching only the outer lips. With a soft moan, she opened her legs to him. He slid one finger into her hot sheath, then another, seeking her center.

"You're already wet for me," he said, desire thick in his voice.

"I know."

Her pulse raced, every nerve firing. Her body, frozen in cold storage for so long, thawed and warmed in the heat of their passion. The feel of his body next to hers was as electric as a live wire. She could feel the definition of his hard muscles, the sweet roughness of the hair on his chest, the silkiness of his hair when he bent his head to her.

Slowly, almost lazily, Cole stroked in and out of her cunt, watching her through slitted eyes. Her eyes became heavy with passion, her breathing ragged. He moved his thumb up to find that so sensitive nub and circled it teasingly. She caught her breath and began to move her hips, urging him to enter her deeper, but he held back.

"Tonight when you come," he said in a low voice, "I want it to be the most shattering climax you've ever had. Don't deny me that."

He curled his fingers, finding the hot spot, and she thrust hard against his hand. When the first little flutters began, he withdrew altogether.

"Oh, god, Cole, don't stop now. Please." Her blood felt like liquid fire and her skin felt too tight. "Make me come."

"I will, sweetheart, but not yet. Definitely not yet."

He slid down her body until he was lying between her legs. Grasping her thighs, he placed them over his shoulders. When she was wide open and vulnerable, he thrust his tongue inside her. She went wild, bucking against his mouth. He teased her with his tongue, with his teeth, with his hands, all the time holding her in such a way as to give him full access to her to her cunt.

Tara couldn't stop moving her body. Her labia and her inner sheath felt hot and swollen, with so many nerve endings sparking, she didn't know why she wasn't burning alive. He was controlling her now, building her tension. Every time she reached the edge, he brought her down a little, keeping her in a constant state of arousal, drawing it out as much as he could.

She felt sensations gripping her body, quivering as he skillfully used his mouth, his tongue and his long, gentle fingers. This was beyond anything she had ever felt before, the tension so prolonged she didn't think she could stand it. She was wild with hunger for him now, wanting to feel the fullness of him inside her. He made love to every inch of her, and she responded with wantonness, a glorious sense of abandonment she'd never thought herself capable of.

"Please, please, please," she begged. It wasn't his fingers she wanted to feel or his mouth. It wasn't enough. She wanted—no, needed—to feel him inside her, filling her.

"Okay, darlin'. Now."

He moved her legs from his shoulders to his thighs. She was juicy wet from her mini-orgasms, her inner muscles soft and unresisting. Slowly, slowly, he eased into her, pulling her toward him so her hips slanted, giving him greater access, allowing him to plunge deeper. There. Now. He was all the way in and the feeling was beyond anything he'd experienced.

He thrust rhythmically in and out, the friction of his cock against her inner walls turning up the heat in her body until her spasms began again, and the muscles of her cunt clenched tightly around him. She knew with every movement he was claiming her, making her his and she rose eagerly to meet him. She was on fire, pulses throbbing, blood rushing hotly through her veins. The need in her rose up and up, spiraling through her like an unwinding coil until she could think of nothing but his thick shaft inside her and the crushing waves of pleasure consuming her.

She was there...almost there...almost...Now! Cole thrust madly once, twice, three times and, with a hoarse cry, carried them both over the edge. Tara's body shook with the crushing intensity of the orgasm. Colors swirled around her, and she felt awash in a velvet liquid. It went on and on until she was sure she couldn't stand it anymore. The spasms shook her until she felt as if her body was breaking into a million pieces. Her nails raked his back, and she could feel the shuddering of his powerful muscles. Someone was screaming. She thought it was her, but she couldn't be sure.

By the time the orgasm subsided, leaving only tiny aftershocks, she lay limp and boneless in his arms, completely spent, utterly sated. This...*this*...was the cataclysmic joining she'd hoped for. The culmination of all those dreams and the tension they'd built. The explosion of lust and desire that had built night after night, leaving her more and more unfulfilled. This was completion beyond anything she could have imagined. *This* was the wild ride down the mountain she'd dreamed about, only it was better than any of her dreams.

She closed her eyes, relaxing in the grip of total satisfaction.

At last. At last.

Chapter Twelve

Every muscle in Cole's body felt as if it had been stretched to its extreme then released. All the strength had been drained from him. It was almost too much for him to realize. In all the years of his sexual experience, he had never experienced this. His body had just exploded with his release, shaking him with its intensity. The wet fist of Tara's delicious cunt had gripped him and hadn't release him until the last vibration died away. None of Cole's vast sexual experience had prepared him for the way this reached his very soul. In that moment, he knew just how totally and completely he loved this woman.

When he could move, he tried to shift his weight to give her breathing room, but she kept her arms wrapped around him, holding him.

"I must be too heavy for you." His breathing was choppy and uneven, and his heart beat loudly against his ribs..

"No. Stay. Don't move." She wouldn't let him withdraw from her, holding him in place with her legs, pressing him into her. Even when he softened, she kept him inside her. When he could move, he rained soft kisses on her cheeks, her eyelids, her forehead, the tip of her nose. "I love you. Do you know that?"

"Yes. I believe I do." She smiled. "I love you, too."

"Was it all right for you?" he asked, his lips against her ear. "I'm a little out of practice."

"I don't think I could stand it any better." She bit her lip. "I worried that I wouldn't satisfy you, that I wouldn't be...experienced...enough for you. Wouldn't know enough."

"You can believe this or not," he said, "but nothing I've ever done before was even close to the feeling I had when we came together." He brushed the damp tendrils of curls away from her face. "Sex doesn't have to be sophisticated to be wonderful, darlin'. I'll teach you anything you want, but believe me, I don't think we can improve on this."

"Yes, I want you to," she whispered. "I want to know everything you like, all the things that make you feel good. I want to be able to give you as much pleasure as you gave me." She lowered her gaze, a delicate blush creeping up her cheeks. "I have to confess something."

He frowned. "What? I thought we were through with confessions for the night."

She refused to look up at him. "I-I've been having dreams. About you."

"Dreams?" He tried to keep his voice even wondering if she, too...

"Yes. Erotic dreams." She turned her head away. "About you and me."

Cole took a deep breath, reaching for control. Was this possible? Had they both been having the same dreams, night after night? God, how many times had he fucked her in his mind? Tasted of her essence, taken her into his mouth?

The Bargain

"I shouldn't have told you," she said when he didn't speak.

"No. I mean, yes, you should." He rolled to the side, taking her with him. He brushed her hair back from her face. "You definitely should have told me, because the same thing has been happening to me. I've been having my own dreams."

Her eyes flew open, and she looked straight at him, an erotic thrill racing through him. "It has? You did? About us?"

"Yes." He smiled. "Almost every night since we made this stupid bargain."

"Why didn't you ever say anything?" she asked.

He brushed his lips across hers, their mouths touching as he spoke. "Why didn't you?"

But he knew the answers to both questions, and the knowledge brought him a fresh wave of self-loathing. Deliberately, he banished those thoughts. Tonight was a new beginning, and he wasn't going to drag the past into it.

"Tell me what you dreamed about," he urged. "About us. Don't be embarrassed," he said when a dark blush colored her skin again. "I want you to be able to say anything to me."

"I don't know if I can." She caught her bottom lip in her teeth.

"Did I do this?" One hand kneaded her breast gently, thumb rasping over the nipple.

"Yes," she whispered.

"And this?" He took the nipple into his mouth, raking his teeth over it and pressing it hard against the roof of his mouth. Her body tensed beneath him, and she arched up into his mouth.

"Yes," she murmured again, her voice thickening.

"And this?" He moved down her body to run his tongue through her curls then trace the length of her slit.

"Yes, yes, yes." She moaned and twisted beneath him.

"Then I must have done this."

He lifted her legs over his shoulders, spread the lips of her pussy wide and thrust his tongue inside. She bucked as his sucked and licked, fucking her with his tongue then moving to lap her clit. Then thrusting inside her again. She locked her legs behind his neck to pull him closer and thrust herself up at him. He felt the tiny quivers begin in her pussy and increased the tempo of his tongue. When her orgasm broke through her, he held her in place, his thumbs keeping her labia apart as he lapped at the convulsing flesh.

When the last aftershock died away, he lowered her legs, massaging the thigh muscles, and shifted so he could kiss her, pressing her own taste into her mouth.

"How did you know that's what I dreamt?" she asked, her voice still shaky.

He nipped at her earlobe. "Because I dreamt the same things." He traced her lips with the tip of his tongue. "But I also dreamt about this."

Positioning himself, he entered her with one swift stroke, pausing only to give her time to adjust to him. This time there was no foreplay, no drawing things out. It was quick and fast and just as cataclysmic. At last, they collapsed, spent, hearts thudding, breath rasping, a fine sheen of perspiration coating their bodies. The heady aroma of musk mingle with Tara's perfume and his aftershave , filling the room with the carnal scent of sex.

The Bargain

"We may not live to see Christmas at this rate," Cole joked, then he tightened his arms around her. "It's a wonder we haven't killed each other tonight with all that pent-up sexual energy." With his mouth against hers, he whispered, "I love you."

"I love you, too," she echoed, so glad to be able to say it aloud. With great effort, he lifted his wrist to look at his watch.

Tara turned her head to check the time with him. "I think we missed our dinner reservation," she told him, and they both burst out laughing.

"No big deal. But I do think this calls for some champagne, although I'm not sure I have the strength to get up and get it."

"Not to worry. I think I can crawl to the bottle." She managed to wriggle out from beneath him to sit up and reach for her gown, but he stopped her.

"The blinds are closed. Don't put that on. I want to watch you naked."

She turned a deep pink, and Cole laughed again.

"I don't think I've ever seen anyone blush all over before." He caught her hand. "You're beautiful naked, Tara. Don't cover yourself, okay? I want to look at you and be able to touch you whenever I want to."

She nibbled on her bottom lip again then nodded. "All right. Then we'll drink champagne in the nude." Her eyes dropped to his penis, still large and heavy even at rest.

As if he could read her mind, he said, "Yes, you took it all. Every bit."

She blushed again.

"I'll get the champagne," he told her. "Stay right where you are. I feel renewed energy."

He brought back the bottle, filled the champagne flutes, handed one to her then raised his glass and touched hers.

"To us?" he asked.

"Oh, yes. To us. No matter what. Right?"

"No matter what."

They clinked their glasses and drank.

"Since we missed dinner, we can always raid the freezer," she told him. "Are you hungry?"

"Not right now." Unbelievably, he was hardening again. "Not for food, anyway."

He reached for her and lowered her back to the pillows. Stretching her out beside him, he let his eyes roam lazily over her body. He was sure he would never tire of looking at her, touching her, discovering her secrets. With Tara, sex was a journey of discovery and a blending of their souls.

"I love you so much," she said.

"No more than I love you."

"Don't you think it's strange that we've both had such...erotic dreams about each other?" she asked.

"I think someone was trying to send us a message. And I think that's why everything tonight has been so explosive. It's been building all this time."

He clasped both of her hands in one of his and stretched them above her head. She looked up at him, totally helpless, and her eyes told him just how much she was turned on by it. He caressed her slowly, tracing the lines of her body.

"Oh, God, Cole," she protested. "I don't think I can."

"Sure you can. Just relax, and let me do all the work." Then he put his mouth close to her ear and whispered, "I love you. You're mine, Tara. You always will be." And that was all it took for the heat to begin rising in his body again.

* * * *

Exhaustion finally claimed them. Tara pulled the afghan off the couch to cover them with. Cole got up twice during the night to stoke the fire then spooned next to her, pulling her tight against him. His semisoft cock nudged against the crevice of her buttocks. For the first time in a long time, she felt content.

She was dozing when he stirred beside her, kissed the sensitive spot behind her ear and flipped her onto her stomach. She tensed at the position.

"I won't hurt you," he promised in his low, husky voice, stroking her back, then running the tip of his tongue along her spine.

He pulled her hips back to him, sliding one of the pillows beneath her, then slipping his hand between her legs to find her hot, open sheath and swollen clit. Murmuring erotic words and phrases to her, he rubbed her clit and massaged the lips of her pussy until she thought she would lose her mind. Jolts of heat speared through her, and throbbing need engulfed her body. At the exact moment she thought she'd screamed if he didn't take her, he lifted her hips higher and entered her with a hard thrust, penetrating more deeply than he ever had before.

This time she climaxed in seconds, violently, pressing back against him as she tried to absorb his entire shaft. Only when she felt the hot gush of liquid from him did she take one last breath and finally collapse on the pillows.

They never actually slept. They would doze then waken and begin to make love again. He introduced her to things she'd never known before, things that assaulted her body with such sensations she couldn't stand it.

He taught her how to pleasure him, to bring him to the peak of arousal. She took him in her mouth and teased him until he wanted to explode, the softness of her tongue stroking his hard, velvety penis. His groan of pleasure vibrated through his body. She tasted the soft-as-satin tip, sucking at the moisture already there, swallowing it with evident pleasure. His sac felt heavy in her hand, and she discovered that by lightly running the tips of her nails over it she could torment him even more. His erection would jerk in her mouth, sending shafts of excitement through her.

Touching him in so many ways made Tara's heart expand. She couldn't get enough of him. Even when they lay panting, spent, still she was drawn by the need to touch him everywhere. She wanted to learn all the secret, sensitive places of his body, as he had done to her. They were intoxicated with each other. Each time they thought they were beyond arousal, a touch, a tease and they would be in heat again.

For Tara, it was an awakening, and she reveled in it. For Cole, it was an unbelievable experience. Nothing he had ever done before prepared him for the wonder of loving her.

* * * *

By the time morning arrived, they could hardly move. They were sore from lovemaking and stiff from sleeping on the floor, but it was a good kind of pain. Neither would have exchanged it.

"Now is when I can use the bath salts Lindsey sent me," Tara said, stretching like a cat.

"Bath salts?"

"Yes." Tara laughed. "She sent me what I can only describe as a full-blown seduction kit." She described it for him.

Cole chuckled. "You should have seen Sean running me around from store to store. I'm sure he thought I was in such bad shape I couldn't make a purchase by myself."

"By the way." She sat up and looked at him. "I think everyone was pretty slick the way they worked it all out yesterday. I mean, Jake just showing up to get Molly and take her to the ranch overnight. Lindsey with her gift basket."

"Sean insisted on taking me shopping so I'd be properly dressed." He grinned at her. "Not that either of us kept our clothes on very long."

"They were all determined to make this happen." She wrapped her arms around his chest. "I think we're lucky to have the friends and family we do."

"I guess we should call them and tell them you haven't thrown me back out on the street."

"In a minute." She leaned on one elbow and gently traced the line of his jaw. "I love you more than I ever thought it possible to love someone. You make my heart full just being with you. I want you to keep that in mind because we still have something important to resolve. I want to talk about it right now before we start our day."

He grinned, a playful look in his eyes. "Are you going to tell me you have me at your mercy, stark naked, so I can't say no?"

"If I need to." She studied his face, looking for some signs that he'd actually hear what she had to say. Was this new beginning too fragile for her to bring it up now? She took a deep breath and let it out slowly. It was now or never, she thought. And maybe discussing it naked would make it a lot easier. "Cole, this is serious. It's really a big deal to me. We didn't resolve anything last night." She stopped and took a deep breath. *Please let me say the right words.* "It's about Molly."

She felt his body tense and saw the protective mask drop into place. He started to roll away from her, but she stopped him, leaning over and raining gentle kisses on his face.

"Don't do that," she pleaded. "Don't close up on me this way. Listen to me. Please. We have to come to some resolution—at least a compromise—or how can we ever build a life together?"

He was silent for so long that she wasn't sure he would ever answer her. Finally, in a flat voice, he said, "All right. I'm listening.

She kept her hand on his cheek, connecting with him while she talked. "I understand what you feel when you look at her, but what happened isn't her fault. You're the only father she's got. Can you understand that? She's getting to the point where she'll start wondering why you treat her as if she's got the plague. Molly didn't do this to you."

"Tara, I..."

She touched her fingers to his lips and shook her head. "No. Last night, you asked me to be quiet and listen to you. Now, I'm asking you to do the same. Molly is a wonderful little child, a treasure. We said today is the first day of the rest of our lives. Can't we find a way to make her part of it, too? It's so important to me."

"You're asking a lot of me," he told her, his voice tight. "I look at her, and I see Maggie's face and hear her voice. I hear those bitter words. I've tried so many times to make it right again, and it just hasn't worked."

Again she searched for the right words. "There's something I probably should have told you before, but the terms of our 'bargain' made it irrelevant." She bit her lip. "I was sure it wouldn't matter so I just kept it to myself."

"What is it, Tara?" Suddenly, he was the voice of concern, shifting so he could reach out his hand and touch her. "What didn't you think you needed to tell me? Are you sick? Is it something we can take care of?"

She shook her head then dropped her gaze. "Not sick. No." Her sigh was heavy enough to split the thick silence. "After my miscarriage, when Mike was killed, the doctors told me I'd probably never conceive another child." She raised her eyes to look at him again. "Molly may be the only one we'll ever share. That's why this is so important to me. I want us to be a family, and we can't if you still shut yourself away from her."

He pulled her into his arms, holding her against his body. "I am so sorry. No wonder you think I'm such a heartless ass. I would do anything in the world to make you happy, sweetheart, but here you may be asking the impossible."

Tara snuggled against him, taking strength from his warmth. "Will you try something for me?"

Although he kept his arms wrapped around her, his body stiffened. "What is it you want, Tara?"

"In a little while, we're going to the ranch to pick up Molly. I want it to be okay that she'll be with us. Can you at least give me that?" She paused. "You know she's growing all the time. Pretty soon, I won't be able to hide her away every minute you're home. And I don't want you to stay away because of it."

Again, he was silent for so long she began to get nervous. Would it all come unraveled now? Was she asking him to take an impossible leap? No. It was past time for that excuse.

Finally, reaching out his fingers to wipe away the tears she hadn't even realized were trickling down her cheeks, he said in a ragged voice, "All right. For you. I will do the best I can." He pulled her close again, nestling her head against his shoulder. "I want to please you, but you have to know this is killing me."

"I know. I really do." A tiny thread of hope surged through her.

"I held that child every day for two weeks when she was born," he told her, his eyes now staring at a point beyond her. "I rocked her in my arms and felt her tiny heart beating against mine. She was my child, my flesh. Then, in seconds, I found out what a cruel joke it all was." His face twisted in pain, remembering.

"You need to find a way to free yourself from this hate, or it will destroy you," she said softly. "And I don't intend to let that happen."

"I promise I'll try, and that's all I can offer. Is that good enough?"

"That's all I ask." She gave him a quick kiss. "I love you, and I'll do whatever I can to make it easier for you. This is a new beginning for all of us. Including Molly."

"All right." He hugged her then grinned. "You may have to give me regular treatments to keep me in line, though." He slapped his forehead. "I forgot the rest of the stuff."

"What are you talking about?"

"Come with me, and I'll show you." He tugged her along behind him to the kitchen where he'd left his packages the night before. "I think these were bribes, in case nothing else worked."

The Bargain

He pulled each box from the shopping bag, watching as she opened each box. The first one held a nightgown, frilly and sheer and made for seduction. The next box contained a soft cashmere sweater with a draped collar and neckline that dipped to a vee, in a golden color that caught the highlights in her hair. She gasped in pleasure and held it against her body, relishing its luxurious feel. It was so different from her other sweaters, all chosen strictly for their utilitarian design and serviceability.

When Cole took out the last package, he stopped to give her a kiss filled with both desire and promise. Then he handed it to her. "This is my heart," he said solemnly. "I give it to you willingly with all my love."

Tara gasped when she opened the jeweler's box. Inside were tiny gold earrings in the shape of hearts, outlined in pearls and diamonds. She had tears in her eyes when she lifted them out. "I will always keep your heart safe," she said, her voice husky, and stood on tiptoe to kiss him.

"And now I'm going to shower," he said. "Why don't you take that bath you want. Then we'll call the ranch."

"All right."

The soothing bath did much for her sore and aching body. She leaned back and let the scented foaming water drift over her as images of the night just past kept floating at the edge of her consciousness. Her body began to tingle just from the memories, and she lay there for a long while with a smile on her face.

Dried and sprayed with her favorite perfume, she dressed in her new sweater and a pair of tight, chocolate, suede jeans she'd bought in a moment of frivolous impulse. They clung to her hips and accentuated her legs. The outfit was so different from her usual dull, functional wardrobe. She smiled as she put on the heart earrings and brushed her hair out until it fell in thick, shimmering waves.

In the mirror, she saw an unfamiliar image, a woman full of life and exhilaration. Her eyes sparkled, and she glowed with passion and joy.

"You're so beautiful you take my breath away."

She looked up. Cole stood in the doorway, clad in chinos and a bright blue sweater that stretched over his powerful muscles and accentuated his dark hair and features. She saw such emotion in his eyes that her heart turned over. She went to him and wrapped her arms around him. "You make me beautiful," she said.

"You should dress this way all the time," he told her. "Except other women would most likely object. They'd pale into insignificance."

She laughed, not used to that kind of compliment. "Let's go make our calls," she said. "The ranch first, I guess."

Lindsey picked up on the first ring.

"Were you sitting on top of the phone?" Tara asked with amusement.

"I've been ordering myself to wait until you called and fast losing the battle. Is everything okay? We're dying out here."

"Everything's fine." She laughed. "More than fine. The gifts were great, but the best gift of all was the maneuvering you all did to get us together."

"Oh, Tara, I'm so glad. We wanted this for both of you. You two are made for each other."

"We're going to stop for breakfast before we pick up Molly, if that's okay."

"Come out whenever you want. Why don't you plan on staying for the afternoon? We're just watching

The Bargain

the football games, and I'm going to fix some sandwiches later on."

"That sounds great."

"Oh and tell Cole that Sean's out here. We'll pass along the good news. He's been about ready to drive back into town and bang on your door."

"You can all see for yourselves in a couple of hours," Tara laughed.

Chapter Thirteen

The day was one of Texas' glorious winter gifts, the sun blazing yellow, the sky a heavenly blue. To Tara and Cole everything seemed newly washed, the way their lives had suddenly become. The air had a fresh scent to it, and even the birds seemed to be singing just for them.

When they pulled up at the ranch, Tara got out of the car and Cole came around to her side, pulling her body to his. He leaned down and kissed her with such thoroughness her knees were weak. He had held back for so long. Now the dam had broken, and he couldn't keep his hands away from her.

"Careful," she told him, "or we night find ourselves naked in the dirt right here."

He chuckled. "At least, it will give those idiots peering out the window something to look at."

As Tara turned, the door to the house opened and Lindsey came out, followed by Jake and Sean. They smiled at the couple in front of them.

"No use to ask how things are," Jake joked. "All we have to do is look."

Lindsey hugged Tara. "You look absolutely amazing. As if you're a whole new person."

"I feel like it," Tara said, laughing.

"But the change in Cole is unbelievable. For the first time in what seems like forever, he's relaxed and at ease. He's actually smiling." She leaned closer and whispered to Tara, "I guess last night really did the trick."

Tara felt heat creep up her cheeks, but she answered, "I never kiss and tell."

"I'm so glad you took pity on him," Sean told her. "Another day and I'd have killed him for sure."

She laughed and hugged him. "You do good work."

Cole shook hands with both men. Nobody said anything, but the emotion that passed among them all was almost tangible.

"The kids are upstairs napping," Lindsey announced, "so we can have a few hours of peace. Jake's got the fire going, and Luisa made something that I don't know the name of, some little rolls that I can't stop eating." She linked her arm through Tara's and led her inside. "We're so happy for you," she said quietly. "Both of you. You deserve happiness."

The afternoon was tranquil. That was the only word for it. They watched football games, Tara and Cole next to each other on the couch so close not even a sheet of paper would fit between them. He held her hand most of the time, the rough texture of the warm skin feeling good against her palm. Even when they ate, he found excuses to touch her in some small way.

When it was time to leave, Tara got Molly ready, but she noticed that Cole, without prodding, put the baby seat in their car and took Molly's things from Luisa. It was the first time she remembered seeing him touch any of her belongings.

The little girl dozed on the ride home and barely woke when Tara took her in the house. When Tara came into her room after settling Molly in her crib, Cole was stretched out on her bed, stark naked, hands behind his head and a lazy grin on his face.

"Tomorrow, I'm moving my things in here," he announced.

They'd both agreed his bedroom held too many bad memories for them to share it. Maggie's aura was everywhere. Any time Cole spent in there was painful.

"We should think about redecorating the room," Tara told him, dragging her eyes away from his swollen, waiting cock. "Something that would personalize it and make it truly ours. New colors, new furniture." She tilted her head. "Does that appeal to you?"

The look in his eyes told her he was only interested in one thing. "Sounds interesting. We'll talk about it in the morning. Tonight, you'll have to be satisfied with just me." He reached out a hand to her. "Come to me, Tara."

She drew her sweater over her head, tossing it to the side, then shimmied out of her jeans. After the previous night, she found herself surprisingly unselfconscious undressing in front of him.

"You take my breath away," he told her as she joined him on the bed.

He gently teased her nipples, and they hardened under his touch. Her skin heated as he traced a line down to her navel, to the warm flesh of her stomach and below that. All her nerve endings woke, sending messages directly to her cunt. When he palmed her opening and slid one finger inside her, she pushed against him.

"Already wet." Desire thickened his voice. "My god, we might kill each other at this rate."

"See what you do to me?" she whispered, her hands moved over the taut flesh of his back. The curling hair of his chest rubbed against her breasts, making them feel tight and heavy.

"Same goes," he whispered.

She let him take her hand and place it on his erection. By now, he was fully engorged, and she relished the feel of it, stroking the silky skin and gently rubbing the tip.

"God, Tara," he groaned. "I can't wait tonight."

"Don't wait," she urged. "Do it now."

Spreading her legs wide, he thrust into her in one powerful motion. She gasped then forced herself to relax to take the thick, full length of him. The time for slow foreplay was past. He began thrusting at once, moving hard and fast. They climaxed together, quickly, but so mightily, it exhausted them both. He collapsed on top of her, the scent of sex surrounding them.

"I hope we get ourselves under some kind of control soon," he muttered, "or we're going to die from happiness."

Tara laughed, a warm, bubbling sound. "They say that's the best way to go."

He rolled onto his side and tucked her up against him, pulling the covers over them both. "I love the feel of you in my arms," he told her. "Sleep, baby. We'll have good dreams."

* * * *

When Tara brought Molly downstairs in the morning to feed her, she found Cole already in the kitchen. She was grateful to see he'd brewed a pot of coffee and poured a cup for each of them, but she wondered if he would retreat to his den until she was through with Molly. Instead, he just leaned against the counter, watching through narrowed eyes as she fed the little girl breakfast.

At least, it's a start. He's trying, just as he promised.

She realized he wasn't dressed in a suit today, even though it was Monday. He'd pulled on gray slacks and a red v-neck sweater. Casual clothes. While she finished with Molly, he called Angela, his secretary, to tell her he'd be out for the day. Tara wondered what that was all about.

"You don't have to stay home today," she told him. "We'll be okay."

"Much as I hate to admit it," he grinned, "I think they'll get along without me. I just hope they don't find out."

Tara settled Molly in her playpen with her favorite toys and turned on the mobile attached to one side. That would keep her occupied while she fixed breakfast for herself and Cole. She could feel his eyes on her as she moved around the kitchen. They were some time getting through breakfast, because it turned into a sensual exercise. Tara made scrambled eggs and sausage, and Cole insisted on feeding her the sausage by hand. As he placed each spicy piece on her tongue, she sucked at his fingertips, touching the edges with her tongue. That made him lean over and trace her lips, licking the taste of the sausage from them. He fed her the eggs one forkful at a time, first himself, then her, his tongue tracing her lips after each taste. When he thrust his tongue into her mouth, she sucked on that, too, loving the mingled taste of coffee and Cole.

Cleaning up became even more of a challenge. She stood at the counter in her nightgown while Cole cleared the table, pressing himself against her back with each delivery, his hot erection probing at the warm flesh of her buttocks. She had barely gotten the last dish in the dishwasher before he swept her up in his arms and carried her upstairs.

Pulling the covers back with one hand, he deposited her on the bed, pulled her gown over her head, stepped out of his sweat pants then mounted her. She was wet, as she always seemed to be now when he touched her. In two days, she had gone from ice maiden to wanton, carnal need consuming her so strongly she couldn't shut it off.

His mouth took hers in a hungry, greedy kiss, his tongue dueling with hers, her own small one twisting against his. He licked the roof of her mouth and the inside of her cheeks, each stroke of his tongue sending sensations straight to the heart of her pussy. She threaded her fingers through the heavy silk of Cole's hair, pulling his head even closer to her.

His hands slid down her body to find her nipples, pinching and rolling them until they stood up in hard, stiff peaks. Her heart raced and her pulse throbbed as her body responded to his touch. He shifted his body back and forth so his cock rubbed against her clitoris, driving her need higher than she'd thought possible.

She slid her hands around to find his flat nipples, pinching them as he had hers and scraping her fingernails over them. Cole lifted his head, the rhythm of his breathing changing and becoming uneven.

"I want you now," he rasped.

She opened her legs as he moved into position. They were both so ready, when he slid his penis inside her, she took the entire length of him in one stroke. They lay still for a moment, savoring the feel of her slick inner muscles grasping at his shaft. Then the room was silent except for the sound of skin against skin, heavy panting and their mingled shouts of joy as their climax crashed through them.

Cole collapsed against her, catching his weight on his forearms as they struggled to drag air into their oxygen-depleted lungs and calm their galloping hearts.

"That was ...incredible," Tara said in a weak voice, when she could speak again.

Cole kissed her softly. "Every time with you is incredible."

"Did we save enough energy to shift all your clothes?" she asked. "That's on our agenda for this morning. Remember?"

"I don't think I could move my body, much less my clothes," Cole chuckled, but he slid off the bed and pulled his pants back on. "All right, woman. I'm up and on my feet. Let's get busy."

When they were finished moving his clothes and personal belongings from one room to the other, Tara surveyed the results with great satisfaction. To her, the sight of their things mingled together was an affirmation of the pledge they had made to each other and the night before.

"Pretty pleased with yourself, aren't you?" Cole wrapped his arms around her from behind and tucked her head under his chin.

"You bet. Now I feel as if we're married."

"Oh, we're married all right," he told her in his deep voice. "Trust me. There's no doubt about that."

"Don't forget, I want us to think about making some major changes in here."

"We will. We'll do something. But I have other things on my mind at the moment." He stood for a long moment, looking at the closet again, scanning the clothes. He had the same speculative look in his eyes Tara had noticed in the kitchen.

Tara hugged herself nervously, wondering if something about the closet bothered him. He turned her around to face him, a somewhat unsatisfied look on his face. Was something making him uncomfortable?

"Is my face smudged?" she asked at last. "Why are you staring at me that way?"

"Because it gives me enormous pleasure."

She could see desire smoldering in his eyes. And something else, something she couldn't quite identify.

"What's going on behind that smile?" she asked. "Are you hatching something?"

"You bet." He grinned at her. "Do you think your folks would take the baby until after supper?"

The baby. Not her name, but at least not *the child*. "I'm sure they would if they don't have plans. They love having her with them. Why?"

He reached for her, resting his hands lightly on her shoulders. "I want to take my beautiful bride shopping, if that's all right."

"Shopping? For what?" She was totally bewildered.

"A new wardrobe."

"But Cole, I have—"

"Not what I want you to have. You need more things like the outfit you wore yesterday. It gives you, oh, I don't know, electricity?" He placed his hands on either side of her face and studied her. "Please let me indulge you." He winked. "And wear that outfit from yesterday."

Cole had other things in mind, too, but he'd need to make a few calls to accomplish them. He'd do it while they shopped, when Tara was tucked out of sight in a dressing room. He had always looked at money as just a means to an end. He'd never had it when he was younger so he'd worked hard to get it. Now that he had

The Bargain

more than he knew what to do with, he enjoyed being able to use it in a manner that give him real satisfaction. He smiled to himself, thinking over the idea that had popped into his mind.

Tara's parents were delighted to babysit, as she'd expected and even offered to keep Molly overnight. Soon, Tara and Cole were headed downtown to the Rivercenter Mall.

"I feel as if I've stepped into a reality television show," she told him, as he moved her along from store to store.

"Believe me, it's real enough," he grinned.

One thing was certain. The man had unerring taste. He sorted through displays, shooing her into dressing rooms, salesgirls following her with arms loaded. There was no question he was in charge today, but he was relaxed and comfortable, a man showing off his wife. He was having fun and so was she.

Tara chuckled in one store at the sight of him lounging in a chair, his legs crossed casually with an ankle resting on the opposite knee, looking magnificent.

"All the women are drooling over you," she whispered when she came out to model an outfit for him.

"If you ask me, I think it's the men who can't take their eyes off *you*." He touched her hand possessively. "I must be sure to let them know you're taken."

They smiled at each other, a smile full of intimate secrets that shut out everyone else.

While Tara tried on clothes, he put the rest of his plan into action. He made calls on his cell phone, speaking in a low voice and watching for Tara to appear. Things were coming together just the way he wanted.

By the time they stopped for coffee late in the afternoon, she was glad to have a minute to catch her breath.

"You must be out of your mind," she protested again. "I don't need all these clothes."

"Yes, you do. You need more color, more...everything. Besides, I love buying things for you, so don't argue with me. I'm a man who knows his own mind. Or so they tell me," he chuckled.

"I feel like a kept woman," she smiled.

"You are," he said. "And I'm the one who's keeping you. For a very long time."

"Where did you learn so much about women's clothes, anyway?"

"Watching my brother. And don't ask me for details," he grinned. "My lips are sealed."

Cole had planned for dinner on the Riverwalk, but by the time they finished at the mall, he agreed with Tara that home looked a lot better. "We can pick up pizza or something on the way," he said. "That okay with you?"

"You bet. I'll be glad to get home."

It took both of them to carry the bags to the bedroom. Tara hung up the things that needed hanging and left the rest for the next day.

"Right now, all I want is a shower," she said.

She was already standing under the streaming hot water, letting it work on her still sore muscles, when she felt someone beside her, a hand sliding the soap along her spine.

"I believe this is my bathroom now, too," Cole said in a low voice. "And my shower."

Her fatigue dissipated as he slowly lathered her body. He made her lean forward, bracing her arms against the wall, while he covered her back from her shoulders to her ankles, up the insides of her thighs and into the cleft of her buttocks, his fingers lingering there and moving in a gentle motion. Then he turned her around and did the same with her front, circling the nipples and sliding lathered fingers into her sheath, paying careful attention to the sensitive flesh inside. As she began to shake with desire, he stopped and handed her the soap.

"Not yet," he said. "My turn."

He stood while she moved the soap over his rock-hard body, covering every inch of it, rubbing his flat nipples until they were stiff, spreading the lather over his erection, running her finger over the tip, watching his face darken with desire. He turned off the shower, dried them both off and carried her to the bed. She had thought herself too tired to want this tonight, especially after making love that morning, but just his touch inflamed her and gripped her with a violent need.

He made slow, careful love to her, drawing out each orgasm until she was sure she would lose her mind, bringing her to climax again and again before entering her.

"Tonight I want nothing from you except to enjoy what I do to you," he murmured in a husky voice. "You make me feel like a man possessed, Tara. I can't get enough of you."

He was fierce and wild, at the same time gentle, claiming her with his love.

At last, he let her rest, tucking her in against him, her head on his shoulder. The last thing she remembered was saying, "We forgot to eat the pizza," and hearing his laugh rumbling deep in his chest. Then she slept.

Chapter Fourteen

"I've been thinking," Cole said the next morning. "I want us to have some time alone away from this house. We never had a honeymoon. I guess it wouldn't have been too appropriate before, but things have changed."

"Yes," she grinned, "they certainly have."

"I'm not talking about some big trip here," he went on. "I just want to hide us away somewhere for a while." He smiled at her. "A client of ours has a weekend cabin up in the hills about an hour from here. Right now, he's taking his family to Bermuda for two weeks so he was glad to give me the keys."

"How long will we be there?"

"Just two or three days. I wish it could be more, but Jake said the Colorado contract's been signed so I need to get back to the office."

"But who will watch Molly?" She tried to think what arrangements she could make. "An agency is out, Nicki has school and I think more than one night would be too much for my folks. She's getting to be a real handful."

"Already taken care of." He sounded pleased with himself. "She's going out to the ranch. With Luisa and Emilio there, Lindsey can manage nicely."

Tara's jaw dropped. "You already arranged this?"

His lips turned up with a self-satisfied smile. "Didn't think I could do it, did you?"

"I guess I think you can do anything," she said, still flabbergasted. "Oh, Cole, what a nice thing for you to do."

"Think we can find something to occupy us?" he teased and laughed as heat crept up her cheeks. "You can bring some of your new finery, although I might not give you a chance to wear much of it." He looked at her with uncharacteristic nervousness. "So, is this okay?"

"It's wonderful." She jumped up and threw her arms around him, kissing him. "When do we leave?"

"Today, as soon as we pick the baby up from your folks. We should pack now so we can leave right from there."

Their arrival in Cibolo created a flurry of activity. Emilio, stolid and implacable as ever, carried in all of Molly's paraphernalia, and Luisa took the little girl off to find Jason. Jake gave Cole the key to the cabin and the directions he'd picked up the night before.

Then, at last, they were off.

* * * *

If Tara had wished for heaven on earth, it would have looked like the cabin in the Hill Country. Although *cabin* couldn't begin to describe their vacation hideaway. Rising majestically on the crest of a hill, its limestone exterior looked as if it had been quarried out of the very ground on which it sat. Guarded by ancient oaks and sycamores, with crepe myrtles blooming in riotous profusion, it had the appearance of a painting on the cover of a western novel.

Deer roamed over the hundred acres that surrounded the house, along with wild turkey, rabbits and hundreds of birds flying in every direction. The air was redolent with the aroma of mountain cedar and Texas sage. A soft breeze rustled the finery of the oak trees and swayed the giant oleander bushes.

Tara gasped in wonder at her first sight of it, stunned by the magnificence the entire scene displayed. She wanted to capture it in a painting and hold onto it forever.

"Like it?" Cole grinned at her, helping her out of the car.

"You're kidding, right? What's not to like? My god, it's unbelievable." She drew in a breath, her nostrils filled with the clean scent of outdoors.

A massive limestone fireplace that soared to the ceiling dominated the center of the house. Tara could almost see the flames crackling in it.

"Great for blazing fires at night," Cole said, coming up behind her and gathering her in his arms. "We seem to do very well in front of fireplaces, don't we?"

Tara blushed at the obvious reference to the night of their reconciliation.

"I like a bride who can still blush," he teased. "I can't wait to see you in the firelight again."

Tara felt her heartbeat accelerate at the anticipation of the evening to come and the rest of the nights in this hideaway at the end of the world. She felt almost giddy with expectation and turned and hugged Cole tightly, pressing her face to his chest.

"Thank you for this," she said. "Thank you so very much." She moved away from him, walking to the front to look at the view again. "This whole place is so beautiful. It's like God's country."

Cole stood beside her, one arm draped over her shoulders. "I know. I get the same feeling when I'm at the ranch with Jake and Lindsey. It's like being in another world. No wonder Jake sold his house in the city when they got married and chose to live in Cibolo. I don't blame him. It's paradise."

They made no plans but just let each day happen, choosing activities as the moment struck them. Sometimes, they hiked the property, which covered a hundred acres. Other times, they roamed the countryside, stopping at out of the way places for lunch or dinner. In the evenings, they hunkered down in cozy comfort with one of the movies from the owner's collection, munching on hot, buttery popcorn and cuddling on the couch as if they were teenagers.

And of course, they made love whenever the mood struck them. They were ravenous for each other, feasting in greedy hunger, driven by their newly acknowledged love. She was always ready for him, hot and wet and waiting. He took her everywhere— in bed, on the couch, on the floor, standing up in the shower. He used every bit of expertise he had to give her total satisfaction, driving them both to exquisite peaks of desire.

One afternoon, lying in front of the fire on thick cushions after having had exhausting sex, he nibbled on her ear and whispered, "I want to try something different."

"Oh?" She was so sated and relaxed she was sure she'd agree to anything. "Different how?"

He bent over her, his tongue tracing circles around her nipples, down between the valley of her breasts and lower to her throbbing clit. "Just...different.

I think we've made love every way possible but one, and I want this with you more than you know."

His fingers sought her clit, massaging it as his mouth sucked each of her nipples. He slipped two fingers inside her, pulling them out slowly and showing them to her, covered with slick liquid. He licked his fingers slowly, drawing his tongue carefully from tip to knuckle. Then he lifted her and flipped her to her stomach, lowering himself to the cushions between her thighs. Before she could ask what he had in mind, he began lapping at her slit, thrusting his tongue inside her cunt and drawing it out slowly.

Tara griped the cushion beneath her head with her fists as sensations spiraled through her. She was sure she didn't have another orgasm left in her, but as always, Cole proved her wrong. One of his large, warm hands moved to caress her buttocks then trail down the cleft to the tight ring of her anus.

She jerked, startled by the thought of his invasion there. Cole simply moved his head and showered kisses on the globes of her ass, all the while letting his finger play in that area between them.

"Don't move," he said, thrusting his fingers inside her pussy then spreading her juices on the puckered entrance to her rectum, rimming it with the tip of one finger.

"Cole?" The word escaped on a long breath.

"Shh. It's all right. Just relax and let me pleasure you."

Did he intend to fuck her there? She had no idea how she would accommodate his enormous cock.

"But—"

"Shh," he repeated. "It will be all right."

As he worked her clit, her pussy and the cleft of her buttocks, she fell into a whirlpool of carnal lust that blocked out everything else. Soon her mind was focused on nothing but the heat spiraling up from her cunt. Whatever Cole wanted, her body apparently was ready to give him.

He pulled her to her knees, spreading her legs wide and placed another pillow beneath her to brace her body.

"Take a deep breath, darlin'." His voice was low and thick.

She did as he asked, drawing in every bit of air she could. At once, she felt the tip of his cock against her anus, pressing, pressing, pressing.

"Let it out slowly," he told her.

As she did, he moved past the tight ring of muscle and partially into her rectum.

"Oh!" she cried out.

He stilled. "Are you okay?"

Yes. No. Ice and heat rocketed through her veins.

"Yes," she said at last in a shaky voice.

"All right, then. Another deep breath, then let it out slowly."

And so it went. Every time she let out a breath, he invaded her even farther, until he was fully seated in that hot, dark tunnel. Flaming sparks fired everywhere inside her and shivers raced over her skin. She had never been drawn to anal sex, maybe because she had never trusted any man enough to give him the opportunity. But with Cole, she was willing to try anything.

An incredible wave of lust roared through her, igniting her pulses, hardening her nipples and making her clit throb in a demanding beat. She wanted this! It excited her in a way she'd never felt before. The dark eroticism of it thrilled her and gripped her in its clutch.

Cole reached around to find her clit, rubbing it until she couldn't stand the stimulation any more. Until her body demanded more than this. Until she wanted him to fuck here *there*.

Now!

She pushed back against him, silently urging him to motion. Wrapping one arm around her waist to keep her in position, Cole pulled back then thrust into her in one swift movement. Then again. In. Out. In. Out. On and on. She was lost in an erotic fog, everything focused on his cock in her ass and the incredible pleasure the friction caused her.

He rode her until the first tremors of her climax began then increased the speed of his movements so they crested and fell together. Tara felt herself whirling in space, her entire body convulsing over and over again, rockets exploding behind her closed eyelids, She clenched over and over again, caught on a plane of desire she'd never known existed. Cole's warm semen filled her rectum, setting off another series of tremors.

At last, when she was sure she could no longer stand it, the last aftershock shimmered over her, and she fell forward, Cole's body a heavy weight on top of her. Silently, he withdrew and stood up. She heard his footsteps leaving the room then returning. In a moment, she felt him cleaning her with a warm cloth. When he was finished, he turned her over to face him, wrapping his arms around her.

"Was it too much for you?" he asked.

She shook her head, unable to speak.

He frowned, concern in his eyes. "Tara, are you all right? Was I too hard on you?"

Finally, she found her voice. "It was the most amazing experience of my life. I've never felt anything like it." She buried her head against his chest. "It was...explosive."

"I worried," he told her, his hand wandering idly up and down her back. "I would never make you do something you didn't want. You know that, right?"

"Cole." She looked up at him. "It was the most intimate moment we've shared. I felt part of you. And yes, I want to do it again and again. And—"

He interrupted her with a deep chuckle. "How did I ever spend one day without you?"

"I don't intend for you to spend any more that way," Tara assured him, feeling his heart beat beneath her cheek as she cuddled against his chest.

* * * *

Three days seemed to fly past them as if they were only seconds. On their last night, after sharing a bottle of wine, brie and crackers, they stretched out in front of the fireplace one final time.

"I want this to work out for us, Tara." Cole's voice was serious. "I've wanted you for so long. You can't know how much I love you. I promised you I'd try with the little girl and I will, but what if I can't make it work?"

"Cole, if two people love each other, they can find ways to work through things. And I believe we love each other enough to do that. You've let me into your life. We've shared our secrets and realize the love we have is strong enough to withstand anything. You'll never lose me. The rest we'll just figure out as we go along." She lifted her face to him. "I'm in for the long haul, cowboy. You won't be getting rid of me any time soon."

"Thank god." He smiled at her lazily. "Let me show you how thankful I am."

He kissed her then. He tasted of wine and the fire and the woods, a strong male essence she wanted to swallow and keep inside of herself forever. She rubbed her hand over the coarse stubble on his chin, loving the rough, uneven feel of it against her palm. She unbuttoned his shirt, wanting to feel every inch of him. She buried her fingertips in the crisp mat of hair on his chest, teasing his nipples with the tips of her nails then putting her mouth on them to suckle as he did so often to her.

She felt cocooned in a warm place in life, free at last from the guilt and misery that had imprisoned her for so long. Now, she had a future with a man who loved her beyond anything, who made her body sing with pleasure and who brought her sunlight and roses. Right now, she was intent on giving some of that pleasure back to him.

Then it was his turn to feast. He took a long time tasting and kissing her skin. He devoted himself to her breasts, teasing her nipples, working at them, not touching any other part of her. He felt her breasts tighten and cupped his palms around the taut mounds. She was so delicious his penis responded with a will of its own and he had to fight for control.

Tara moved restlessly against him, and Cole slid one hand lower on her body, palming her mound, moving his fingers against her. He used his lips and tongue and fingers expertly, touching all the right places, drawing out each sensation.

She moaned against and he took it as a sign to him that she wanted more.

"Is that good, darlin'?" he asked, his voice raw with desire.

"Yes, yes." She could hardly speak.

He kissed her navel, swirling his tongue, pulling at it with his lips. And all the while, his fingers worked their magic between her legs. Little feathers of sensation chased up and down her spine and the pulse deep in her center began to thrum again. Her body didn't belong to her anymore. It was his, and he was totally possessing it.

He held her suspended, his tongue tracing patterns everywhere, his fingers tormenting her. She wanted him inside her, needed his thrusting to help her reach her peak, but he deliberately held her back. When he slid his fingers, wet with her juices, into the cleft of her buttocks, she gasped and a little spasm rippled through her.

"Right now," she panted. "Please, Cole. Now."

But he just continued to tantalize her with the tips of his fingers, circling and provoking. She tried to urge him inside her, but he shook his head.

"Slow, darlin'. Very, very slow. We have all night."

She took a deep breath, forcing herself to relax. Her body was turning into one gigantic nerve, humming with anticipation.

"Tell me," he ordered.

"Tell you what?" She couldn't think. Her mind was fogged.

"Tell me," he commanded, harsher this time, and she knew what he meant.

"I...love...you."

"Again. Say it again."

"I love you," she screamed. What was he doing to her? She could hardly form words, so intense was the desire coursing through her body. "I love you," she gasped.

The Bargain

"I love you, too, Tara. You are my life. You're mine. You belong to me. Say it." His mouth claimed hers in a demanding kiss.

"Yes, yes, yes, I belong to you," she panted against his lips. "Always, always. Please, please, please."

He held her teetering on the edge so long he knew every nerve in her body screamed for relief. She strained for the release that eluded her. Sweat made her skin shine in the muted light, and she fought to catch her breath. Her entire body trembled and shook with need yet he kept on and on.

He watched her through glittering eyes, captivated by her look of total abandonment, thrilled that the look was for him. Her head arched back, and she pushed against his hand as he used all his skill to draw her orgasm out as long as he could. Her entire body shuddered and shook.

"Please, please," she begged again, wanting more, wanting him to fill her.

Then, when he knew she could stand no more, he gave her what she needed and entered her. She convulsed around him, and his climax came almost at once. They both shook from the intensity of it, consumed by the fierce joining of their bodies.

He collapsed on top of her, drained, every bit of breath sucked out of his body. When he could raise his head, he looked into her eyes and was captured by what he saw there. He had always been a man of great sexual appetites, but for most of his life, what he experienced had been little more than a physical exercise. With Maggie, everything became a perversion. But with Tara, it was a blending of souls as well as bodies. A shared giving. Not even in his dreams had he thought he would find this kind of happiness. He swore he would do his best not to lose it.

"I hate to think of leaving tomorrow," Tara said. "This has been incredible."

"You like it here?" he asked.

"Oh, yes. No wonder Jake sold his house in town. This whole area is magic."

He leaned down and kissed her. "I agree. Let's enjoy every minute we have left here."

Tomorrow, he'd have another surprise for her, and he hoped she'd be as excited as he was.

Chapter Fifteen

Tara looked through the car window with mixed regret and excitement as they pulled away from the cabin. She felt sure that these few days had really cemented the marriage and turned a bizarre bargain into a real relationship. Too bad, they couldn't have stayed longer, maybe have brought Molly out to be with them. She had a distinct feelings that, in someplace other than that house filled with bitter memories, Cole would be able to find his way back to the little girl.

Closing her eyes and giving herself over to the motion of the car, she jolted upright when she realized they had stopped. She had no idea where they were except they were parked off the road between huge oaks. Nothing looked familiar.

She looked at Cole, confused. "Where are we?"

"About two miles from Lindsey and Jake." He grinned at her. "I told Jake what I wanted and had him scout it out." He went around and opened the car door for her, then urged her forward until she realized they were standing at the top of a hill. "Ten acres, with a creek running through it and plenty of space for a home, a yard, maybe even a couple of horses. You've got a horse farm to the right and a small cattle ranch to the left." He turned to her, anxiety written on his face. "What do you think?"

She was stunned. "I love it. Didn't you think I would? But—"

"I don't want to remodel the house, Tara. I want to be out of it. Start fresh, with no memories of any kind."

"Any kind?" she teased.

"Well," he drawled, "maybe a few. Listen, I had Jake tell the real estate agent someone might be interested. Would you be happy with this?"

Tara threw her arms around him. "More than I can tell you."

A house of her own, built just for them. She couldn't have asked for more.

By the time they reached the ranch, Tara could hardly contain her excitement. And when she went into the room where Molly sat in a playpen and the child reached out her arms for her, her heart was so full she had to turn away to hide her tears.

"Was she good?" she asked Luisa.

"As gold," Luisa answered. "I told Lindsey she should order a baby girl just like this one."

"She's been great," Lindsey said, "but she's been looking for you every day."

Tara hugged the little girl to her and rained kisses on her cheeks. The little girl smelled deliciously of cookies and chocolate and baby powder, a scent that made her heart turn over. Molly patted her with her chubby little hands then shifted in Tara's arms as she spotted Cole walking in behind her. Bouncing up and down, the little girl lifted her arms out to him, cooing.

Everyone in the room froze. No one made a move. Tara couldn't breathe, terrified that their newfound relationship would flounder in this situation. Cole had promised to try, but this might be asking too much too soon.

Molly squirmed, trying to reach Cole. Tara held her breath.

Cole stood for a long moment, such a look of agony on his face that Tara wanted to cry for him. Then, so stiff he looked as if his body would break, he reached out and took the little girl in his arms.

Jake broke the tension in the room. "Luisa packed all of Molly's stuff," he said. "I'll just take everything out to the car."

Tara barely noticed them leave the room. She just stood where she was, mesmerized, watching. "Do you want me to take her?" she asked at last, trying to ease this strange situation.

"No," Cole said, his voice sounding as if his throat were paralyzed. "It's all right. I'll carry her to the car. We should say our goodbyes and get going. And we need to thank everyone for doing this."

On the way out to the car, Lindsey pulled Tara aside. "By the looks of things, I'd say the delayed honeymoon exceeded expectations," she whispered.

"Better than you can imagine. We still have some hurdles to get past, but we'll get there. Everything between us is so wonderful, Lindsey."

"I'm so glad for you both. He's such a special person."

"Yes, he is. I'm very lucky."

"No," Lindsey said softly, "Cole's the lucky one."

"So did you give her the nickel tour?" Jake asked.

Cole nodded. "Call your agent and set up a meeting. It's a go."

Lindsey clapped her hands. "How wonderful. We'll be so close together."

"Remember," Cole warned, "we have one house to sell and another to build before this all happens."

"But it will." Lindsey kissed his cheek. "That's for luck."

They drove home in silence, but not a bad one. Not strained. A thoughtful quiet time.

While Cole carried all the suitcases into the house, she took Molly up to her room. Luisa had fed the little girl lunch, and her eyes were drooping now. When Tara put her in her crib, she popped her thumb in her mouth, closed her eyes and was asleep at once.

Tara went into the bedroom to unpack. She had no idea where Cole was. In the doorway of the room, she stopped, frozen. He was lying on the bed, eyes closed and one arm thrown across his forehead.

Slowly, she walked over to him, and what she saw made her heart ache. He made no move or sound, but tears ran unchecked down his face. It destroyed her to see this man, who had such great strength, coming apart this way. Not knowing what else to do, she sat down next to him and laid her hand on his chest.

He jumped as if she'd touched him with a lighted match then lay his head back down again. Tara sat with him, unmoving, for the longest time, not even offering to wipe away the tears. At last, when the torrent ceased, she smoothed away the dampness on his cheeks.

"It's so hard, Tara." His voice was tight with misery. "You're right. She's adorable and a child anyone would be proud of and excited to claim as their own. Holding her in my arms was unbelievable joy. Then I remembered. How can I get past this? Help me, Tara. I don't want to be this way."

She lay down next to him, nestling her head on his shoulder, touching his face. "I'll help you all I can, but

The Bargain

somehow, you have to come to terms with this yourself. But I am always here for you. You have to know that."

Cole held her to him as if he'd never let her go. She wanted to weep herself, for all the pain one person had caused. Instead, she molded herself to him as tightly as she could and let her hand rest on his muscular chest, trying to infuse his body with her warmth. After a long time, they dozed, clinging to each other.

At supper, she saw him making an even greater effort.

"I'll run out and get some Chinese so you won't have to cook," he told her, brushing her lips with a soft kiss. "It won't take me a minute."

When he returned, she had Molly in her highchair and was fixing her food.

"I'll be through with her dinner in just a few minutes," she told Cole. "She's not ready for bed yet, but I can see if she'll tolerate the playpen long enough for us to eat. Unless you want to wait until she's down for the night, and I'll just heat everything up."

"No, that's all right." He busied himself putting things on the table, not looking at either her or Molly. "I'll handle it."

The meal definitely had a strange feel to it. Cole dished out the Chinese food to Tara and himself then concentrated on eating. Molly sat in her playpen, making baby noises as she played with the soft toys Tara had placed in there. Tara was so tense she could hardly chew, but Cole plodded doggedly ahead with the meal.

This is the same as going to the dentist but without anesthetic.

The dinner seemed to last forever. She breathed a deep sigh of relief when at last it was time to give Molly her bath and put her to bed. Cole retreated to his den, and Tara left him there to battle his demons in private. She was more than thankful that the next day was Monday and Cole could leave for work. They all needed some space right now.

She crawled into bed, excited about the land they were buying and hoping the whole situation with Molly could be resolved before they moved into the new house. She had barely closed her eyes before she heard Cole come into the room and strip off his clothes. The mattress dipped as he lowered his body next to hers. His warm hand cupped her cheek, turning her face toward him.

"I'm sorry I'm such a difficult ass to live with." He kissed her eyelids, her cheeks, the line of her jaw.

"I know you're trying," she whispered, barely getting the words out before his mouth came down on hers.

There was nothing tentative about the kiss. His tongue traced the seam of her lips before forcing them open and thrusting inside. He fed on her, tasting every inch of her.

Tara wound her arms around his neck, pulling him closer, wishing she could make the demons go away. She met his tongue thrust for thrust, tangling with him, tasting him, silently urging him to more. When she slid her hands down his back to his buttocks, she encountered bare flesh and realized he hadn't left his boxers on.

"I enjoy sleeping naked with you," he murmured against her mouth. "You can forget about wearing nightgowns anymore. I sleep better when I can feel every inch of your skin."

"I don't think sleeping's what you have in mind," she teased as he maneuvered her gown over head and tossed it to the floor..

"Damn right."

He lowered his head to her breasts, sucking each hard nipple until it swelled and throbbed. His teeth grazed the pebbled flesh, tugging each one until she moaned with pleasure. His tongue laved them, soothing them, before his mouth moved farther down to her navel where he traced feathery circles.

Tara shifted restlessly beneath his assault, her skin hot, her blood racing. Just one touch from him could ignite every nerve in her body. Her pussy vibrated with need, demanding his cock. She slipped her hand between them and tried to reach down for him, but his position kept it just beyond her grasp.

"Please," she murmured.

He lifted his head. "Please what?"

"Please let me touch you." The words escaped her on a sigh.

"Do you want to suck my cock, Tara?"

"Yes." Heat flashed over her at the thought. She'd become much bolder with him. "I would."

With lithe movements, he shifted until he was flat on his back, one strong arm urging her up and forward until she leaned over him.

"I love it when your hair brushes my skin." Desire thickened his voice. "It's like silk."

He sifted his fingers through it as she bent and took the head of his shaft into her mouth, her tongue brushing the velvety slit. The drop of liquid sitting on the dark purple flesh coated her tongue, a deliciously musky taste. She pulled back to run her tongue back and forth through the weeping opening, eliciting a heavy groan from Cole.

Her fingers closed around the base of his cock, squeezing gently, as she lowered her mouth, taking in the length of him. In a natural tempo, her hands and mouth moved up and down his penis, fingers squeezing rhythmically, the edge of her hand pressing into his swollen balls. She raked her teeth over the steel-hard shaft the same way he teased her nipples, and his entire body shuddered at her touch.

"Enough," he groaned, lifting her head with his strong hands and pulling her towards him. Instinctively, she positioned herself over his cock, knowing she was more than wet enough to take him. He guided the head to the opening of her cunt then gripped her waist as she slowly lowered herself onto him.

Electricity shot through her, sparks of lust that this connection with him always ignited. He'd shown her the way he enjoyed it, and now, she began that rhythmic up and down movement, bracing herself on his chest, fingertips pinching his nipples. His hands tightened on her hips, using his grip to increase the speed of her movement. His cock flexed inside of her and his body tightened at the same time. Her own climax approached, and she lifted herself one last time then lowered herself, gripping him with the muscles of her pussy, threw back her head and let the orgasm overtake them both.

She collapsed forward onto his chest, utterly spent but loving the unbreakable connection between them. His unsteady lips brushed against hers as his arms came around her, holding her tightly to him.

"We'll get through this," he promised. "Just hang onto me and don't let go."

As if she would!

* * * *

The Bargain

Obviously tired from her three days of excitement, Molly slept later than usual the next morning and so did Tara. When she came downstairs with the freshly diapered child, Cole was already at the kitchen table, drinking coffee and talking on the phone. When Tara looked at him, he held up one finger signaling to wait, he was almost through.

"All right," he said into the receiver. "Tell them that's the best offer they're going to get. I'll be at my office in an hour. Call me back as soon as you get an answer." Disconnecting the call, he leaned back in his chair with a self-satisfied look on his face.

Tara raised an eyebrow as she settled Molly in her highchair. "You sure look like someone who won the lottery. What's going on?"

"I called the real estate agent on that property and made an offer. He's going to call me back at the office, but I think they'll take it. It's close enough to their asking price that I think they won't bargain."

"What happens then?"

"As soon as we close on it, we need to hire an architect, meet with him and get some plans drawn up."

"Wow!" Tara tucked her hair behind her ears and sat down to feed Molly. "Moving at the speed of light, are we?"

He reached across the table to touch her arm. "I can't get out of this house fast enough, if you want to know the truth."

Tara was silent for a moment, working to get more food in Molly's mouth than on her chin. An idea suddenly took root in her brain. When Cole returned to the table, his own coffee mug refilled and carrying one for her, she turned to look at him.

"I have an idea in that direction," she said slowly.

"Yeah?" Cole sipped the hot liquid in his mug. "Okay, let me have it."

"We could move into my house. No one's ever lived there but me," she hurried to assure him. "You've had the landscape and cleaning services there once a week so it's in good shape. I know it's a lot smaller than this place, but it would do for the short term. We can sell it when the new house is ready."

When he didn't answer, she glanced at him nervously. He was staring at her.

"Bad idea?" she asked.

"No, it's a great idea. Why didn't we think of this before?"

"Because before," she said very carefully, "it didn't matter where we lived. Now it does."

"You'd sell your house?"

She shrugged. "It's only a building. No memories. Someone new will make their own. We'd have to put all this furniture in storage."

"Get rid of it," Cole bit off. "Sell it with the house. Burn it. I don't care. How soon can we move?"

Tara laughed. "As quickly as I can air out the place and call the movers. We need to take Molly's stuff, our clothes, the things from your den..."

"Buy something new. Order it today and have them deliver it and set it up."

He came to stand behind her and placed a kiss on the top of her head. "Do it. Call today. As soon as I get to the office, I'll call a real estate agent we've done a lot of work with and get this place listed." He drained the rest of the coffee and put his mug in the sink. "I'd better get going. This is shaping up to be a busy day ahead."

* * * *

The Bargain

Everything kicked into fast forward. In less than a week, they finalized a listing agreement, hired an architect and moved forward with their plans. Tara's parents were delighted when she told them, although not too excited about having them living farther away.

"It won't be that far, Mom," Tara assured her. "I still have to be close enough so Cole won't have a long drive to the office. And we drove it yesterday. It's only twenty-five minutes between our new place and yours."

"Well, all things considered," Ellen said, "I do think getting out of that house will be good for both of you. Forgive me for saying this, sweetheart, but being the second wife sometimes has its drawbacks. It never helps to cook in another woman's kitchen."

Tara had never told the McKees the Maggie story nor did she intend to. It was Cole's secret to share, not hers. But Ellen, with her uncanny intuition, had sensed an air of imbalance in the house that she couldn't quite define. Tara could tell she was pleased that they were going to make a fresh start in a new place.

* * * *

Cole was home earlier than usual the following night, looking very satisfied with himself. He dropped a large envelope on the counter.

"An early Christmas present, darlin'. They accepted our offer. We now own a big piece of land in the middle of somewhere."

"Oh, Cole. Really and truly?" She leaped up and threw her arms around him. "But that's wonderful."

"All you have to do is sign these papers tonight, and I'll have someone drive them to the agent's office tomorrow. The seller has already signed."

"I've been busy, too," she grinned. "The nursery furniture will be delivered and set up tomorrow and the movers will be here Wednesday. They'll pack up everything I tell them to, including our clothes and we'll just leave the rest." She frowned at him. "Are you sure that's what you really want to do?"

"You don't know how much." His face was suddenly grim. "I just want to walk out the door and never look back." She saw him glance at Molly in her highchair.

"I'll get her upstairs and bathed in just a minute," she said hastily. "You came home a little early, is all, so I'm running just a bit behind."

"It's all right, Tara," he said. "You don't have to hide her just because I'm in the house." His face took on a conflicted look. "I've touched her, and it hasn't killed me. It's just very hard, that's all. But I think it's time to move ahead. I guess I'll just keep doing my best with it and see where it goes."

"Oh, Cole." She hugged him and laid her face against his chest. "You don't know how much I want to make the past go away."

"Me, too, sweetheart." He patted her fanny. "Now, why don't you go do whatever it is you need to do and I'll get rid of this jacket and tie. I brought home some champagne so we could celebrate before dinner."

* * * *

She drove Lindsey out to see their property the next morning.

"This is gorgeous." Lindsey's eyes sparkled. She turned to hug Tara, somewhat of a problem with her now bulging stomach and Molly in Tara's arms, but they managed. "I'm so very happy for you. Both of you. Cole deserves every bit of happiness you bring him."

"We still have some bumps in the road," Tara said, "but we're getting there, one step at a time."

The Bargain

Wednesday the movers showed up on schedule and by five that afternoon, juggling a cranky Molly whose naps had been hit or miss, Tara walked back into her house where the furniture fought for space with piles of cartons. Several of them were stacked in her garage and wouldn't be opened until the new house was ready, but her house was half the size of Cole's, which doubled the problem. Plus the fact that her rooms were a miniature of the ones Cole was used to and likely to give him a case of claustrophobia.

Well, no matter. We'll be a little crammed, but we can make it work. We just need to get the plans finished, settle on a builder and get him in high gear.

She unpacked some of their clothes and Molly's things, fed and bathed the little girl and put her down for the night. At last, she collapsed on the couch, catching her breath. She was still sprawled in the same position when Cole showed up promptly at six, carrying pizza and sodas.

"My hero," she told him. "Just what the doctor ordered."

"You're an amazing woman," he said, looking around. "I can't believe how much you've gotten done." He leaned down and kissed her. "If you're not too tired, maybe later, I can show you just how much I admire you." He winked and leered at her.

She was sure she was too worn out to respond to anything, but when she came out of the shower, he was waiting for her, holding a towel.

"I thought we should christen the bed." His voice was hoarse with passion, and desire glittered in his eyes.

He began to dry her with gentle pats, his touch so intimate that she was instantly aroused. She felt the familiar race of her pulse and the throb between her legs.

When he leaned down and kissed the tender spot at the hollow of her throat, a steady thrumming there reverberated against his tongue. His lips moved over her jaw line, feathering light kisses, until his mouth came down on hers, his tongue probing, tangling with hers and feeding on her mouth. He swept the hot, dark recesses of her mouth, drinking her in, tickling at every nerve, the in and out thrust mimicking the movement of his penis when he penetrated her.

He held the kiss as he dried her breasts with great care, teasing the nipples with the roughness of the towel. The feel of his hand alone was enough to start a pulse thudding deep inside her womb, turning her knees to jelly.

He tore his mouth away from hers at last, picked her up and carried her to the bed. His eyes raked her body as he tore off his own clothes and lay down next to her. As if it were all new to him, he kissed every inch of her, touching all her sensitive places. Not an inch of her skin evaded his marauding mouth and hands. He felt her tremble with the anticipation of his movements.

Her breasts were hot to his touch, the nipples a dark rose already pebbled and waiting for his mouth. He loved to suck them and press them against the roof of his mouth with his tongue. Feel them harden even more. Feel Tara arch her body into him to give him greater access.

He touched the insides of her thighs and found them damp with her liquid. His probing fingers discovered a pussy deliciously wet for him. His warm breath blew on her soft curls as his fingertips touched her swelling labia, parting them and kissing the exposed skin with the softest touch. She pushed down at the gentle glide of his lean fingers into her vaginal canal. Cole couldn't believe how responsive she was, how hot their sex continued to be.

"You're wet for me," he whispered. "God, I love the slick feel inside you, Tara. I love to feel your liquid in my hands." He took her hand and placed it on his thick, distended cock. "See what you do to me?"

She moved her hand along the thickness of the shaft, loving the feel of it, teasing the velvety head. Sliding the tip of her finger across the drop of moisture on the top of his penis, she brought her hand up and rubbed it on her lips. The erotic sight made him groan, and he nudged her legs wider apart.

"You like my taste, don't you?" He was so aroused he could hardly get the words out.

"Yes." Even her words were becoming bolder. "I love it, just as I love taking your cock in my mouth and sucking it until you come."

"I have to be inside you," he whispered. "Now."

But as he'd done at the cabin, he flipped her onto her stomach, using pillows to brace her and lifted her to her hands and knees. Using his fingers to scoop her juices from her cunt, he painted the tight opening of her anus, sliding one finger inside to lubricate her for his penetration.

When he was sure she was ready, panting with need, he spread the cheeks of her buttocks, positioned himself and slid into her by increments. She was still learning the pleasures of anal sex and the last thing he wanted to do was hurt her. But god, she was so hot and tight there she nearly blew the top of his head off.

He rolled his hips, setting the rhythm, coaxing her to breathe in and out as he fucked her ass with slow, steady strokes. He moved one hand around to find her clit, rubbing and pulling at it until she moaned with arousal and need. He was at the edge, and he knew it.

"I can't wait, Tara."

"Neither can I. Don't wait. Do it now."

In seconds, he was pouring into her, pulling her hard against him, feeling her clench around him, spurting again and again until he filled that hot, dark channel. Finally, reluctantly, he pulled from her body and went to the bathroom. She heard the sound of running water then he was back with a cloth to clean her. When he climbed back into bed, she spooned against him, her body softening. When he reached between her thighs to find her pussy, a shocked gasp slipped from her mouth.

"Cole?"

"We're far from done yet, darlin'. I think this house has given me renewed vigor."

Cole had no idea where either of them found the strength to last the night. He kept her in a constant state of arousal, building the tension, holding her on the edge, then backing off, soothing her and starting all over again.

There was a difference in their lovemaking, a freedom and a newness. This was more giving than possessing, tender in its fierceness. Tonight, once again, he was focused only on her pleasure. He teased at her with his fingers and his tongue, using his thumb to draw the lazy circles around her clit and felt her body shiver beneath him. When she tried to reach for him, he clasped both of her hands in one of his and held them in place over her head, arching her body toward him.

He devoured her. That was the only word for it. At last, he gave her the release she sought. Plunging into her with one swift movement, they tumbled through space, pulsating waves of pleasure flooding them both. Afterwards, they lay still in each other's arms.

Cole stroked the side of her face, her shoulder and her arm. He'd never expected to fall in love with such total commitment. He felt it in every nerve and muscle of his body, and his heart was full to capacity. Every one of his senses was more alive because of her. The air smelled cleaner, the sky was bluer, the sun brighter. The soft cadence of her voice whenever she spoke to him had the soothing quality of a lullaby. He gave thanks constantly that she'd given him a second chance.

"You were different tonight," she said faintly, as the moonlight filtered through the curtains.

"Except for the cabin, tonight is the first time we made love that I didn't feel a phantom hovering over my shoulder. This house is clean, Tara. The only spirit in it is yours. And now ours."

"I feel as if we've closed one door and walked through another."

"That's the plan, my love. That is, indeed, the plan." He hugged her close to him, molding her against him, and they fell easily asleep.

Chapter Sixteen

Although they slept later than usual, Tara expected to be exhausted when she got up in the morning. To her surprise, she felt refreshed and rejuvenated. She commented on it to Cole, who just smiled.

"Dr. Cassidy's magic fingers." He leered wickedly.

"Dr. Cassidy better keep his magic fingers to himself this morning," she told him as he reached for her. "I have a lot to get done and I want to make something special for our first dinner here. So go to work and keep your magic fingers busy until tonight."

As the days moved along, they all adapted to the house much better than she'd expected. Cole suffered from claustrophobia for the first week or two, but before long, he adjusted to the more confined situation. She gave him the tiny den to use, realizing he still needed a room to hide himself in now and then. That seemed to increase his comfort zone.

Molly was consumed with delight. She had new corners to poke into and new areas to explore. The problem was her inquisitive nature propelled her into all sorts of trouble. Tara had Cole remove the inside door from the enclosed back porch and turned it into a playroom for Molly. It gave the little girl a place to expend her energy, and Tara some peace of mind.

They managed, after a fashion, but she'd be glad when the new house was finally built.

* * * *

The house had only been listed for a week when the real estate agent called to tell them they had a buyer. The people had made an offer, asking if the furniture went with it. Tara called Cole at the office, barely able to contain her excitement.

"The agent has a buyer." She was almost dancing with glee. "The people from the Sunday showing. Almost the full price, too. And guess what? They also want all the furniture and stuff."

"You're kidding." Cole laughed. "I think you're right. This was meant to be."

She cleared her throat. "It will be nice for you to spend Christmas someplace else."

"You are so right," he said after a moment of silence. "And it will be our first together."

Our first Christmas. I have to make it special for him.

The day they closed on the sale of the house, they left Molly with her parents and went to dinner to celebrate. Cole took her to the Italian restaurant they'd eaten at before, and they took a long time over dinner.

"This is the beginning of everything new." Tara touched his hand gently, praying silently that she was right. "A new door is opening for us."

"You're good for me." He rubbed his fingers across the back of her hand. "If I hadn't been such a fool, we could have had this a long time ago."

"Forget about that. We have it now. That's all that matters."

Smiling at each other, they toasted their new life.

The Bargain

* * * *

The meetings with the architect went better than either of them had expected. Deciding not to build his own house and borrow trouble, Cole chose a homebuilder he had high regard for. They met with him to finalize arrangements and everything was a go for the first of the year.

Determined to fall in with the holiday spirit, especially now that they were in new surroundings, Cole took two days off and went shopping with Tara for a tree and ornaments.

"Not much," she reminded him. "Next year, we'll decorate in the new house. But I can't let the season go by unnoticed. And it will be good for Molly."

They hauled the tree to her house, and Cole helped her decorate.

"I haven't had a tree since my folks died." His eyes were suddenly sad.

"We'll more than make up for it." Tara hugged him. "From now on, every Christmas will be special."

Christmas was a joyous celebration. They opened presents in the morning, watching Molly's unrestrained pleasure in everything. Then they all, including her parents and Sean, trooped out to Cibolo for a holiday feast at the Varner ranch.

They celebrated New Year's very quietly, not wanting to share this first one with anyone. At midnight, they toasted each other with champagne.

"To our wonderful life," Cole said.

"The best," Tara agreed.

They looked at each other with feelings of deep satisfaction and pleasure, aware of how blessed they were with a love that grew more each day.

"The land is cleared," she told Cole one night after a trip out to the property, unable to contain her excitement. Her eyes danced, and she couldn't stop smiling. "Oh, it looks so wonderful. And they have the house staked out to give us the best view. Right on the crest of the hill."

"Did the builder say when they'd be pouring the concrete?"

"Tomorrow." Tara felt like a kid at Christmas. "It's going to be just fantastic."

Two or three times each week, she bundled Molly into the car and drove out to the site, checking progress and meeting with the builder. And of course, there was a never-ending array of things to select—paint, flooring, fixtures, counters, appliances. The list went on and on. Cole was busier at the office than ever. Alamo had three new projects going. Still, he managed to steal time here and there when Tara needed him.

Some nights, they were so tired they just crawled into bed, looked at each other and fell asleep. But Tara was never too tired to be conscious of the tension that was still their companion where Molly was concerned. Cole's stoicism when he was with her was almost painful to watch.

Sitting at the kitchen table one morning, sipping the last of her coffee, she tried to search her mind for some solution. The house was quiet. Cole had gone to the office for a rare Saturday meeting, and Molly was with Nicki. The teenager had picked her up earlier to take her to a birthday party for one of the myriad Varner nieces and nephews. Tara had looked forward to this time to do some uninterrupted work, but her mind kept wandering.

Since the week in the cabin, their marriage had been incredible—warm, passionate, loving. Cole was more open with her in every way than he'd ever been to anyone in his life. He had torn down walls he'd spent years erecting, reaching out to make her a part of himself. It was everything she could want. Almost.

The subject of Molly was still an invisible barrier between them.

"I'll try," he'd promised.

He really was making the effort, but Tara could see how painful every contact was for him, how he nearly dreaded it. Knowing he did it for her made her heart ache twice as much. How awful that his love for a tiny life he'd thought he'd created has been brutally destroyed by a few careless but well-chosen words.

The whole situation was still a ticking time bomb. The older Molly got, the more she'd sense Cole's feelings for her and wonder at the distance he created. What new problems would that bring? Tara could see herself placed squarely in the middle of a no-win situation.

In the midst of all her newfound happiness, she wanted to weep at the unfairness of it all, at the legacy of a spiteful woman.

Damn Maggie, anyway, for bringing such pain to such a wonderful man.

At last, sighing, she drained her coffee cup and placed it in the dishwasher. The answer was some place. She'd just have to be clever enough to find it before it destroyed them all.

* * * *

Time seemed to be passing so swiftly now with the activities that consumed each day. Before they knew it, their first anniversary was approaching and Cole wanted them to do something special.

"Not go away," he said quickly. "I know the timing isn't right for that. But think about some place you've always wanted to go for dinner. Or something we can do that's always been on your wish list."

"You spoil me." She kissed him. "I'll give it some thought, okay? And try to come up with some suggestions."

At that moment, though, she was so tired nothing appealed to her. And deadlines were looming. The house was nearly complete. All it needed were the last finishing touches. Then they would call the movers and put her house up for sale. They'd decided to take their time shopping for furniture, using hers in the interim. She knew Cole was anxious to actually be settled at last, and she was doing her best to get ready.

Tara was so relieved he was willing to wait on the furniture she could have wept. The thought of more shopping, more choosing, exhausted her. A fatigue enveloped her that she just couldn't seem to shake. She'd felt it for days. Then one morning, she woke up and couldn't drag herself out of bed.

"I think I have the flu." She had just thrown up for the third time. "It's been going around. Remember when Nicki had it? What with all the moving around and everything, I just realized I forgot to get my flu shot. I don't think I'll be up to much celebrating on our anniversary. I'm so sorry."

Cole, concern lining his face, brought her some tea and made her lie down with a cold cloth on her forehead. "The important thing is for you to get well. You've worn yourself out with moving and working on the new house. I should have seen what was happening and put the brakes on."

"It wasn't a big deal," she protested. "If I had just gotten that stupid flu shot, I'd be all right."

Molly was bouncing up and down in her crib, babbling her familiar sounds.

"I have to get up." Tara tried to sit up without much success. "Molly needs to be dressed and fed."

Cole forced her back down to the pillow. "I'll manage. You're in no condition to do anything."

"But you don't..."

"I can do it." He smiled at her thinly. "I run a company with massive projects.. I should be able to take care of one small child."

"Come get me if you need help," she called in a weak voice.

He headed down the hall, his body unnaturally stiff. She worried about how he'd deal with being forced into the situation, but she was too sick to care. She put her head on the pillow and fell asleep at once.

When she woke, she was nauseous again and stumbled to the bathroom. Cole must have heard her because he was upstairs and beside her in what seemed like seconds. He helped her back to bed, wiped her face and gave her some water to drink.

"Can you hold anything in your stomach?" he asked. His face was taut with worry.

"Some tea, maybe. I'll come downstairs if you'll help me."

"Not on your life. I can fix a cup of tea and I'll bring some crackers—one thing my mother was always good at was treating the sick. Crackers and tea, her cure for everything. Then I'm going to take you in the shower with me, and when we get out, I'll change the sheets. You have to feel sticky."

"Where's Molly?" she asked, her forehead creased with anxiety.

"In bed asleep."

"Did you find everything for her okay? What did you do about breakfast and lunch? And how did you handle her all morning?"

"Everything was fine. She's very good, which helps a lot. I may not have fed her what you would have, but we made out all right. And look." He gave her a weak grin. "I haven't had a nervous breakdown."

She tried to smile at his mild attempt at humor. "Nicki can come in after school and help," she reminded him.

"Let's wait and see how you feel tomorrow. If you're still sick, I just might call her."

The shower felt good. She was grateful to have the sour feeling of nausea washed away. Cole was very gentle with her, holding her while he bathed her, sitting her on the vanity so he could dry her and put on a fresh gown. He placed her in the slipper chair while he did a hasty job of bed making then carried her over and laid her down with the pillows fluffed under her head.

"I know I'll be better tomorrow." She tried to subdue the nausea that never seemed to leave her. "And you have to go to work. I know how busy it is when you take on new projects."

"I do believe they're learning how to get along without me." He grinned. "What a blow to my ego. Jake doesn't miss a beat, just picks up whatever slack he needs to. I told them to expect me when I show up. Quit worrying about everything, and let me take care of things. That's an order."

She sank back on the pillows, thankful to leave everything in his hands. She drank another cup of tea and promptly fell asleep again.

But the next morning, she wasn't any better. The nausea hit her as soon as she opened her eyes. Cole held her head, wiping her face and holding a glass of water so she could rinse her mouth. She kept down tea and crackers then slept. She couldn't seem to keep her eyes open, which was a blessing because when she was asleep at least she didn't throw up.

The Bargain

In moments of wakefulness, she wondered how Cole was surviving with Molly. He was out of bed instantly each morning when he heard her voice, his face set in granite but determination in every line of his body. He had taken her advice and called Nicki, who blessedly came in each day after school.

Tara strained to hear the noises of the house, expecting disaster, but all she heard was Molly's familiar giggle and Cole's deep voice. She wanted to get up and help, but she barely had the strength to make it to the bathroom and back. Nicki was now coming in right after school and staying until Molly was in bed for the night.

"Are you doing okay with her in the morning?" Tara asked one evening, full of anxiety. She had been sick for four days now and didn't seem to be getting any better. She knew Cole was increasingly worried about her.

"We haven't had any disasters yet," he told her. "Everything is fine."

She knew what a supreme effort it was for him and ached for the internal struggle she was sure he was having. What a situation.

By the fifth day, she was beginning to feel a little better. She wasn't racked with nausea all the time, and she could keep down some broth as well as tea and crackers. She was lying on the pillows in the late afternoon, wondering if she should try and get up, when she heard a crash and a scream from downstairs. Her blood chilled and panic clutched at her. The scream was Molly's.

She forced herself up from the bed, found her robe and made her way downstairs, clinging to the banister and hoping she didn't pass out. Molly was still screaming and over that sound she heard Nicki's scared voice and Cole's, tense but in command.

She leaned into the doorframe in the kitchen, supporting herself and shaking at what she saw. The highchair was lying on the floor, glass and blood were everywhere, and Cole was holding Molly. Blood was spurting from her arm at an alarming rate. Nicki had grabbed dishtowels and was trying to apply pressure.

"That's arterial blood," Tara whispered, her voice shaky with fear. "She needs a tourniquet."

Dizzy and weak yet somehow finding the strength to move, she grabbed another towel and twirled it to form a wide strip. With Cole helping, she placed it around Molly's arm, tying it over the other towels to form a pressure pad.

"Hold her arm up," she ordered. She tried not to look at the long, deep cut on the little arm. "Did you call 9-1-1?"

"I'm taking her right to the emergency room," Cole said, his jaw clenched. "The hospital isn't very far."

"I'm coming with you," Tara told him.

"Tara, you're sick and you can hardly stand up. Besides, you can't run around in a nightgown. Please get back in bed."

"Nicki." She turned to the terrified teenager, forcing a strength she didn't feel. "Grab my raincoat, would you? It's spring, for heaven's sake. It's already balmy here. And my shoes, too. Hurry. I'm going. I want to be with her. Nicki. Go now." Somehow, she found the strength to hold it together, but barely.

"I'm so sorry, Mrs. Cassidy," Nicki said, twisting her hands. "It's all my fault."

"No, it's not," Cole insisted. "I was here, too. But right now, we need to get to the emergency room. Help me get them both in the car. You'd better come, too."

The Bargain

Cole drove like a madman, honking his horn at every vehicle in his way. Nicki was wedged in the front seat between them, helping Tara with Molly, keeping the bleeding arm raised. They both tried not to notice how pale the little girl was. Tara's own discomfort was forgotten for the moment as she focused on the emergency at hand.

"I was irresponsible," Cole said, anguished. "I should have paid better attention. We had her in her highchair, but I didn't check to make sure she was securely strapped in. I know she tries to stand up in it all the time. I've seen her do it."

"Did she just fall?"

"I had a glass of soda on the counter," Nicki said miserably. "Molly reached for it. Lost her balance, and she and the highchair both fell, pulling the glass with them. When she landed, a jagged edge cut her arm." She was caressing the little girl's face, wiping her tears, trying to soothe her. "I'm a terrible baby-sitter. I wouldn't blame you if you fired me."

"Nicki, accidents happen with children." Tara tried to sound reassuring, but she was fighting back a new wave of nausea and dizziness. "You do the best you can and pray about everything else."

Cole pulled up to the emergency entrance, slammed the car in Park and ran around to take the baby from them. He was already racing into the reception area when Tara struggled out of the car.

I will not faint. I will not be sick..

Tara clenched her jaw and exerted as much control as she could muster. Cole could worry about her later. The baby came first.

Nicki helped her inside, and she collapsed into the chair nearest the door.

The emergency room was in chaos, people hurrying everywhere, voices raised. Although the seating area was full of people waiting their turn, rules and regulations didn't exist for Cole Cassidy. People seldom argued with him about anything. With his usual expectation of compliance, he carried Molly up to the desk, corralled a nurse who yelled at once for a doctor and they all disappeared into a curtained area.

Tara sat huddled into the chair, letting the noise swirl around her, holding her coat to her for warmth. Nicki stood next to her, wringing her hands, unsure what to do next. Tara could see the teenager was running on nerves at this point. She wondered if anyone would come and tell her anything.

The combined odors of illness and medicine were threatening her fragile hold on her heaving stomach. She kept her eyes closed, calling on what little strength she had to survive this without passing out or throwing up on the hospital floor. Cole was right, she shouldn't have come, but she couldn't have let him take Molly without her.

All she could think was *what a mess*.

Tara was leaning back with her eyes closed, willing the nausea to go away, when a gentle hand touched her arm and a soft voice said, "Mrs. Cassidy?"

She pried open her eyes.

A nurse was beside her with a wheelchair. "Mr. Cassidy is worried to death about you. He says you have a bad case of the flu. It's sure been going around. He wants a doctor to take a look at you. Come on, let me help you into the wheelchair." She smiled reassuringly. "If you pass out on the floor here, it doesn't make us look too good."

"Molly?"

"Your little girl's being taken care of. The doctor's with her and so is your husband."

"The bleeding?" Tara was almost afraid to ask.

"They've got it under control. I'm just going to get you into an area here, then tell them where you are. Someone will come and let you know what's happening real quick."

"Is it all right if I go call my mother?" Nicki asked, after helping the nurse with Tara. She was fighting back the tears that threatened to spill out of her eyes.

Tara nodded as she was wheeled away. In a minute, she was lying down in a treatment area, being covered with a blanket, the privacy curtain pulled around her. She felt the nausea rise again and with great effort fought it back. She was trying to get herself under control when someone pulled the curtain aside, and Cole was there with the doctor.

"Where's Molly?" she asked, her voice thin and thready.

"She'll be fine," the doctor said. His nametag read R. Moreland, M.D. "The nurse is with her at the moment. We've stopped the bleeding and put an inflatable tourniquet on her. I gave her some light medication for the pain so she's more comfortable. While she's calm, I thought we'd come here and bring you up to date. Nasty, nasty cut, but we're taking care of it."

Cole stood next to Tara and gripped her hand. She could feel the nervous tension vibrating through his body.

"We have a plastic surgeon coming to stitch her up," Dr. Moreland continued, "so she won't have much of a scar. We will want to give her a general anesthetic, though. Otherwise, the suturing can be quite traumatic for her, since the cut's so deep. Your husband wanted me to check with you before he signed the papers."

Tara could only nod.

The doctor handed Cole a clipboard with forms attached, and Cole scrawled his name.

"We also will need to give her some blood. She's lost quite a lot, and we don't want to run into other problems during the surgery. We prefer to check the parents first before using our own supplies. We always prefer family, if possible." He looked at Tara critically. "Not you, my dear." It was apparent he was unaware of the situation. "I think right now you need all you've got."

"Molly isn't my biological child anyway," Tara told him, "although our blood type might be compatible. I've never checked."

Cole's face tightened in embarrassment that he didn't know this simple fact. "I'm sure it's in her medical records at the pediatrician's, but I never paid attention enough to ask."

"No matter. You're wife's in no shape right now to be a donor under any circumstances. But the lab tech is right here, so Mr. Cassidy, I guess you're it."

Cole opened his mouth to say something, closed it and swallowed hard. "Actually I'm not her biological parent either," he said, harshness edging his voice.

"Then this is an adoption?" the doctor asked. "Well, let's test you anyway. If you have the right blood you can still be a donor."

He nodded, his face rigid, and Tara squeezed his hand weakly, trying to give him assurance. He looked so uptight she was afraid he'd break apart any minute.

A technician entered with all his paraphernalia. He was quick and efficient and, in just seconds,

The Bargain

handed a vial of Cole's blood to a waiting lab messenger.

"I'm going to see if the surgeon's come down yet." Dr. Moreland looked at Cole. "The nurse has been with your daughter since we sedated her, but you might want to come with me, Mr. Cassidy, in case she's at all aware. Just to reassure her until we take her to surgery."

Cole was torn, wanting to be two places at once.

"I'll be all right," Tara told him. "Please go be with Molly."

The lab tech had moved to the bed to stand next to Tara.

"We're going to take a little blood from you, too, Mrs. Cassidy. I need to run some tests before we try to prescribe anything for you. And the nurse will come and take your vitals. We'll be as quick as we can. I know you're in rough shape. Can you handle it until then?"

Tara moved her head in a weak nod. "It will be all right. Just go. Molly needs all of you more than I do right now."

Cole kissed her forehead then turned and followed the doctor.

After everyone had left the area, she dozed, rousing only when the nurse came to check her blood pressure and other vital signs. She was vaguely aware of the activity around her beyond the curtains, but as long as she lay perfectly still, she was all right. She wondered when someone would come to tell her more about Molly. An icy knot of fear curled in her stomach as dozens of unpleasant possibilities flashed through her brain.

When she opened her eyes again, Cole was beside her bed, holding her cold hand in one of his large warm ones, reassuring her with his presence. But who was comforting him? she wondered. The harsh lines of strain cut deeply into his face, and tension vibrated through his body.

"They're just waiting for the lab results," he told her. " Meanwhile, the medication's put her to sleep."

Before Tara could comment, they heard footsteps enter the room.

"Oh, good, you're both here." Dr. Morehead moved the curtain aside and entered the treatment area. "Mr. Cassidy, I'm somewhat puzzled here. You say Molly is adopted?"

"Not...exactly." Cole's face flushed a dark red. He didn't want to tell this doctor about Maggie and her lies. "Why do you ask?"

"First of all, your blood type is a match. You're both A Positive, and while that's not a particularly rare blood type, it is a little uncommon. Secondly, with a child this young, we try to match the blood as much as possible so we do something called the HLA test. We routinely use it for tissue compatibility, as well. It determines certain proteins found in the outer coating of nearly every cell in the body. Everyone has a small, relatively unique set inherited from their parents."

"So what are you saying?"

"I'm saying that while it doesn't prove paternity, it can disprove it. If father and child do not have one antigen pair identical to each other, it rules out paternity." Dr. Moreland paused for the space of a heartbeat. "This test shows you and the little girl have matching pairs, which means you definitely could be Molly's father. I don't mean to pry into your business, but..."

Cole's face was frozen in shock. He had to force himself to speak. "But I had a DNA test done that proved the opposite."

"Where did you have this done, if I might ask?"

Cole named the lab, and Dr. Moreland shook his head. "I'm sorry to say, that lab is under major scrutiny right now. They hired unqualified lab technicians and many of their test results were incorrect."

Tara thought Cole was going to have a heart attack. The blood drained from his face, and he staggered, falling into the chair next to the bed.

"We can do another test if it would reassure you," the doctor went on, "but right now we need you to give blood so we can get your daughter into surgery."

Dazed, Cole let himself be led away.

Chapter Seventeen

Tara roused a little when the nurse came to check on her again and let her know the doctor would be back very soon. They would give her something for the nausea as soon as her test results were back, if she could just hold on.

The next time, she awoke she felt a warm hand touching her. Opening her eyes, she saw Cole sitting upright in a chair beside her, his eyes glazed, his breathing slightly erratic. Shock, she decided. But a good shock, after all.

"You are not allowed to say I told you so," he said, when he noticed she was awake.

"I told you so." She tried for a faint grin. "You can't hit me when I'm sick."

He bowed his head, rubbing his temples with the tips of his fingers. "I can't believe this. All these months, I've been so miserable to her, shutting her out, withholding love. What a bastard I am. I don't deserve her. Or you. Either of you."

"Stop that." Tara summoned what strength she had. "You had no way of knowing the test was flawed. You could only go on the information that was given to you."

"You don't know how terrified I've been, watching them take care of her." He wiped his hand over his face as if brushing cobwebs away. "I looked at her lying there, so panicked at the sight of her still, little form and realized, in the end, it didn't matter what any of these tests show. You've been right all along. Biology has little to do with it."

Tara blinked her eyes against the tears crowding her lids. "You've always loved her. I sensed it, but you were just in too much pain to show it."

"Selfish pain, Tara." He gently squeezed her hand, holding it as afraid to break the contact. "I took out my own damaged ego on a child who was the innocent bystander in this little melodrama. She's my daughter—our daughter—and just the way it happened with you, it took a near disaster to show me what a damn fool I've been." He leaned back in the chair, eyes closed, lines of anguish scoring his face. "God, what if something goes wrong, and I never get to tell her how much I love her?"

"She'll be fine," Tara reassured him. "You heard the doctor. You got her here in plenty of time; she's got a full medical team taking care of her. Please stop beating yourself up. Children survive worse things."

"I love her, Tara." His eyes were bright with unshed tears, and the hand holding hers shook. "I love both of you. I'm going to spend the rest of my life showing you just how much."

"Loving us is all we ever asked of you, you know." Her voice was soft, and she squeezed the hand holding hers with what strength she had.

"What agony that woman put us all through."

Even in her weakened condition, Tara found the strength to silently curse Maggie. "She wanted to strike back at you, hurt you the only way she knew how. She saw how much you loved Molly and knew that was where she could strike at you to cause the most pain."

"How can I ever make it up to Molly?" He visibly fought the tears now, his throat muscle working reflexively.

"Children know things, Cole. They sense things. It will be fine. I promise you."

Tara wanted to say something else, but she couldn't make herself think straight any more. The nausea was coming in waves, swamping her and receding. She wished someone would come back with her test results so they could give her something to keep it at bay.

Cole, fidgeting in the chair, glanced through the curtain toward the door. "Can I leave you for a minute, sweetheart? Are you okay here? I'm sorry. I just have to know how she's doing."

"She's doing fine." Dr. Moreland came through the curtain before Cole could move. "She's out of surgery and doing very nicely." He made some notes on one of the charts he held. "She had no adverse reaction to the anesthetic, but she's got quite a lot of stitches in that arm. I'd prefer to keep her for a couple of nights, just to monitor her and give her some IV antibiotics."

"Of course," Cole said, standing up. "Whatever's best. Can we see her?"

"As soon as they get her set up. Right now, she's in pediatric recovery, and I need to discuss with you where we're going to put her."

"I don't understand." Cole was instantly alert, ready to take command. "Is there some problem?"

"No. There are just a few other things we need to address." He made one last note on the second chart then flipped it closed.

"What things? And what about my wife? What have you found out about her? Can't you do something for her?" His voice rose as the worry he'd been battling surged to the forefront. "She's had this virus or whatever you want to call it for five days now and doesn't seem to be getting much better."

The doctor nodded and opened the chart again. "Mrs. Cassidy, have you ever been told you have a major hormonal imbalance?"

"Yes, I know about that. I had a miscarriage several years ago, and my hormones haven't been right since then. I used to take a low dose of birth control to try and straighten it out, but the pills made me sick. Why?"

"I'm sure that's the reason you're having such severe nausea. You don't have the flu, my dear. You're pregnant."

Tara and Cole stared at him as if he'd grown an extra head.

"Pregnant?" Tara managed to croak. She had a sudden urge to laugh hysterically.

"Yes, your lab tests confirm it. About two months, I'd say. I always run the test before we medicate, just in case. Don't want any problems, you know. But the hormone imbalance has exacerbated what we usually call morning sickness and also made you drowsier than normal. So." He closed the chart and smiled at them. "I'm assuming this is good news."

Tara was the first to find her voice. "Yes, doctor, thank you." She clung to Cole's hand with a fierce grip. "It's very good news."

"You'll need to see your own obstetrician as soon as possible. With your condition and history, you should be monitored carefully. Meanwhile I'm going to keep you for a couple of nights, too. You're severely

The Bargain

dehydrated from all the vomiting, and your blood pressure's a little low. We discussed it and thought you might want your daughter set up in the room with you."

Cole swallowed several times before he finally managed to speak, although his voice was barely recognizable. "Yes, we'd appreciate that very much. Thank you."

"All right, then. The nurse will give you something for that nausea now, Mrs. Cassidy and set up an IV. Then they'll come and get you as soon as the room is ready." He shook hands with Cole and left the room.

Cole lowered himself back into the chair beside the bed, still clutching Tara's hand, still unbelieving. The tears he'd been trying to hold back were now rolling down his face and his throat was so tight he couldn't say anything. The look on his face made Tara's heart ache.

"A baby," he said. He was having trouble taking everything in. First the news about Molly. Now this. "I don't deserve all this good fortune." His voice was thick with emotion.

"I think everything was meant to happen the way it did." Tara managed to summon a smile. "We are truly blessed."

He raised his head, and they looked at each other, stunned by it all.

They were still trying to absorb it all when the nurse came in carrying a tray with several items on it.

"These shots should make you feel better real quick. And I'm going to start an IV drip, so we can get some fluids into your body. That will help a lot, too."

Cole moved out of the way until the nurse was finished then he was back at Tara's side in an instant. He laid his hand over her lower abdomen.

"That night right before our anniversary." His voice was quiet, loving. "I knew there was something different when we made love. I swear that's when it happened."

"I think so, too. My periods have never been regular since the miscarriage so I didn't suspect anything unusual. I just thought this was the flu," Tara told him. "Everything happens for a purpose, you know. We can put the past behind us now once and for all. Life is good." She grinned weakly. "And I'm even starting to feel a little better."

"I love you so much, Tara."

He leaned over to kiss her, wanting to hold her but afraid of dislodging something.

"Mr. Cassidy?" The nurse was at the curtain again. "You're daughter's doing fine. It will be just a few minutes now, and we'll get both her and your wife upstairs. There's a young lady out here in great distress, though, who wants to see you. Is it all right to bring her back here?"

"It must be Nicki," Cole said. "Yes, please. Go and get her."

It was a tear-stained and shaken Nicki, who appeared, with her mother behind her.

"I told her everything would be all right, but she's been a wreck," Mrs. Varner said.

Cole went to her and took her hands in his. "Nicki, if it's anyone's fault, it's mine. I was right there and wasn't paying attention."

Tara wished she could hug the unhappy, scared teenager. "Molly's fine," she told her. "Accidents happen. Please don't keep blaming yourself. You take such good care of her. We trust you, honestly. And she's doing fine. They've already finished stitching her up. They'll keep her a couple of nights as a precaution, but I promise you she's okay."

Nicki burst into tears again. Cole looked at Tara helplessly then put his arm around Nicki and moved her over closer to his wife.

"You'd better pull yourself together because we're really going to need you now," Tara smiled, reaching for Nicki's hand. "We're going to have a baby."

Nicki looked up through her tears. "Honest? A baby?"

"Yes and we need your help before it comes and afterwards. You'd better get in shape for this."

"She was so worried you wouldn't want her to sit anymore," Mrs. Varner said. "I told her it's all right. She should know about accidents. She and her brothers and sisters kept the emergency room in business when they were younger."

When the orderly came to get Tara, Cole sent Nicki and her mother home. He walked along beside his wife, still clutching her hand, as they rolled her toward the elevator.

In minutes, Tara was settled in the hospital room, her IV checked and her vitals taken once more. When the nurse had finished with her, they rolled in a hospital crib with Molly in it. She looked so white and still both Tara and Cole panicked.

"She's fine," the nurse assured them. "She woke up from the anesthetic with no problem. She's sleeping normally now. We'll be checking on both of you throughout the night. Doctor wants regular reports. I'll be back after a while."

Cole stood at the crib, motionless, his eyes fixed on Molly. She looked so small, so fragile. Her dark curls were tousled around her pale face. Her left arm was bandaged from wrist to shoulder and an IV needle was taped to her right hand.

Why hadn't he looked at her more closely before? Now he could see his own features stamped on her tiny face, only softer. He saw the same dark eyes and thick lashes, the same straight nose and high cheekbones. He'd been so blinded by anger and rage he'd seen nothing except his love for this child ripped from his heart by hateful words.

His eyes moved to Tara, drowsy from the medication, her eyes closing as she drifted off. What an incredible woman she was. He'd hired her as if employing a servant, and she'd stepped in where others would have fled. She was a loving mother to the daughter he'd refused to acknowledge, and she'd given her heart to him willingly, despite how little of himself he'd given back to her. When he'd turned to her for love, she had accepted him without reservation.

He thought agonizingly of all the time that had been wasted, time when he and Tara could have had a real relationship. Time he could have spent as Molly's father. He was more fortunate now than any man had a right to be. He would spend the rest of his life making it up to both of them and to the new little life that he and Tara had created.

He watched them until he was sure they were both sleeping then tiptoed from the room to find a place to use his cell phone. He needed to call Jake and Lindsey as well as Tara's parents. He was sure the McKees, in particular, had called the house and been worried when no one answered.

Ellen McKee burst into happy tears at the news then handed the phone to her husband who had a hard time controlling his own emotions. Jake and Lindsey could barely contain their excitement. Cole told

The Bargain

everyone, when they asked, that they could check on his family in the morning. His family! What a nice ring that had to it.

Both Tara and Molly were still sleeping when he returned to the room. Torn between finding a place next to his daughter or his wife, he finally solved his problem by moving the crib even closer to Tara's bed. Situating himself in the chair, he reached out one hand to touch Molly and placed the other on Tara's arm. He sat for a long time, his heart so full he thought it would burst. At last, the specter of Maggie had been chased away.

* * * *

When Tara opened her eyes, light was pouring in through the window, the sun casting shadows against the wall. She turned her head and smiled at what she saw. Cole was slumped in the chair between the bed and the crib, rumpled and unshaven. One hand rested on her arm and one of his large fingers was clasped tightly in Molly's tiny ones. The little girl was still sleeping, but Tara could see her breathing was even and regular and her color much better.

She shifted a little, and Cole came awake at once.

"Are you all right?" He lifted his hand from her arm and rubbed his eyes. "How do you feel?"

"Better, I think. How's Molly?"

"Pretty good. She woke once during the night. I think her arm was bothering her, so they gave her some baby aspirin. That's why she's still sleeping now."

"Not any more. Take a look."

Molly had her eyes wide open and was trying to sit up. Cole bent over the crib and lifted her gently.

"They showed me how to hold her," he explained. "The bandage on her arm is so big because they want to protect all the stitches. But they took out the IV early this morning, so she can move around better now. They took yours out, too. They said you were pretty well re-hydrated, and you could now take medication by mouth. They want another twenty-four hours, though, to see if you can keep food down."

Cole settled Molly on his lap, taking care with her arm and showered her face with soft kisses. He couldn't take his eyes away from her. He touched her hair, her cheeks, her tiny mouth, kissing her over and over again.

Molly, reveling in the attention, giggled and reached up to pat him with her good hand.

Tara felt tears gathering in her eyes and blinked them away.

"I called Lindsey and Jake and your folks," Cole informed Tara. "And Sean. I figured Nicki's mother would have passed the word on the Varner grapevine. And I didn't want your folks to worry when we weren't home, knowing you'd been sick."

"Did you tell them we're fine now?"

"Yes. They said they'd probably come by later today. I expect to see my partner and his wife this morning, though and maybe even Sean."

A nurse's aide bustled in, carrying a tray that she put on the bed table. "Breakfast for the ladies," she called out. "Mrs. Cassidy, your orders say you should try some weak tea and dry toast. How's the nausea this morning?"

"Much better," Tara told her. "And I don't feel quite so dizzy." She didn't. The room had settled around her, everything staying in one place even when she moved.

"Good." This from the nurse entering the room. "Here's your morning meds and baby aspirin for your daughter. She'll need this for a few days until the worst

The Bargain

of the soreness is gone. Doctor will send you home with some medication for the nausea, Mrs. Cassidy, but he wants you to see your obstetrician as soon as possible."

"We'll take care of it right away," Cole stated, his voice firm.

"I'll let you get started on your breakfast." The nurse smiled at Molly. "I'd say you need a highchair to feed this little angel. I'll send one in right away."

Cole shook his head. "I'll hold her on my lap and feed her."

* * * *

The doctor had put a rush on the preliminary DNA test the night before, and the day seemed to drag by while they waited for the results.

"I'm convinced it's positive," Cole said at one point. "Not a doubt at this point."

"Even if it's not," Tara pointed out, "it won't make a difference."

"It will be positive." Cole's voice was firm and confident. "I just know it."

He helped Tara eat and fed Molly. Then, while Tara dozed, he held the child on his lap, crooning to her, until she, too, fell asleep. He knew he should put her back in the crib, but he couldn't get enough of holding her.

The nurse arrived with the evening medication, and the doctor walked in right on her heels.

"First things first," he said. "I have the results back on the preliminary DNA test." He grinned. "Good thing you said cost didn't matter because I think they charged through the nose to rush it. However, there's no doubt you're Molly's father, Mr. Cassidy. I hope that pleases you."

Cole could only nod, so gripped by emotion he couldn't speak.

"Well, everyone seems fine here. I'll just check my patients over, but I think both can go home tomorrow."

Finished with his exam of mother and child, he made notes on the chart then told them he was writing discharge orders for the next day. He wanted the two of them there one more night, but they could all go home in the morning.

Cole collapsed back in the chair, still amazed by the turn their life had taken.

Tara, feeling immeasurably better, grinned at him. "Life sure is good, isn't it, daddy?"

"Better than I deserve." He leaned over and kissed his wife firmly on the lips then picked up Molly and sat back in the chair. Nestling the little girl against his chest, he reached for Tara's hand and twined his fingers through hers.

And that's how they were, Cole feeding Molly and Tara sipping at her tea when Jake and Lindsey appeared in the doorway. Tara looked up and saw them and waved them in.

Lindsey came over to the side of the bed and hugged her. "Cole called last night," she said.

"I figured he would. We're fine. Honestly."

"He told us the good news, too. Oh, Tara, we're so very happy for you. For both of you. It's a shame it took this kind of an emergency to turn things around, but I knew everything would work out sooner or later."

"The best news is we had another DNA test done, and it proves without a doubt that Cole is Molly's father." Tara beamed.

"Oh, my god," Lindsey gasped. "That is just too much." She kissed her friends soundly, while Jake shook Cole's free hand. Emotion was very thick in the room.

Tara turned her head and looked at Cole, cuddling his daughter. Then she looked at Jake, with his arm around Lindsey, glowing with her own pregnancy. Two of the best friends in the world.

Their marriage might have begun as a bargain, but it had certainly turned out to be a good one for both of them. Tara touched her abdomen where the baby was growing, the child she and Cole had conceived with their love. *A new home, a new child and a new life.*

And she smiled.

Epilogue

The scene could have come straight from a painting. The blue Texas sky, dotted with puffs of cloud, was a backdrop for a golden sun. A soft breeze fluttered the leaves on the oaks and sycamore and drew ripples in the little stream. Next to the barn, in a paddock fenced with white split rails, four horses nickered gently as they nuzzled one another. The aroma of hay and horseflesh drifted on the air.

The house of gleaming limestone and weathered wood sat on the crest of the hill. Huge windows, that filled the house with light, reflected the sun.

On the wraparound porch, two cats snoozed on the wide railing, tails curled comfortably around them. In one chair was a large, muscular man in jeans that molded to his strong thighs. A denim shirt accentuated the breadth of his shoulders and on his feet were scuffed boots. A graceful-looking woman sat next to him. Her golden sweater picked up the tawny highlights of her thick coffee-colored hair and soft suede jeans clung tantalizingly to her hips.

The man held a little girl about two years old, her head with its tousled curls nestled happily against his chest. The woman, her hair loose about her face and cascading over her shoulders, held a tiny baby against her body. Her cheek rested against the soft, downy head, her lips pressing against the skin.

They rocked in rhythm, unwilling to disturb their sleeping children. Their faces held a look of total peace and serenity. And a love that was so strong it shut out everyone and everything else. People who saw them envied the strength of what they had.

They sat and rocked as the sun began to dip from the sky and the light of day faded. Their children slumbered peacefully in their arms. They had weathered a difficult journey, but now they had reached nirvana. Life was good.

About the Author

Desiree Holt has lived a life of excitement that brings the color to her writing. She was a summer fishing guide, a summer field hand where she was one of only three women working, a member of a beginning ski team that skied in competition (and no, no broken bones!). She spent several years in the music business representing every kind of artist from country singer to heavy metal rock bands. For several years she also ran her own public relations agency handling any client that interested her. She is twice a finalist for an EPIC E-Book Award, a nominee for a Romantic Times Reviewers Choice Award, winner of the first 5 Heart Sweetheart of the Year Award at The Romance Studio, and is published by four different houses. *Romance Junkies* said of her work: "Desiree Holt is the most amazing erotica author of our time and each story is more fulfilling then the last."

You can find her at www.desireeholt.com and www.desireeholttellsall.com

Thank You!

We appreciate your purchase of this Resplendence Publishing title. We hope your reading experience was a pleasurable one, and invite you to take 10% off your next electronic book purchase from website.

Visit www.ResplendencePublishing.com, select any title, and enter the following code when you check out: **ReadRP10**. This code is valid only on our website, for electronic book purchases only.

During your visit to www.ResplendencePublishing.com, you can enjoy Free Reads from RP's hottest authors, obtain information on our Read Green charitable donation program, or sign up for our quarterly newsletter and our RP Reader Rewards program, which awards loyal readers with a $10.00 gift certificate for every $100.00 spent.

You can also join us on MySpace, Facebook, and Blogspot. You will find regular updates, information on upcoming releases and appearances, as well as contests for free RP titles. We love to hear from our readers, and hope to see you there.

Thank you again for your purchase, and we look forward to becoming your number one resource for high quality electronic fiction.

Best,
The RP Team

Available from Resplendence Publishing

Carnal Reunions

Training Randi by Tessie Bradford

Miranda Ellson graduated from college with a degree in design in one hand and a ticket to London in the other. Ten years, five job changes and three boring, unfulfilling relationships later she's back at WIU to reconnect with old friends, enjoy the campus activities and take a break from...oh who the hell is she kidding?

Jeff Briggs, former college neighbor and best bud, now successful gym owner, lives in town. He's the only guy she has ever known who could set her panties on fire by simply walking into a room and Randi is sick and tired of only hooking up with him in her dreams. This may be her only chance to discover exactly what kind of personal training he has to offer.

Smokin' Ace by Regina Carlysle

A college reunion and seeing her best 'gal pals' is just the thing widow and single mom, Chloe Wells needs to put a little oomph back into her boring, routine life. For her, those carefree years and the friendships she made with six other women in the old Victorian were unforgettable and, hey, what's wrong with revisiting a past that was fun and full of laughter? But when she bumps into Michael "Ace" Banner other memories surface. Memories of hot nights and rumpled bed sheets. Memories of the loss of the one man who burned her to ash.

Former college tennis star, Ace Banner, now a renowned sports photographer, has just one chance to regain the love of pretty, sweet, very sexy Chloe. Yeah, he blew it years ago by walking away but he's a man now and not about to let her get away again. Ace is prepared to pull out all the stops in reclaiming what he lost all those years ago. It'll take a slow hand and an easy touch but he's up for the challenge.

***First and Ten* by Fran Lee**

What Fran Jamison and Jack Gerrard have in common, you could balance on the head of a pin. And to make things worse, Jack blew his chances to hell back in High School with the BBW.

Neither goes to their 10th college reunion expecting sparks to fly, but when they collide in the airport, painful old memories quickly evaporate to make way for two people desperately needing to scratch 12-year-old itches.

Jack royally blew it when he let other people's opinions stop him from pursuing the 5'11" bombshell so many years back, and by the time he realized he was a jackass and tried to apologize, a traumatized and hurt Fran had shredded his ego in public, leaving him to lick his wounds and move on.

She thought she would hate him on sight. She didn't. She thought she could walk away. She couldn't. She certainly didn't expect to find herself making out like a madwoman on the hood of a borrowed car in the airport parking ramp. But she did expect one thing...she was not going to walk away again. Not when he was so damn good at scratching those itches...

Nailed by Cindy Spencer Pape

When shy scientist Karen Sikorski meets up with her college crush, Warner Beckett, sparks fly, but she knows the handsome contractor would never fall for a plain nerd like her. Warner, though, has other ideas. Smart, voluptuous Karen is everything he's ever wanted in a woman, and this time around, he's enough of a grown up to appreciate it. Now all he has to do is convince the lady he really does want her—in every way possible.

IOU by Paris Brandon

The morning after her final exams, Bliss Harper woke up in her own bed wearing only her underwear. She's never remembered how she got there or why she found an I.O.U. tucked into her panties for one night of "Bad Boy Sex," signed by her favorite pizza delivery guy, Nick Santucci. But she had a ten-year plan that didn't include any more bad decisions and handsome men. But all work and no play make for a dull life and she's headed to her ten-year college reunion with every intention of collecting on a debt that's long overdue.

Ten years ago, bad boy Nick hadn't usually looked twice at shy, thrift-store fashion reject Bliss Harper. He just hadn't been able to avoid it when she'd started doing a tabletop, drunken striptease at a frat party the police were raiding. These days Nick's not delivering pizza, he's delivering deals and he's headed to his ten-year college reunion determined to negotiate one night into many with the woman who holds the marker on his heart.

Prisoner of the Heart by Anny Cook

When Rebecca Iversen graduated from college, she headed home with nothing on her mind but wedding plans. Less than a month later, her plans were in ruins when she discovered she was pregnant the same week her fiancé was arrested for selling drugs. Anxious to provide legitimacy for her child, she married Tom while he was still in jail. Years later, Becky finally divorced him, resolved to make a peaceful life for her children and herself.

When the reunion invitation from Karen arrived in her e-mail, her Aunt Mary urged her to take the time to enjoy a little adult time at the reunion.

Young Joe Harris lived across the street from the old Victorian where Becky lived during college. He spent those years secretly yearning for the "older woman". Now that Becky is back and single, Joe plans to do everything in his power to convince her that he's exactly the man she needs.

G-Spot by Taylor Tryst

Lily Sutherland—no—Detective Lily Sutherland, a title she worked her ass off to earn, has returned to Heartwood Indiana for her ten-year college reunion. An ex-Lady Hawk, and a star athlete on the volleyball team, Lily used her competitive edge to win on the court. She dove into the male dominated world of law enforcement where she once again rocked the foundation and shot up the ranks to homicide detective in record time. As far as Lily is concerned, she's just one of the boys until she reunites with Dakota Reese, the love of her life.

Special Agent Dakota Reese has always been too smart for his own damn good. Specializing in serial cases, Dakota attends his college reunion at Western Indiana University for what he believes will be a reprieve, only to discover that his life just became much harder...literally, when he see's Lily Sutherland at the grand old Victorian down the street. Dakota and Lily had split amicably ten years prior, each of them marrying for all of the right reasons. Unfortunately, they married someone else, and were now both divorced. There's a natural animosity between the cops and the feebs, but can Lily put their differences aside long enough for her 'G Man' to find her g spot and rock her world, forever?

Also Available from Resplendence Publishing

Binding Gillian by Melinda Barron

In college, Brad Claybourne and Gillian York were soul mates. But their relationship could not survive the manipulations of a conniving woman, and ended in heartbreak.

Now Brad is a world-famous journalist and Gillian is an on-the-rise author. When her agent unwittingly sets Gillian up to be interviewed by Brad, Gillian vows that she will not allow old feelings to surface.

But Brad has other ideas. He intends to remind Gillian of how good they were together. All he will need is a little bit of holiday magic...and a few feet of rope.

Punished by Brynn Paulin

Prim Natalia Cooper lives life on the straight and narrow, never veering into naughty territory. But she wants to. One night, years ago, her boyfriend gave her a few swats on the rear as part of their sex play and she loved it. She wants more. But he's long gone and she hasn't been spanked since. When she learns of a club where she can get exactly what she needs—anonymously—she's so turned on and ready she can hardly bear it.

For Ethan Tavish, The Dungeon has served as a place

to exert his dominance without making lasting commitments. He can hardly believe his eyes when he enters the play area to find his secretary, Natalia, bent over the spanking bench in a schoolgirl uniform. They're both masked, but he'd recognize her anywhere. In an instant, he has a plan to give them what they both want...and perhaps a whole lot more.

Red Ribbons and Blue Balls by Tia Fanning

After Nicolas punishes her for being naughty, the usually nice but now sexually frustrated Winter arrives at their secluded mountain cabin bearing gifts—special gifts that will ensure his submission and her revenge.

With only seven days left until Christmas, Nicolas expects to spend the night decorating the house for the approaching holiday, but Winter has other plans... Christmas might be coming, but if Winter gets her way, Nicolas won't be.

Body of Art by Bronwyn Green

Art professor Seth Granger has two problems—an absentee life drawing models and a case of unrequited lust. Luckily his troubles have the same answer—his colleague, Dr. Callie Sullivan.

The trick will be getting her out of her clothes and into his studio...and hopefully into his bed. However, she's intent on keeping her mind on her art and ignoring him. Now he just needs to convince her she should be his body of art.

Transparent Illusions by Melinda Barron

Freelance writer Saffron Tyler needs work. When she offers her journalistic skills to Steele Publications, they suggest that she spend two weeks as a submissive at Fingertip Fantasies, an exclusive BDSM resort that caters to the ultimate fantasies of any customer willing to pay for the high-end service. She's been tasked to come back with a titillating exposé guaranteed to enthrall the readers of Steele's underground magazine, *Salacious*.

But when Saffron arrives at the resort, she realizes nothing is as it seems, from the fact she doesn't know where the resort is located, or anything about the man she is submitting to—except she's to call him Master, with a capital M.

What starts out as an undercover assignment soon becomes so much more. Immersed in the lifestyle, Saffron finds herself no longer acting the role of the submissive, but actually wanting to be the perfect sub her Master believes she can be. When all is said and done, will Saffron take her experience and her story and never look back? Or will she choose to stay with the man who commands her mind, body, and soul.

Chance Encounters by Mia Jae

Seven short, erotic stories to whet your appetite, packaged in one collection. Whether the couples meet on a glance, make a split second decision or take a chance to be together, the encounters change their lives, for a minute, or for a lifetime.

You'll find a plumber who gets into more than a little hot water, a housewife tangled up in a cyber relationship, a cowboy trio attempting to brand a bartender for their very own, and a woman experimenting with a same-sex relationship. Then there is naughty Rose, who dances naked in front of her bedroom window, a chance sexual encounter in a taxi that turns the tables, and a woman who finds herself doing exactly what she thinks she shouldn't...and liking it.

Find Resplendence titles at the following retailers

Resplendence Publishing
www.ResplendencePublishing.com

Amazon
www.Amazon.com

Barnes and Noble
www.BarnesandNoble.com

Target
www.Target.com

Fictionwise
www.Fictionwise.com

All Romance E-Books
www.AllRomanceEBooks.com

Mobipocket
www.Mobipocket.com

Printed in Great Britain
by Amazon.co.uk, Ltd.,
Marston Gate.